Becoming Lawrence

T. H. FORTITUDE

CONTENTS

Chapter One

THE CUSTOMS AGENT

The customs agent leaned back, slowly crossing meaty forearms. He looked down his nose at me standing before him as I wondered what was he was thinking.

Those arms, crossed under his perfectly round head, made me think of the skull and crossbones on a pirate's flag. Not a good vision. A tad unsettling you might say and, indeed, proclaiming that this would not likely be a cursory glance, a quick once-over of the passport, a thump of an entry stamp, and a wave to the next in line.

What the... ?? Was I being profiled?

After a long pause he picked up my passport and his thumbs flicked the pages. He asked, in that low growl familiar to those who know how big Caribbean men can speak in deep bass tones that rumble against your eardrums, "What hotel you be stay'n at?"

No-one at a customs desk had asked me that before, and I hesitated in doubt before stumbling over an answer: "I... I don't really know yet; I have to find one."

His voice rose, "You got no hotel? You come to dis country wid no hotel?"

This small matter – to me anyway – hadn't been considered before I boarded the flight from Miami, and now I stammered, which is precisely how one raises the suspicions of a border agent.

"I... I... came on... rather short notice. You see, I was in Miami sitting on this bench, and...."

That's as far as I got before his large palm, quite pale compared to his arm, thrust forward in the universal sign for "shut the hell up." That big hand hung in front of my face while a hush seemed to fall on the noisy room as if it had been meant for everyone within a fifty-foot radius. Then he turned and pointed at a doorway behind him:
"Go in dat room. Sit on de chair, and wait for de captain."
I did as told, not sure what I'd done wrong, just wanting to get into town and find a hotel, not 'go in dat room'.
'Dat room' was small, with paint on walls as rough as the airport in general. A fan, unmoving, hung low and out of kilter from the middle of the ceiling. A wooden swivel chair behind a tortured wooden desk, with 'TOBY G' etched into its top, waited for "de captain."

The clock on the wall read 9:28 p.m.

Exactly two hours earlier I had been in Miami sitting on a wooden bench at a bus stop in a contemplative mood, pondering a daylight moon hanging faded in the blue sky above a huge billboard, bothered by nothing more than the decision about whether this was a car night or hotel night.
On the odd day I would find a bed in the art-deco-

style, rather decrepit Shelbourne Hotel in Miami Beach. It was as Art Deco as one could find - complete with ninety-year-old men in wicker lobby chairs and old ladies shuffling behind walkers at the pace of once-across-the-lobby-per-afternoon, as if they had come to Miami to see the Rat Pack playing the Fontainebleau in the '50s and had never found their way back to Jersey. However, my budget often allowed only one or the other, so some nights I rented a car, and other nights I rented a room. After all, a car can shelter as well as a hotel, and for many people a car would have been an upgrade to their accommodations. I sat on that bench, gauging time against the rise of the moon over the billboard, trying to decide my next move. Hotel? Car? Hotel? Car?

The billboard, all of fifty feet wide intruded on my view of that moon-laden blue sky, colourfully depicting frangipani and allamanda petals, a smiling man with an armful of lobster and exotic fruit on a bed of bougainvillea.

"It's Better in the Bahamas" the sign proclaimed in ten-foot letters, and across the bottom of the billboard: *BAHAMAS AIR, Flights to Nassau. $ 39 dollars one-way.*

The Bahamas? Nassau? If I recall correctly, the homeport of Blackbeard the pirate, the only place in the Bahamas I'd ever heard about other than Freeport.

It was fate. I was taking a break from a long walk on a bench that happened to be a bus stop, and just as that billboard caught my eye, a bus approached. I got up, so the driver wouldn't think I was waiting for him, and turned to leave. But, as I turned away, my eye caught the route sign on the front of the bus:
MIAMI INTERNATIONAL AIRPORT

I froze midstride, my head involuntarily cocked to one side, understanding immediately that this was beyond perfect timing; it was a twist of fate of the uncommon variety known as the stars aligning. The sort of fate one does not mess with.

Nassau; the name itself an exotic word, where lobsters ten feet across float pink and ready to eat on a bed of flowers in the arms of a smiling man in a bright shirt, exuding welcome. Better yet, just thirty nine dollars away. And, the icing on the cake: it was *better* there. What was better had yet to be determined; perhaps *everything* was better, and for thirty-nine bucks one way, I could see for myself.

Yes!

I spun on my heel and looked at the driver in the approaching bus. It stopped, and the doors opened. I thought to myself,
"Why not get on? When a bus stops, and its destination is the international airport, and a ticket to some exotic-sounding place is at a price you can afford, you must get on." Rule number one for spontaneous living: when omens speak, you must listen. I stepped aboard.

Seventeen minutes later I was out the rear door into Terminal One. Five minutes after that I was buying a ticket to Nassau, and 63 minutes after that I was in the arrivals hall of the Nassau International Airport, looking at new surroundings with David Bowie singing in my head, "This… is not…. America…."
The airport covered the spectrum of the pastel shades known as tropical colours, with open walls from the baggage carousel to the sidewalk and waiting taxis, and the only thing between me and my island adventure was this customs agent pestering me with details, like "What hotel

you be stayin' at?"

I'd been travelling for three months, and up to now, answered to no one. But here I was, committing no offence, but under suspicion because of my choice to follow rule number one. I sat before the desk and empty swivel chair waiting, and waiting, and becoming very tired of waiting, when finally the door behind me swung open and in came the man, the chief customs officer. He sat down behind the desk, set his elbows firmly on its scarred surface, and leaned forward with a hard stare into my face, obviously not at all amused that he'd been called in at this late hour of the evening.

Short on patience, he got right to it, "Why you come dis island? Tell me de real reason and save us trouble."

I hadn't expected to have to explain, but I had to say something, "I was at a bus stop in Miami, and I saw this billboard that said, "It's better in the Bahamas."

His tone of voice went up a few decibels, "*What* is better?"

"I don't know. The sign just said *it's* better, and I wanted to find out what that is."

He leaned closer, now almost above me, and said, in precise, clipped English, "I asked you once, and I am only going to ask once more, and you'd better answer wit de troot, or we be here for de looooong time. And stop dat ting about a bus. I don' wan' hear no nonsense about de bus. Busses don' ride over de watah from Miami. Who you workin' for?"

I hesitated in confusion. Currently, I was in fact unemployed, but reluctant to admit it as I knew border agents don't like unemployed people coming into their country, especially those of the sunburned, unkempt variety.

De Captain saw only one possibility - drug mule.

This was October of 1983, and this island was a central point of transfer for Colombian cocaine. I had to make him understand that I was not there to move drugs. I opened my mouth to speak, but before I could get out a word, he screamed in my face, spit flying to speckle my forehead and cheeks,

"Tell me! Tell me now, and we won't have to throw you in jail. Save your skin!"

My mouth snapped shut. My head went back at the shout in my face at a loss for words as I realized nothing I said would make a difference. He was certain I was working for a drug cartel. In his eyes I would only be more guilty if I had sacks of cocaine taped to my body.

Again he barked at me, "I give you one more chance, make it easy on yourself, who you be meetin', and where are you to take it? If we give you to the US DEA you will be going to hell for a loooong while."

He emphasized the words hell and long by shouting that slowly and more loudly than the rest of the statement.

I sat immobile, my brain frozen, in terror of saying the wrong thing. Somehow I'd become a drug smuggler, and no matter who I was working for, or not, or what I said to the contrary would change his opinion. This had become serious, and I was becoming very nervous.

Then, in such a voice that anyone else in the airport would have heard him clearly, he screamed in my face,

"Tell me now! You get maybe five years, here in de New Providence Penitentiary. But, if you don' tell me, *right now*, we give you to de DEA, and you'll get twenty five years...in dere prison, not ours."

I was wide awake, shocked, and struck dumb all at the same time. I had stumbled upon something unfamiliar and extremely unpleasant. I'd heard of things like this happening, but never thought it would happen to me.

Sweat ran down the undersides of my arms. Our eyes locked. His piercing stare was crushing my resolve, causing me to question, who did I think I was, coming to a place unknown, without making arrangements ahead of time?

I was ready to break when a crystal clear solution came to me, "What if I just give it up?" Yes, I could admit to everything. I would give him what he wanted. Why not negotiate, like at the street market in Guadalajara? Five years was like, what, 20 percent of 25 years? I would have to handle that, and maybe even try to get time off for good behavior. I can't be going to Sing-Sing, or the state pen in Alabama or wherever they send drug smugglers. Maybe better in the Bahamas meant the government prison was better in the Bahamas. I don't know. Maybe that is what the billboard was saying with that infinitely ambiguous statement.

As I tried to think up a starting point to my confession, I realized I would have to lie through my teeth. I wasn't a drug smuggler. I would have to make up some sort of story.

Think fast, dammit, save 20 years!

I didn't know where to start. What should I say was my fictional big boss's name? Tony? Jose? Or maybe I worked for Pablo?

I suddenly felt like a failure. Drug smuggling was one more of the things I hadn't done in my life so I had no idea about how to even begin a credible story.

Then I gave my head a shake. What the heck was I doing chastising myself for not being a criminal? It occurred to me now, in a big way, that the jovial fun, the spur-of-the-moment, get-on-a-plane to destinations-unknown freedom could have consequences.

What was this place? And how could I have been so arrogant as to believe I could go anywhere, anytime, like I was in my home country, and things would be the same?

Panic welled in my throat. I looked for my bag that had been by the door, and was surprised – and not in a good way – to see that it was not there.

What?

Was I being set up? Perhaps my bag was now stuffed with drugs, and now I was, indeed, a smuggler. Was this why I had to wait so long for de captain?

Was something being planted while I waited?

Was this some sort of shake down?

Could this be extortion?

I'd heard about such things happening in Mexico, but I could hardly believe it from the Bahamas, even though I'd never been here before.

But, that could be it. I knew nothing about this place, why should I assume it to be any certain way?

I couldn't help but panic. This was no joke. I could be in handcuffs and facing rats and bats and real criminals in a prison cell and the better in the Bahamas thing was just a ruse to get naïve travelers to drop on by and become extortion targets.

I had to let it all out. Right now!

The panic was in my voice; I was beyond controlling it. I stammered as I started to speak and it all poured out almost beyond my control,

"Wait. Wait. Wait a second. Hang on here. I can't tell you what I don't know. I can't give up my contact and boss and meeting point because I don't have a contact or boss or meeting point. I just got on a plane because it was leaving and coming here. I had no idea I might be smuggling drugs. I don't even know how to smuggle drugs. I wasn't supposed to meet anyone here let alone anyone smuggling drugs. I was just wandering around in Miami and saw this big sign with a lobster that comes from the ocean already cooked with butter on the side and got on a bus that said airport and ended up here." The sound of my voice was foreign to me, tinged with fear, and I knew I was sounding like a grade three schoolgirl but couldn't help it.

De Captain glared at me, leaning slowly forward, stopping only when his big face was inches from mine. I looked up at him, unable to say anything, unable to think fast enough to put together any lie that might work better than the truth that just spewed uncontrollably. Our faces were suspended inches apart. A long pause ensued. Then a longer one, and then, he blinked. I saw it.

Warmth seemed to radiate from him, as if a precursor to an explosion or an indication of blood pressure rising.

The blink had been a sign of what he didn't want to reveal: the uncertainty he was feeling. He pulled back, straightened up, then sat down with a deep sigh and resumed a silent stare. A full sixty seconds later he shouted toward the closed door, "Eustatious!"

The customs agent appeared at the door, carrying my red leather bag. "Whar is dis young man's belongin's?"

"Here, Captain." He lifted the bag.

"Eustacious, put dat bag here, on de desk. Open it up, and let's see what is dere. I want you to be witness to the inspection of dis bag."

I almost lost control of my sphincter. A lump rose in my throat and began choking me, my stomach became hot and memories of Mexico and the numerous washroom visits.

Will I have to ask to use the washroom, or risk an 'accident'?

Did they plant something in my bag?

Was it now filled with cocaine?

What have I gotten myself into?

He placed the bag on the desk and unzipped it, extracting my meager belongings, item after item, laying them across the desk. Shorts, t-shirts, camera, five socks, two pair of not-so-clean underwear, one pair of jeans, but, thank God above, no bags of planted drugs.

Captain looked everything over carefully, "Dis be how you travel? You expeck me to believe you travel like dis?"

I tried to explain, even surprised myself my belongings looked this bad in this light, "I don't like to carry more than I have to and I've been carrying it a long way."

He looked it all over once more. My passport sat to one side, tattered and yawning as if inviting a look inside.

He picked it up as if it was contagious and went through page by page, slowly turning it around, squinting closely at the stamps, his brain working, setting up dates of ins and outs of countries.

"Mexico?" he asked. "Where's that stamp for Columbia?"

"No, no Columbia, and yes, Mexico. But nothing to do with drugs, other than a pound or two of Imodium." I replied meekly. He set the passport down and tried closing it a couple of times before giving up.

"Eustatious, make sure dis young man stays for a week. He's not about to fool me wid a quick delivery. Make him stay a week to slow him down. Keep an eye on him all de time. Who he meets and what he picks up. Now, get him out of here."

With that, he stepped around the desk and left the room. Eustatious motioned me back to the customs desk, opened my passport, and with a slam of an entry stamp allowed me entry.

He said, "You book de room for de week, as Cappy say, but *I* tell you where you go."

I had to guess what that could mean. "I have a pretty low budget."

He said, "Yah, mon, dat is where I call de bullshit, mon. You play dis game, and you and I bot' know boss man in Miami have plenny big budget. You just don' wan' spend what he give you for de rent."

He stopped to lean into my face once more, "I tell you whar to go. I keep an eye on you, so I tell you whar to go. You don' like dat idea, you sleep dere, on de chair, to wait for de return flight to Miami. Dat is not till tomorrow, mon, and you can't leave dis room, even if you got to piss. You hear me? It's your choice."

"OK, I'll stay at the hotel, not on de chair."

He nodded slowly, "For one week. Seven days like Cappy say, and when you leave in one week you have to pass *me* on de way out, so forget about takin' anyting back. I tell US custom to watch for you reeeeal close."

'Is it even legal? Could they do this?' was going through my head. But, I was the last person in the airport, it was late at night, and I had no idea who to contact to help me. After the yelling in my face, this seemed a relief.

I nodded to confirm, yes, seven days. OK.

He walked to a phone and made a call, then led me through the now-deserted arrivals area. I followed him as he carried my bag out of the airport into the darkness of the quiet night to the only remaining taxi. He opened the back door, tossed my bag in, and said a few words to the driver.

My hotel for a week, like it or not, was booked and arranged. Probably not, but what was I going to do? I was now committed, almost hostage to the suspicions of Her Majesty's Border Protection Agency, to the hotel of their choice. The BPA mandated by the government and pestered by the US to stop the flow of drugs through the Bahamas and trying to do it one traveler at a time.

Chapter Two

THE MANOR

The street the taxi traveled was narrow and very dark, with only a few cars parked along one side. The hotel the driver had been instructed to deliver me wasn't a hotel at all, but rather a manor house or former estate. We stopped in front of what must have been a grand entrance.

Set off the sidewalk stood two gate posts, discoloured with algae, where hung brass plates with coats of arms, or some semblance of as corrosion now obscured their features. The branches of an ancient banyan overhung the sidewalk, much narrower than it once would have been.

On one side a rusty, off-kilter gate, hung by the top hinge alone, the opposing leaf permanently in it's open position, embedded into the sidewalk.

The driver did not speak nor move from his place behind the wheel. I had to take this as my cue to get out, this had to be my destination. The door closed as he pulled away, leaving me in the quiet street, this suddenly very quiet, very foreign, very warm and humid and very fragrant street. After the short flight followed by the eventful hours in the airport, this seemed unnerving. The airport I knew, this I did not.

I had to force myself to step forward, the smell of the warm air and the trees draping down to the sidewalk reinforcing my feeling that I was indeed in a new place. I walked hesitantly up the sidewalk and approached the house and wide staircase, where each tread was worn smooth, and each riser bore only a mere vestige of paint.

I stood for a moment before the door, and then as I raised my hand to rap on the frosted window, it opened.

There stood an elderly - very elderly - woman. She was small, and her back was bowed to the point that she had to turn her head to look at me. She peered at me over the top of her narrow eyeglasses and did not say anything as she slowly looked me over from head to foot.

Over her I could see into the dimly lit front parlor of this once-grand mansion. The room was faintly lit by bulbs covered by shades of various colors, set close to walls of heavily textured wallpaper. In the middle of the room was an ancient red velvet armchair within which was deeply ensconced what must have been the former master of the house. His eyes stared blankly somewhere to my right and he remained still, his arms resting on the arms of the chair. He sat deeply into that chair as if it had conformed to his lean shape so much that even each of his arms had created an indentation. The small woman put out her hand and said in a surprising strong voice,

"Hello, the customs authority called. I am Mrs. Papadopolous. Call me Mrs. P. Mr. P is unable to greet you at the moment; he is resting."

She moved her head slightly to nod in the direction of the armchair, occupied, apparently by 'Mr. P'.

I looked, discreetly, as he appeared not alive at all since

his skin was an ashen grey. But something was moving. The fingers of his right hand were twitching slightly and had scratched a hole in the fabric and were detaching tufts of white stuffing from the arm of the chair. It was tufting slightly around his fingers and some had fallen to the floor below.

I had taken this look, and then had to look away out of respect as Mr. P. proud strong, virile - at some long distant time, was this no longer, and something about his rather sad condition had me knowing that staring would have been nothing less than rude.

"Follow me young man, I will show you to your room."

She led me up the stairs and down a hall. The progress was slow, so I had time to look over the rail into the parlor below to observe the red armchair with Mr. P. facing the huge front door; a massive, carved china cabinet filled with gold-rimmed tea-cups and plates in the pattern of Old Country Roses; petite-point in oval frames, bottles set as decoration by virtue of their timelessness of shape and colour, all of this being overlooked by an almost life sized oil painting of a rather stern, though still teenaged Queen Victoria on the day of her Coronation. This had to have been a grand colonial mansion at one time.

I turned from this living diorama as the tiny matron of the house moved down the hall. At a door to a room she paused. Time had not been any better a friend to organic things of bone and muscle than it had been to the house around her. Mrs. P. probably had had no idea she would still be above ground paying taxes well into her old age for herself and for her heart-still-beating though barely breathing husband, who spent his days propped upright in that chair facing the door. She had bills to pay and no choice but to rent spare rooms in the upper floor, where the children had grown and left to some distant place, and, as I was about to discover, to a fate unknown.

She was at the door of the room but before entering, turned to face me and got to the business at hand. "Twenty dollars. Per night, my dear boy." She said this in such a matter of fact tone I was taken aback. It seemed a little steep for a room in an old house when I was paying thirty dollars for a hotel – albeit a crumbling one – in the South Beach area of Miami, but I had no choice. The customs agent was watching me, or so he said. I pulled out my money and handed her the 140 dollars.

The door was paneled, with a brass passage set, and she reached and turned the handle and swung it partway open with a screech. She wavered at the threshold and stood for a long moment. An almost imperceptible draft blew across my ankles. I might have imagined it, but given the surroundings, with the quiet that had fallen upon us standing in that doorway, this was most foreboding.

She hesitated before entering, then turned her bowed head toward me. In barely a whisper she said,

"You can have Lawrence's room," as the door swung open, "He's away for a while."

This came in a very sweet voice, cracking slightly at the words 'his' and 'room' and my thoughts turned to how long 'a while' had been.

"Lawrence?" I said, "he won't be back within the week? Are you sure? I would hate to put Lawrence out of his room."

"No, I don't think Lawrence will be needing it this week. My dear Lawrence left on some sort of adventure, back in 1952. Perhaps he kept going all the way to Africa or around the world with just the shirt on his back and hasn't made it around yet, I don't know. Regardless, I don't think he'll need his room this particular week. If that grand event should befall us, I could ask him to stay downstairs until we can move you to a different room."

The door swung open further with the screech of metal on metal. The hinges probably hadn't seen oil since the last time they had seen good old Lawrence. Mrs. P. reached inside and flicked on a light switch, then stepped aside to let me in. I stepped around her head, as it was a good ways in front of the rest of her body, and as I did she said,

"You should find everything in order and everything you need. I had Missy dust now and then, but she passed on a few years back, so there might be a smattering of lint and a few cobwebs about. No harm. A few swats with a towel, and they'll be as good as gone."

She stepped back, gesturing to the waiting room with a wave of her arm then stepped out, pulling the door closed as she went.

A wave of dread rose within me at the sound of the latch. I looked slowly around the room, filled with relics, like a museum paying homage to a lost life. Lawrence had walked the face of the earth like all of us, and left this room to face the world without a thought that as he closed the door behind him he was closing a door to a room to which he would never return. I stood there, imagining him standing in the same spot, taking a last look before taking a short trip.

It was an almost panic-inducing thought, beginning to pass the tolerance point on the creepy scale. This was not worth it. I couldn't stay in Lawrence's room, even for one night, never mind seven. Forget it. I would get my money back, go back to the airport, go to the bathroom first, for sure, and spend the night in *dat* room and wait for the next flight to Miami. I would be OK being officially deported after one night spent in 'dat room' in the Commonwealth of the Bahamas, and that would suit me just fine. Even if I had to forfeit the 140 bucks, that too would be fine. I'd chalk it up to experience and go to that bus stop and that billboard and swear aloud at the man holding the lobster on a bed of flowers that he was full of crap and *nothing* is better in the Bahamas.

I reached for the doorknob. It spun uselessly three times without retracting the bolt, so I spun it harder until finally the gears caught. I stepped back into the hall.

There, at the door, was the bowed head of Mrs. P., her eyes on me as she peered over her glasses. I was startled, but after a moment I said to her in quiet tones, as if to not let Lawrence hear,

"Ma'am... ma'am..., I think I've changed my mind. Maybe you should keep Lawrence's room for Lawrence. He's sure to be back any day. I think I will go back to the US, maybe this trip to the Bahamas was not a good idea."

She looked up at me in silence and did not reply for a long moment. The two cataract-dimmed eyes looking up at me over those vintage eyeglass frames moistened. Tears welled. A vibration came over her, then more, finally culminating in a shiver. Her mouth opened to speak but for a long pause nothing came out, until, in a barely audible 94-year-old whisper she said,

"But, my dear... but my dear young man...," her eyelids fluttered to clear the tears from her eyes,

".... you must understand, the man at the airport, that border agent, he...., he...., will still demand his half of the $140 dollars you gave me, even if you don't stay a week. I already owe him that."

What? So that was the gig. He was taking half the week's rent for sending me here. What commission was that? Fifty percent?

So that's why he and Cappy insisted on a week's stay.

This was their own tax on drug–couriers-passing-through? A creative tax they'd dreamed up for themselves?

I wanted to say to her right then that I would not expect her to have to refund the 140 dollars, and she would still be getting that, but what came to me next was the sadness of it. The sadness of desperation, of getting old and frail and dependent on others, and the sadness of this woman whom her god would not take, who left her there with a long-departed son and a husband to bury one day when he finally stopped breathing in his armchair facing the door. The sadness of life, where the descendants of the plantation owners, the ruling class in a sugar cane society, should have to take on boarders to stay in food and water, at the mercy of border guards who make profit on misfortune. The sadness of the moment, and how her lowered head seemed to fall lower and she seemed shrink even smaller, overcame me. In this darkened hall outside this room, I felt her sadness like an embrace.

My next thought was that I had no choice but to make myself at home for a week. At least I would make that border agent follow me around for a little for his seventy dollar fee.

I nodded silently as I backed slowly into the room and closed the door. I stood with the door at my back until I could hear her faint rustling footsteps recede down the hall and stairs. Before I moved, my feelings for her tempered, and with resignation I accepted, at least for the short term, that this would be my room, and I might as well make the best of it. Turning slowly from side to side, I took stock of the room, my home for the week.

Apparently, Lawrence liked cricket and was an ace in track and field too, judging from the ribbons tacked to the corkboard: red for both the 100 and 200 meters in track, and tri-color lanyards supporting medallions for 50 and 100 meter freestyle swimming. So, he was fast on the ground, and in the water. Unconsciously, my hand went to my chin and I felt respect for him for the kind of athlete these awards represented. I immediately felt a kinship as one who strived to compete at a high level, and I could understand what dedication and hard work it took to accomplish such victories. "Kudos to you, dear Lawrence, if I may be so fortunate as to count you a friend."

The top of the dresser bore various mementos and dust almost as thick. It was obvious Missy must have departed more than just a few years ago. I turned my face to the top of the dresser and blew gently, in response to which clusters of dust bunnies rolled like tumbleweeds over the edge and down to the floor. Over the back of a wooden chair near the dresser hung a folded sweater. I was hesitant to touch it at first, reluctant to handle my new compatriot's possession. It was a thick varsity sweater, with a large A on the left front, proving Lawrence had to have spent time in an American college. The size of the A meant he had to have been on at least two senior teams. This relic was prominent amongst the other relics in the room, and knowing how hard-won a sweater like this would have been, it inspired a special reverence within me.

On a bookshelf next to the dresser were a number of classic novels: Robert Louis Stevenson's *Treasure Island*, and another with gold embossed calligraphy on the spine, "*A biography of Captain Henry Morgan*" and a worn copy of "*The History of Port Royal, the Jamaican Jewel of the Caribbean.*" The most impressive and well-worn was the reference book with, "*Buried Treasures of the Caribbean Islands*" emblazoned across its leather cover. It had to be at least a hundred years old but contained no dates or records of copyrights. I flipped through this book full of sketches, rough and foreign, in what looked like quill pen, with captions describing who was purported to have hidden what, after whichever Spanish galleon was taken or recovered and my heart skipped slightly as childhood thoughts of treasure hunting and finding hidden loot had my imagination transposing me from this room to some distant past and my impressions of what a pirates life was like, right or wrong. It was clearly the oldest of the books, and the spine crackled as I opened it, such that I was afraid the dry pages would fall out. I closed it carefully and set it back where I'd found it gently out of respect for this museum piece.

I stepped to the single bed with it's depression in the middle and loose folds in the blanket. For a second I imagined that maybe Lawrence wasn't gone at all, maybe he was hiding in the closet waiting to come out and say "Boo," that he and Mrs. P were playing a prank on me and would laugh and say, "Your room is down the hall; hah hah, silly man." I looked down between my sandals at the threadbare carpet, which was red like the velvet of the armchair ensconcing Mr. P but of coarser weave, Turkish or Moroccan. I looked closely, thinking there might be crumbs there, or lint from the varsity sweater, or some other evidence this room had just been used, and thought, "Maybe *I am* just using Lawrence's room for the week, because he really is just away on vacation."

However, reality intruded and brought me crashing back as I caught my reflection in the mirror. I was wearing one of my two sets of clothes. The glass was more silver than most mirrors, and had to be almost as old as the house, possibly fashioned during the early nineteenth century, if they even had mirrors in the 1820s. I dropped my bag on the bed and opened it to retrieve my camera to take a self-portrait of the mirror's reflection. Not sure why I would need a self portrait, when each exposure on 35 mm film was so precious, but my gaunt look was unusual to me. I had lost quite a few pounds due to, well, due to….Mexico, and what Mexico can do to a stomach, and I felt a need to save the image reflected in that faded silver mirror, as if the patina of the glass was in me too. I was thin; it would be kind to say my clothes had seen fresher days, and I could've shaved that morning. But the reflection in the mirror, being that I and this old house looked to be in the same state, was as worth saving on film as any random photo of a sunset over a beach

I sat on the edge of the bed and surveyed the room once more. Then, as I am not one to believe in ghosts or be afraid of a little dust, I decided to change my attitude. Just being in such an old house was an experience. If these walls could speak, what would they say? What happened when this was a plantation house, and slaves came and went and owners came and went and prosperity came and went? Prosperity tied to the market for sugarcane. The human lives that came before me had stories to tell, and there had to be some fascinating ones amongst them. That is how one has to drive crazy thoughts from one's head, and they were crazy thoughts of ghosts, of old men who didn't speak or move, sitting almost buried in a hundred-year-old armchair guarding the front door. Haunted houses? Hah! Who said, 'damn the torpedo's?' I wish it were me, I can do this.

So…. fine. I was to spend a week, better make the best of it. First, find some water and dust the place down. Who knows what that dust contained, and whatever it was my lungs didn't need it. I found the bathroom down the hall and forced a rusted tap open. After a rush of brown water, it ran clear and appeared acceptable. Not drinkable or even toothbrush-worthy, but for wiping a few decades of dust from antique furniture, it would do just fine.

Back in the room I began to tidy up after Lawrence. Muscling open a window obviously unused for decades, I shook the blankets, the sheets, and the pillowcase vigorously in the warm breeze. If the ghost of Lawrence was in those sheets he would've needed a strong grip to stay another night. I said quietly, "Pleasant roaming brother, don't forget to write this time." Eventually I settled in, lying on top of the bedding, not up to crawling between the sheets, trying to fall asleep without inhaling.

The next morning came with the sun on my face through the eastern window. The sun, the eyes opening, the thought, 'where am I?' all in logical succession. My belongings spread before me on the dresser, then the varsity sweater over the chair, and I immediately knew where I was.

"Good Morning, Lawrence" I said to the silent room.

I opened the window again to hang my head out and get some idea of where I was. The house was surrounded by an unkempt garden and yard enclosed by a tall rock wall. In one direction I noticed buildings in the distance that stopped a half-mile or so away, so I had to assume that direction was the waterfront.

I left the house in search of something to eat since meals were not included in this 'hotel'. As I was leaving I once more had to pass Mr. P in his overstuffed chair where little by little he was reducing the stuffing as he pulled out small tufts.. He was ghostly pale, and I realized it wasn't a nervous twitch, or some obsessive compulsion, this was his sign of life. He must have had a stroke and this was now his only form of expression. It was his way of saying to Mrs. P.: "Keep feeding me; I live."

I stepped along the street, past a blue church of Greek Orthodox, past a green house with red shutters, and as walked I felt invigorated. Here was a new adventure; here was a place so foreign just 12 hours before. My senses tingled with anticipation of what lay ahead. I now had a week to study the town of Nassau and the island of New Providence, not by my choice, but now that the duration of the trip was determined by others, I might as well make the best of it.

By the end of the day I'd found a museum filled with wild Junkanoo costumes and a stone fort on the highest point of the waterfront with defunct bronze cannons pointing at the strait beyond the dock. I found the heart of the sixteenth-century town with jewelry shops and day tourists from cruise ships on Bay Street looking for duty free booze and watches being sold by island women, impeccably dressed and Miss World beautiful. I wandered around and settled in at the 'Fish Fry' one of a series of island grill restaurants with not much more in the way of furnishings than a few rickety tables and chairs, and in the way of food preparation equipment nothing more than some charcoal in a barrel cut in half lengthwise.

The fish was fresh and good and I was satisfied, full of fried food and cold beer and suddenly felt indebted to 'de Captain' for making me commit to at least seven days.

Chapter Three

THE BAR, BUDDY, AND THE PLAN

On the third day I found a rental motorcycle and made a trip around New Providence. On a narrow back road I came across a number of men walking, carrying plastic jugs. On my left the men going one way and on my right the other. Those on the right were walking with full jugs and wore happy grins while the ones on the left bore empty jugs and somber faces. I continued for a number of miles and discovered a rum distillery. I stopped to inquire and was informed that the locals could fill a plastic jug from a tap on the wall for one dollar. I soon started to look for a wayward jug to join those men on the right.

But then I decided against it since I had no helmet, no proper shoes, and was riding a motorcycle on bumpy roads, so I'd better not be too happy on practically free rum. Practically free rum goes down waaay too easy.

It was in the evening that third day of exploring New

Providence that I ventured into a local's bar. I wondered as I approached the door what adventures, or misadventures, this would lead to, considering what boarding the bus in Miami had led to. Who could know what entering this bar would mean? I stopped before entering, unsure of myself.

This little bar was plastered in rough stucco painted lime green. A wooden door hung crookedly in the middle of the wall along the bumpy road, under an equally crooked sign, "BAR," painted in crude brush strokes.

Not even a name? It was like having a child without naming it, but much more likely shortness of paint or patience on the part of the artist. I looked left and right, the pleasantness of the afternoon and the lack of any threats spoke to me, making me question why I stood there, not going in.

I stepped ahead, now thirsty for a happy hour treat of island rum. As I entered, every person present, all fifteen or twenty of them, turned to look at me. Some stared, some turned away quickly, a few smiled. I was surprised that at this time of the late afternoon the bar could be almost full, and so boisterous. The room was almost completely black, and in the far corners those who grinned were apparent only by crescents of white teeth.

I crossed to the bar itself, trying to not bump tables and chairs as my eyes adjusted to the light, then ordered a rum, neat, no ice. It arrived and I was presently surprised when the bartender said, "fifty cents, you wanna run a tab?" I smiled, yes, I can afford more than one at that price.

Two men, sitting across the width of the room from each other, were rapping. One man would sing out a string of words together to a rhythm and end it so it would rhyme, then the other would reply with an answer to the question or statement, or a comeback with a comparable insult. A voice sang out of the back corner of the bar in a lilting melody,

"Mon got no car no job no dope, he come from de hill and got no hope."

In answer the other voice would come back from across the room,

"But yo sisters so ugly she can't wear shoes, they run away in ones and twos."

It would go back and forth, and if either used a line heard before the others would shout insults at him in waves of catcalls, upon which he promptly lost his turn and another patron would rap a line. Most wanted to take a turn, and in many cases the rap was just a criticism of how bad the previous line had been, which caused the rap to be self-perpetuating, as each patron, in waiting his turn had time to come up with responses. It was unfortunate for me the language was so strange. I couldn't understand a lot of it and needed an interpreter.

I had to listen carefully and try to figure out the rap, sorry to miss the joke when after one line the entire place burst into howls of laughter for a prolonged period, and I was the only one *not* roaring with laughter. I just sat there smiling, trying not to stick out too much, hoping white-guy-at-the-bar-with-the-silly-grin was not the object of that last hilarious line. So you want to fit in? So you want to be smart and go into a local's bar at the end of the street, where a non-local probably hasn't stepped foot in years, if ever?

But the rum was cheap, and good, smooth and mellow from casks possibly brought by wooden sailing ships. Rum that lubricates and elucidates and emboldens and relaxes and spawns creativity and softens features and hides tensions and apprehensions, rum that makes stupid jokes funny and soon forgotten and pain disappear. They called it the demon, the demon rum, because only the devil or some demon could be so sweet and so bitter, so generous and so cruel, so smooth and warm and yet so cold and hard in so short a time.

As a third glass was set before me, up and down it went, and despite the fact I was beginning to feel the effects of the first two shots, I continued sipping, my justification being that it was just 50 cents a shot, and I'd never tasted such good rum for so little money. The demon rum was working through its magic phase as I was beginning to feel that these strangers were warming up to me. This thought gave me pause, as I realized I had a smile on my face for no other reason than that it felt good.

But then, despite my smile, a faintly ominous feeling washed over me that I had a lesson coming my way, but then quickly brushed aside with the help of the demon. I'd become very relaxed, and those barriers or self-protections a weary traveler creates, were falling by the wayside as if a curtain was being drawn in my brain to hide the thing called common sense.

As I gazed around the room with shiny new eyes, all was good in this strange place, all was happy, life was short, live for the moment, danger or threats or the nasty part of the dark side of human nature were miles and miles away. In my euphoria I congratulated myself because I had done it; I had entered a bar without a name on a street on an island I never been to before, and settled right in.

For one long moment this feeling lasted. But, like all of those fleeting moments of innocent bliss we occasionally have in our lives, it lasted for just a moment, and then real life came back to me.

It came in the form of a man who sat down on the bar

stool next to me, then inched it in really close, cutting short my blissfully naïve contemplation. I looked into his face, at how closely he sat to me, then I looked at my glass, trying to gauge how many more sips were left before I could set it down, turn and escape through that old wooden door, before the demon half of the rum took over.

I was unsure of my new compatriot, who looked at me for a few moments then said something while sticking out his hand for a shake. After a few fumbled attempts, - even handshakes can come in different dialects; up around the thumb, over the hand as usual for home, a finger tug, a partial finger loose handshake - it was hard to tell what he was doing, and this confirmed to us both that I was green as green gets and hadn't been on the island long enough to know how the men shook hands.

'What am I doing in this bar?' is the thought that crossed my mind. In answer I recalled it was fifty cents for a glass of good rum as opposed to the four dollars a measured shot of bad rum cost on the other side of the toll bridge on tourist-trap island. Oh, that's why.

As a consequence, here I was with this stranger beside me. I thought about what was left of the few dollars I'd brought that day, leaving the balance of my stash in the care of Lawrence's mattress. I thought about what could happen if I entered into conversation with this man. I could lose my few bucks and get beat up or, even worse, tossed into the Caribbean.

Roddy, or something, his name was, which morphed into Buddy, which he was OK with. Buddy, or whatever, he didn't seem to care. The main thing was, he wasn't about to spoil the moment by correcting me. He wanted something and I just had to wait to find out what that was.

He spoke fast, and I nodded as if I understood. I got the answers to most of his questions wrong, so he would have to ask again and again. Ultimately, I figured out that the gist of it was simple: what was I doing in that bar, on that island?

"I was waiting at a bus stop, the bus came; I got on, and here I am."

He seemed to understand me perfectly, as if the Queen's English only went one way.

"Yah mon, you da firs man ever to take de bus to da Bahamas. I gotta take de boat. I got nooooo bus ride from Miami to Nassau. But I got keys to de fas boat!"

I shook my head, "No, I took the bus to the airport, I took... I took...."

It didn't matter, really, how I got there and I realized he wasn't listening. Apparently, he felt the need to tell me everything I would need to know about life whether I wanted to hear his opinion or not, and he had this compulsion to tell me about some boat, a 'fas boat' that he kept going back to it regardless of how little interested I showed in hearing about his 'fas boat'.

"I got de boat, mon. De fas boat, mon. Big mon leave de boat for me to care for, I look after de fas boat, mon."

I nodded, "Good for you. You look after a fast boat, good," not knowing what else to say.

"I can take out de boat mon, no problem for me to take out de fas boat." I nodded as he went on. Then came the reason for his being on the barstool next to me,

"You buy de groceries, and we take out de boat."

I nodded at this too, as I had at everything else.

"We go to Eleuthera; we barbeque flamingos on de beach mon. You give me fifty dollars, and I will get two girls to go to cook de bird on de beach...among other tings dey do, hah!" He broke out in a big laugh.

After another twenty minutes of drunken knee-slapping and further explanation I got the message. He had the keys to a boat and for fifty bucks we could go to Eleuthera, to a private beach, with women and supplies for the day. Sounded like a lot of fun.

"Yeah sure, when do we go?" I said, not believing it.

"Tomorrow, mon, tomorrow we go. I tell de girls

tonight. You like dem skinny or wit some cushion?"

I was drunk and getting into the fun, so I went with it, "I don't like them too fat; they sweat too much; bring me a skinny one."

"No problem, mon, plenny skinny ones wanna ride de fas boat. Plenny. Hah! You don't like dem fat 'cause they sweat too much. Mon, you crazy. Skinny girl have no cushion for de pushin. Skinny girl hungry all de tiiiimme, mon. All de time dey wanna eat, and den we gotta kill two flamingoes, mon."

He slapped his knee, then mine. His laugh was throaty in my ear. I'd never heard of eating flamingo before, so I had to ask, "How hard is it to catch a flamingo?"

He sat back with an incredulous look, "Who knows? We don't gotta do dat, mon. Dats for dey women. Dey catch em and skin em and cook em. We just gotta make fire to get some coals, den eat. Dah women, all out on de sand, with booties popping will be dessert. Hah!"

He slapped his knee, folding at the waist with laughter only to roll back and reach toward me for one more elaborate handshake that comprised manipulations of the arm and wrist, leaving me wondering what the hell 'booties popping' was supposed to mean.

He put his hand up and spittle flew as he said, "I know two right now mon, one fat and she do what I say, mon, she always do what I say, and wit de skinny sista. You might not make her too happy, she be used to de black men, but you can try all you wan...all you wan, mon, hah!"

Every sentence ended with that same laugh and a head roll. Soon his big hug and handshake accompanied everything he said, like we'd become brothers or partners and his sweaty shoulder and arm were beginning to dampen my shirt as well.

He had the perfect plan: I pay, he drives the boat and arranges the girls, and the girls cook a flamingo or two. I could have thought what a great new brother I'd found, but there is no amount of rum, demon or otherwise, that could completely ease my suspicions.

But, I was enjoying it to some extent, and once I decided to leave and bring this comedy to a close, I began to have fun with it. No doubt, this was quite the experience.

So I continued to play gullible, even to the extent of agreeing to go with him the next morning, all the while having no real intention of doing so. We joked and laughed for a while longer, neither understanding the other all that much, until, like too much of a good thing, I was getting tired of him, and the more rum he had on my tab, the more irritating he became. I had quite the glow on and had to wrap it up, as I still had to find my way back to Mrs. P's, and uncertain of the direction.

I put my hand up to halt his narrative and the smoke he expelled with each word. He had a rude habit of taking a drag from his cigarette then talking loudly into my face. He was saying something in a singsong rap sentence, which was not making sense, and I had to make him stop. The smile that comes from rum on an empty stomach only lasts so long. Without having a cigarette I'd probably smoked the equivalent of half a pack in the time I was there; smoke which had previously been into and out of the lungs of Wally or Holley or Robby, or whatever my new best friend's name was - the guy with the shiny face and big, bucktooth, spit-gap grin, and keys to a boat, and the pirate adventure - yeah, that guy.

I had my hand up, and he smiled and stopped mid-sentence like he knew he wasn't saying anything worthwhile and might as well stop.

"Listen, Wally…" I said.

"Roddy. Rod-dee, me, I'm Roddy," he said.

"Right, sorry," I said, "It's so loud in here. Listen, I got to go, OK? Time for me to go."

"Yeah, mon, you gotta go, mon. No problem. You come back here in de morning and we take out de fas boat. But, you gotta give me de money now, so I can buy de things we need."

I looked back at him, not too surprised he was trying to hit me up for the fifty. I knew that was coming. "I don't have fifty bucks on me. I don't carry that much around. I'll give it to you tomorrow."

"No mon," he said, "We go to your hotel, and get the money now, den I can get the groceries in de morning."

I sat back and opened a little neutral space between us. I didn't think even he would consider me that stupid. I thought he had at least a little respect. Apparently not.

"No can do." I said. I'm staying at an old lady's house, and I don't want to disturb them coming and going to get the money. I will meet you here in the morning, and then we get groceries."

"No, mon, better you give me de money tonight, mon. When I show de girls de fifty, dey will get so hot dey will be ready to go right away. I know dees girls, dey smooth and sweet, dey like islan' honey but day like islan' money better. Best you give me now to show you got it, mon and not just talkin'."

I had to look away. That ain't going to happen.

I picked up my empty glass and held it in front of him, "My rum is gone. I need to go and I have a long walk ahead of me. Unless of course, you want to buy me a drink before I go, I couldn't say no to that." That was enough for him to let me leave without reminding me one more time how early it was and how we still had time to drink and be merry and talk about tomorrow.

So, with that and a number of convoluted handshakes, a couple of greasy hugs, and promises of meeting in the morning, I was out the door and into the dark.

Chapter Four

THE CABBIE AND THE CRACK DEN

I stepped into the sudden fresh air and quiet of the tropical night, and had to focus my thoughts to recall this street as I'd last seen it in the slanting sunlight and rising dust of early evening without a rum-induced glow. All that happened with Buddy in my face made it seem quite a while since I was last outside the bar.

I stood under the sign that simply said "Bar" and looked up and down the street. It was as almost as warm outside as inside the bar but the air was fresh with humidity and the scent of fresh flowers, perhaps magnolia, not sure, but certainly far from the Marlboro Red I'd been inhaling for the last while.

The street was bumpy as a goat trail and paved with cobblestones that glistened with a bluish tone in the faint light, as if polished by tires. A few parked cars lined either side of the narrow, relatively straight road. It was so quiet I suddenly felt alone, but this was not an uncomfortable feeling since being alone meant no one would ask why I was there. I had to ask myself, "How did my wanderings lead me to this street?"

Nothing was familiar, but I knew I was quite a long way from where I needed to be.

It was dark and only a series of yellow circles of light leading into the distance at each cross street could help me to decide which direction I should go. Wrong or right, I was going to follow this road. At least I was away from or Robby or Roddy or Buddy, and his promise of being a pirate for a day with booty in the form of two island girls and barbequed flamingo.

I began to walk. First destination: the circle of light at the next corner, then take it from there. I walked briskly, feeling good about the blood flowing again after prolonged sitting on the barstool, and I began to think about what Buddy said and whether I should I show up the next morning. A complete stranger, met just hours before, was offering to take me on an adventurous journey to an exotic island to party and swim and eat barbequed flamingoes on a beach, in the company of smooth-skinned native girls fat or skinny, my choice. I was not in any fit state of mind to make a decision, and at that moment it was an internal struggle influenced by the most dangerous combination of factors known to a young man, alcohol and testosterone. that same fuel that powered two hundred years of pirates marauding around these islands.

And here I was, an escapee from the frozen tundra, with a pittance to sustain me facing the promise of being, in essence, a pirate for an entire day. I would not be waving about a cutlass, or have a hook for a hand or a peg leg that made me tippy, but the prospect of being a pirate for a day was on offer. I'd come for adventure, and here it was. How could I let some moment of clarity stop me? Was I, who had come all this way, in any position to say no?

I looked back in my mind to the bar through the rose-coloured glasses of that liquid courage known as rum and recalled the dark recesses of the black corners where something unknown could have been hiding. History spoke to me, the history in the walls that hosted the pirates that had come before.

Life is nothing if it isn't short and glorious, and one thing that is definite is death, while life will always be a definite maybe.

The booze I'd consumed gave me an inner strength in equal proportions to an inner foolishness, and I said,

"Yes, I will pay for the groceries, and the girls, fat or skinny. I can have it all, and we will go cut the throats and skin and barbeque a few flamingoes on Eleuthera. I will indeed be Captain of the Pirates for a day."

I wondered if I should tell Buddy flamingoes had feathers? Skinning not required.

But, why not? Go with this smiling man, Buddy, my compatriot, and his island honeys, go for the pirate tour!

I was moving full speed ahead in an alcoholic daze. Brainpower was running low, energy high, foolishness recklessly rampant. But could anyone ever have done anything without saying yes to a proposition, to an invitation? Would there be any human endeavor or accomplishment if nothing was ever chanced, or tried?

Like the first European who stepped on these islands, when it was suggested that he should sail west and keep sailing west until maybe, *just maybe*, he reached east. Was he about to say, "Hell, no. I won't go."?

And here I was, in the land that Columbus found, home the Lucayans, with my own two-bit barely reasonable facsimile, but as close I would ever likely come to a pirate tour, ahead of me. Could I say no? I decided, yes, try it. Tomorrow.

I walked the dark street, trying to get my bearings. One foot in front of the other, by the light shining from the joints and gaps in the walls of the houses on either side. I had no real fear, or if anything, a fear of how far I still had to walk. There was nothing so far about the evening that felt threatening. To get back to my bed I had to keep following these blue-tinged cobblestones. Seven houses or so farther along, near the street, perched on a wall of rough stones, under the yellow light on the corner, two man sat quietly.

I saw them and reacted as if I was driving beyond the legal limit for alcohol. I did not want to talk to or interact with anyone at that moment, but I looked straight at them. One wore a blue-striped t-shirt and the other a white rag of a t-shirt with holes on the front. Neither one seemed to be a threat. I gave them what I thought was a confident glance, not a look of hello, nor of apprehension, but a look of acknowledgment. I turned eyes forward again, pulling back my shoulders almost unconsciously. Suddenly, I felt it, I didn't mean to do it, but somehow I could not help it. I was in their territory, late at night, a complete foreigner, in short pants, and a colourful shirt that waved a flag or like fireworks let off in a quiet night. The fireworks wrote these letters in the sky, 'I am a tourist and an easy target'.

I looked straight ahead with a smile. I was just in their local pub, the one they could not go into for lack of the fifty cents it took to buy a drink, and I had just created a lifelong pal of one of their own, some guy with keys to a boat and a few girls to go to Eleuthera with in the morning. Leave me alone boys, I have connections.

The sound of two voices came from the wall. Each repeated it. "Pussy."

They called me pussy when I passed them. They were calling me pussy to get a reaction, to instigate something. Then, clearly in my head I heard those lyrics:

"I was walkin' down the street
Concentratin' on truckin' right
I heard a dark voice beside of me
And I looked round in a state of fright

And over and over the most poignant line…

"A lonnng waaayyy from hommme."

I had to shake my head. I was suddenly in a 10CC song. I could hear it so clearly in my head, and as much as I could hear the words, I could almost see these two men hop down off the wall and start playing guitar and bongos, cradling a mike stand with dreadlocks dangling to their knees wailing out those lyrics,

"A looong way from hooooome, a long way from home… "

I grit my teeth to stop the song in my head. I kept putting one foot in front of the other, but in my head a dialog was playing:

"This is what you call me! I've come to visit your island, to take nothing away but memories and pictures. I buy your brothers drinks and pay for an adventure to an island, and this is what you call me?"

I wanted to stop and face them and say just that. But I am not an idiot; I am not that stupid. I had to take it. I was on the darkest of streets with only a couple of bucks in my pocket, and with only a vague idea of where I was. Was I to stop and challenge the two of them? Was I to say, in a friendly tone, "Where I come from, they don't call strangers foul names, pussy." Then I wondered how many extra punches would that get me.

I had a choice. I could stop and face them and take a few shots to the head or a kick in the ribs in exchange for my pride or I could walk on. But there was no saying were they would stop. They were picking the fight, and there were two of them. I would get in at best two good shots, but more likely only one, before being lambasted. Even my rum-fuddled brain could reason well enough to understand that my best course of action was to keep putting one foot in front of the other and perhaps, if need be, to run, run like hell. Fun is fun, but maybe I was crossing a line that shouldn't be crossed wandering in a dark neighborhood in a foreign place, and challenging two men in their dark neighborhood just might be that un-crossable line. Four, five, eight, ten steps. Yeah, right, lucky for them they didn't follow.

I kept walking, not quickening my pace, and they didn't follow me. I was relieved, yes, but seething inside at the insults and for not being able to retaliate, all the while knowing it was the right thing to do. The head and face and ribs were fine, not punched or bruised, the pride not so much.

At the next corner a solitary street lamp seemed to flicker under the attack of flying insects mindlessly bombarding the lens. It cast a circle of light that became my destination. The street to the left went up a jumbled road, so I decided my best bet was to keep going down toward the next light in the distance. Uphill was dark, downhill had one light and perhaps the waterfront. I knew that if I found the water and took a left, I would end up downtown. Just one landmark, like the old fort on the hill or the lights on the bridge, would be enough to guide me to the old house on West Street.

As I walked, the breeze freshened and brought with it a slight cooling of the air. I looked up at the dark sky, roiling indigo overcast with the fresh scent of rain now palpable. This unsettled weather pattern, thick with sudden squalls, had dominated the past two weeks, continuing relentlessly. Now it was returning once more with these dense, rain-soaked, purple clouds. From behind me I heard a car approaching slowly. Except for the two thugs on the wall calling me names, the people of the island seemed non-threatening, but still I wondered why this car had slowed beside me. If this was another threat, fast as I was, a car would be hard to out run. I turned to look, as it had matched my walking speed.

Surprisingly, it was a taxi. Not a real taxi, but a car with a sheet of paper on the dash with the letters T A X I scrawled in pencil. Miracles of miracles: a taxi. I nodded toward the windshield, yes, I need a taxi.

I crouched down to the open passenger side window to speak to the driver, who I thought I saw as one of those a I'd seen earlier on that narrow road leading to the rum factory. But this driver had somehow found his way there and back and was now looking to be my salvation. His glassy-eyed face wandered its way in my direction. I said,

"I need to go into town. Anywhere near the Colonial Hotel."

He looked at me from little brown pits within pools of yellow. His face was bristled with tight curls of forgotten beard on cheeks that were pimpled like blisters from uprooted candles on a chocolate cake. I could see this driver was not a sober man, but he had a car and knew the way, which was all that mattered at that moment with rain coming and me without hat or jacket.

He looked at me with a dull gaze and nodded slowly. I asked, "How much?"

He said, "What?"

"How much to take me to town?"

"OK, mon, not much. Get in, mon. We go."

I reached for the handle to make sure he wouldn't drive away without me, but I still wanted the fare settled,

"I have two dollars. You take me to within sight of the Colonial Hotel, and I'll give you two dollars. OK?"

He nodded and then reached up until his hand finally made contact with the gear shifter, which I took as my cue to get in. Two dollars, enough, negotiations complete.

I climbed into the seat next to him and sat down and down until my tailbone hit floorboard. I did not want to get into the back, as it was clearly too far from the steering wheel to administer any course correction that might be needed to prevent the sideswiping of stationary objects. He pulled the shifter into drive, and we started off, bumping through potholes that could have been avoided, awakening a chorus of complaints from rusty springs and worn shock absorbers. The bouncing seat sent jolting impulses up my spine. Searching in vain for a seat belt as we made our way down the hill, I scanned the blackness for anything I might recognize from my walk earlier that day.

A minute into our trip, out of the darkness, an arm waved us down from the side of the road. Apparently, my driver, my taxi was the only one on the island that cruised the suburban areas so, of course, driver pulled over without a glance at me, the paying customer. Did I want to share this ride? Did I want to take another passenger in my hired car? I got no opportunity to offer either approval or denial because the question wasn't asked.

I was not a local, but I understood that this is the way it's done. Ride sharing was a natural and quite sensible thing. The taxi came to a stop, the back door opened in a rush, and in flopped the new passenger, sweaty, breathing heavily, smelling pungently of sailor-on-liberty.

He yelled out at the top of his lungs from mere feet away, "Yo, mon! I'm de king of de world! I'm de president of the U S of Bahamas, mon. I got money, and I need rock. I got money, and I neeeeeed rock!"

He was as full of himself as I'd ever seen anyone, practically changing the course of the car with his bouncing in the back seat. "I got cash money, mon. I need rock, mon, and I need rock now. Take me to some rock."

Cabbie/Driver, formerly my driver, could not have forgotten about me quicker. I had ceased to exist now that "King of the World" with cash in hand had entered his cab. Here was a real fare. No dickering involved over a measly two bucks, not a Cheap Charley tourist that has to negotiate before entering. Here was a true-blue, rock-seeking, cash-in-hand fare. My yellow-eyed driver pushed the gear shifter up into P, set his left arm on the seatback behind my neck and slowly turned to face the loudmouth in the rear seat saying,

"You no king o' dis island. Show me dis cash."

The man in the back – punk being what he truly was – seemed to love the challenge and laughed hard and yelled again, even louder, "I am de king of dees islands, all o' dem, mon. I *am* de king. I got a clean straight fifty of US of A dollars on me, and you can see that right here. Right here."

With that he pulled a folded note from his pocket. The cab smelled like sweat through humidity, the dome light that the driver had turned on revealed spots of algae on the headliner of the car, and in the faint yellow light appeared, being snapped a few times for emphasis, a real-looking US fifty dollar note.

"Dis is what makes me king, dis here fifty."

The driver was convinced. He turned face front and reached for the gear shifter. With his foot on the brake, ready to move, he looked in the rearview mirror and said to his new passenger,

"Rock? You want rock? OK, we go get rock."

We jolted forward. At the next corner the car wallowed through a U-turn, back up the hill toward the bar I'd just left. I understood it would be pointless to question our sudden change of course or remind him I was still in the car. My two-buck fare had been trumped by a fifty dollar note. It was clear to me that if I wanted to chance another cab, which probably didn't exist, I could get out at the next corner or, it was my choice, I could ride along and wait my turn.

With the realization that we were headed in the direction he required, renewed energy further enlivened the loudmouth in the back seat. He would not shut up. He was blathering and singing like he'd just gotten out of prison or won the lottery. Yap, yap, yap, some incoherent nonsense even more irritating than Buddy who I'd just left in the bar. He was the king of de world. Superman.

Cabbie ignored the clamor by staying more or less focused on getting to wherever it was we were going, as if this new destination lent some clarity of mission. He was going somewhere up the hills and over the bumps and through the potholes to get this self-proclaimed king separated from his US fifty. We passed houses in the dark that in the glare of this taxi's dim headlights grew progressively more dilapidated. At one point we swerved around a rusted well-drilling rig, resting on its frame, abandoned for so long the wheels were part of the road. From houses with bars on windows, to houses without bars on windows, to houses with no glass in the windows, or doors, just rags hanging in doorways. Some of the houses were concrete block, some were rough boards where the light from inside shone through in horizontal lines. Oh, the beauty and simplicity of the islands. The emancipation of the slaves held promise but had proven no relief from poverty to a great many. The neighborhoods we were passing through were rough and getting rougher.

Ten turns, maybe less, but each turn was like a corkscrew in my gut, as I was determined to watch and remember the route up the hill in case I needed to get back down on my own. Each left or right and each fork in the road complicated the maze. In a few places trees had overgrown the road so we had to swerve to avoid overhanging branches and not hit the trunk. I glanced at Cabbie and noticed he seemed a bit more clear-eyed. He was not listening to the yammering from King Loud Mouth in the back seat, and I couldn't help but notice he had a gleam in his eye. Something was up, and he was excited about it. He reached under the seat and extracted a small bottle, a half mickey, the poor man's version of a decent bottle. When the going gets tough, the distillers knew to break the bottles into smaller, cheaper portions. He tipped the bottle back and took a long swallow that I tried not to see – better not to know at this point.

The smell of rain came through the open window seconds before it began to fall in huge drops, building steadily. Within moments the downpour was so heavy the wipers could not keep up. A flash of sheet lightning brightened the surroundings with a momentary white glare followed a second later by a mighty boom of rolling thunder that made me flinch. The windshield fogged over almost immediately, but Cabbie, on his mission, and perhaps accustomed to this, made no hint of motion to turn the defroster on to try to clear it. Not only did the wipers clear only ten percent of the rain on the outside, but the inside of the windshield was opaque. Within moments he had to stop the car, unable to see through the befogged glass. The rain pounded a chorus on the roof of the cab, and another flash of lightning stobed white light through the car. The yapping in the back seat quieted as we sat listening to the rhythm of the downpour on the roof.

It was as if the mission Cabbie and the King were on and the excitement of the night ahead were momentarily on hold as we all contemplated the drama of the storm around us. This had to be standard operating procedure for this region, as there was no expression of impatience or disappointment, or even wonder about when life could resume. It was simply: hold everything, this will pass, wait for it…wait for it…. Outside my side window I could see the street below us, now a shallow river of paper and plastic bottles and bits of Styrofoam take-out containers.

We sat quietly as the beads of sweat grew on backs, chest, and arms. Every breath we exhaled became one more bead of sweat tickling its way down underarms and chests and sides.

But then, as abruptly as it started, the rain stopped, as if someone turned off the shower prop on a movie set. Cut, can it. The water on the street however, didn't stop, nor did the flow of garbage over the cobblestones. Apparently this short respite was just long enough for back-seat-guy to straighten out, or level off the high he was on, because he sat there in the back looking straight ahead without saying a word. Good, I thought, he is quiet; I hope he stays that way.

Cabbie looked blankly at the frosted windshield. I had to reach for the controls of the fan and heater. I reached down and yanked the heater lever to the right. The cable snapped in my hand with a pop. So much for that idea. The fan however began to whirl when I turned the dial. A small pattern, like butterfly wings opening slowly cleared on the fogged windshield and the three of us crouched down to peer through these wings of clear glass. I looked at the faces of my two cab-mates, and if it weren't for the fact that I was lost, I would have laughed out loud. It was comical to see three men, one totally drunk, one semi-drunk, and one stoned and drunk, with their heads together all trying to peer through a tiny defrosted opening just above the dashboard. It was probably going to take a team effort to guide that car farther up the bumpy road, all three needed to help navigate the car past any trees, walls, cars, stumps, or whatever else might be in the way.

After a seemingly very long few minutes, the windscreen cleared enough that the stones of the road were visible ahead of the dim headlights and Cabbie started us off again. We rounded a bend at the top of the hill and finally pulled to a stop facing a distant memory of a house, without lights, paint, eaves, or shutters. Close observation of the window openings of this wreck revealed faint light that gradually brightened, as if someone had noticed our approach and adjusted a lamp in greeting.

The house appeared to once have been blue and white or grey, but now was somewhere in between, without glass or shutters in any of the openings in the wall, or a proper front door. As my two cab-mates reached for door handles, I asked, "So what are we doing? We were going back to town."

Cabbie had lost all awareness of me and had to think about what this stranger was saying to him. It was as if he heard a ghost voice from the front seat, and he had to reconcile mysterious thoughts to put it all back into context. He looked at me as if for the first time and said, "You wait. You wait here, mon. We go inna de house and be right back."

"What? How long?"

He kept reaching for the door handle.

I said, "We had a deal," as the door swung open, "Two bucks to take me to town."

The door closed with a thump. I watched, suddenly alone and silent as they departed, leaving me in this beat up car that was blending into the neighborhood as naturally as garbage blends into a landfill. There they went, my cabbie and his preferred customer, making their way up a broken sidewalk to a house with an opening where a front door should have been, and all I could do was sit and wonder what was next.

I sat still and my breath started the windows fogging over once again now that there was no fan to keep the butterfly open. I was uncomfortably aware of how strange this evening had become as I sat waiting in that rusty cab at the top of this unknown hill in the complete darkness.

The windows fogged over completely within a minute, and I was enveloped, unable to see out. I sighed, took a deep breath, and resigned myself to waiting as patiently as I could. But I waited, and waited some more. I waited as calmly as I could. After several more long minutes I thought I saw the shape of a person passing between the car and the dim light of the doorway of the house. Then another ghostly shape morphed out of the blackness. There appeared to be at least two, maybe three men around the car.

I reached across to the driver side door and pressed down the lock button, then locked the rear doors as well. The shapes against the diffused light kept circling. They might have noticed that I locked the doors, and this might what have set off what I had avoided earlier with the two men sitting on the wall: the chase instinct. Within a few seconds a sharp rap on the window to my left startled me. I flinched at the sound and turned to look. It came again, this time harder and louder. It was the end of piece of pipe tapping against the window. I reached up with my arm and rubbed the steamy window, clearing a spot in the mist that was as long as my forearm. As I lowered my arm, an unsmiling face appeared in the opening – not my Robby/Roddy/Buddy pal/confidant, nor any island welcoming party, just big, mean, and stupid ugly.

The eyes focused on me, and I suddenly felt very alone. A shout came from the pug-like face,

"Hey!" The pipe tapped the window again.

"Hey!" he shouted again. Then louder, closer to the window,

"You got a lead pipe in dere?"

I heard it but didn't understand. He shouted again, and this time he rapped the side of the car with the pipe, harder than on the glass. "I said: you got a lead pipe in dere??" I looked at the face and shook my head, "No." I wanted to say more, to say something more in line with what I was thinking, something like, "Why in the hell would I need a lead pipe?" but "no" was all I could muster. He pressed his face closer to the window, as if I was a zoo animal, and from his bearded face another shouted question: "Well den, what you going to defend yourself wit?"

Oh, so that's what he's getting at. Did I have a lead pipe like his.

I didn't know what to say. I was alone in a taxi, waiting for a drug deal to go down so my drunk and soon-to-be-stoned driver could take his newly rich but soon to be poorer but happily-wasted-on-rock second passenger somewhere else. I had no lead pipe, or copper pipe, or even a crack pipe. I had nothing but my sorely-tried and getting slower by the minute wits with which to defend myself. How do I tell him that? The face in the window was becoming agitated. He had the decision to make. He had to break the window or back away.

He seemed to realize that I was unarmed, but just as he was winding up to hit the window with the pipe I heard a voice shouting,

"Hey!! Leave de white boy alone. He got nuttin for you and don' be breakin' my car."

It was Driver/Cabbie, car owner and part time taxi driver/drug buyer. Big Face in window was ugly and mean, but one thing about the islands, if an elder speaks, you listen. Big Face backed away. The arm-length spot on the window immediately began fogging up again, but I had absolutely no desire to wipe it clear again.

Then the door handle on the driver side rattled, and knuckles rapped on the window. Reluctantly, I reached up to wipe it clear. This time it was glassy-eyed Cabbie, and I was relieved to the point of letting go a deep breath. He waved his hand, "Come on, you comin' wi' me, not safe for you out here."

Not a bad idea. The cab was putrid with the essence of anxiety. I needed to get out and opened the door to a rush of fresh air. The air was cooler and infused with negative ions from the lightning, a welcome relief from the stuffiness of the malodorous old car.

He stepped forward ahead of me, and I could just follow his darkened shape up a path of broken concrete. We passed around the cloth hanging in the doorway into an almost bare room, where there were just one rotting sofa and matching chair and a spindle from a roll of electrical cable, which acted as a coffee table upon which sat a battered kerosene lamp flickering weakly. The walls were covered with chipping plaster, falling off in flakes to reveal a series of colours that might have been festive and quite 'island' at one time, but now were just flaking paint on the walls of a woebegone crack house. There were two doors in the room, other than the front door, one of which seemed to lead to a bedroom and another to what would have been the kitchen. A dark hallway led away from the left corner to a rear entry.

Cabbie gestured me to sit, which I did as an eerie feeling crept up my spine as the tattered sofa depressed about me. I set my hands on my knees and tried to do what bugs do when a light comes on and reveals them on a white floor: don't move, maybe no one will see me if I don't move. King sprawled at the other end of the sofa, and Cabbie stumbled about the room. He stopped at the doorway on the right and said unintelligible things to someone for a long moment, gesturing, smiling, becoming animated. He called the person by a name that might have been Barbra, or Babba, or something similar, but with his accent it sounded like Bubba to me, and I thought a man named Bubba would appear. After a minute Cabbie stepped back into the room and moved to the sofa between King and me. He sat down between us and, as he did, an enormous woman clad in a Hawaiian muu-muu of circus-tent proportions entered the room.

She was only slightly taller than she was round, and she was plenty tall. Pendulous breasts swung low, too visible for my liking, swaying independently and randomly from each other beneath the thin fabric. Her button nose and downturned mouth perched over brown marshmallows that were her chin and neck and appeared to have been inflated by a tire pump. Her body had the shape of a pile of inner tubes covered with a tarp and her hair looked like a bundle of black steel wool.

I'd never seen such a specimen. She shuffled to the middle of the room to the armchair, and turned to back in like a concrete truck preparing to unload, turning her head slightly to ensure her co-ordinates were correct before starting the downward shift of her weight. As she bent at the waist, two huge mounds of gluteus maximus billowed against the draping cloth of her muu-muu and it looked like a baby elephant was butting his head, trying to escape the circus tent. She tilted forward and leaned back until gravity took control and this mass of humanity fell into the armchair with a great whummmpphh of air expelled forcefully from protesting stuffing and a cloud of dust jetted away like shooting stars through the dim light of the lamp. Upon settling she exhaled a deep breath then turned her attention to the two men with a sly smile and a mischievous look that said, without words,

"See what momma has for you, boys?"

She lay opened her puffy palms on the arms of the chair to reveal the goodies they'd come for. One hand held a now empty cigarette pack, in one corner of which a small piece of aluminum foil was fitted over a cut-out square. The foil had been placed into the space to form a depression and holes had been poked through the foil with a needle. In the opposite corner an equal-sized hole had been cut, but without any perforated foil covering it. In her other hand was a small plastic baggy which contained the reason for our visit to this house, three sizable chunks of rock cocaine.

I looked at the two men I'd arrived with, both now completely entranced at the sight of the paraphernalia and the white lumps of rock cocaine. Neither seemed even to be breathing. At that moment I could have, not evenly deftly, and without the assistance of the aforementioned lead pipe, lifted the car keys, their wallets, watches, shoes and maybe even their socks, if I was so inclined, so enthralled were these two in the contents of that little plastic bag.

The big woman, Bubba, picked the largest rock from the bag and placed it on the foil in the corner of the box. She then set the bag down, reached into the top of her muu-muu – could anything have a more fitting description? – and extracted a small lighter. She sparked it and placed her mouth against the square hole in the side of the box. As she drew air through the hole in the box, a long flame whisked over the rock of cocaine, and it crackled as it vaporized down into pure white smoke. This smoke she drew through the box into her lungs. She closed her eyes tight and sat back as she swung her arm, box in hand, toward King sitting nearest her. He greedily accepted it but had to pry the lighter from her fingers. They were latched tight shut, and she was completely unaware of it.

King repeated her movements, setting a rock on the foil, lighting it, and inhaling a long draw of white smoke. The hissing died slowly and he shut off the flame. Then, as with Bubba, he closed his eyes and sat back. Cabbie greedily pawed at King's closed hands to unlatch his fingers and snatched up the lighter and baggie. In his haste the last rock, from within its little bed of crumpled baggie, tumbled out to fall into a fold of the King's pants directly between his legs. Cabbie suddenly became completely aware, having watched his rock fall into that usually forbidden space directly between King's legs. He scoffed aloud and said something like ' n------bastard' and without a second thought began to dig violently in King's crotch to retrieve the wayward rock. King didn't move, apparently not even noticing the scrabbling that was taking place in such close proximity to his genitals, or if he did, he didn't care. After a moment Driver/Cabbie extracted his hand and held something up to the flickering light to inspect it, or perhaps to ensure it was not just some dead bug he'd found. Satisfied he had indeed found the small crystal of cocaine, he repeated the procedure of torching the cocaine and within 30 seconds he too sat back with eyes closed.

The three were as silent as three marble statues - capable of sweating, until finally, after displaying the endurance an Olympian swimmer would have been proud of, with a great whoosh like that of a breaching whale, a dense white stream of smoke was expelled through Bubba's lips. With that her shoulders, face and even her inner-tube neck seemed to relax fully, and whatever little human shape she had before now diminished. She became one with the chair. Neither she, Bubba, nor it, the chair, had more consciousness or humanity than the other at that moment. Eventually her eyes opened slightly to stare vacantly upward.

King was next to let go his gaseous breath of white smoke, and once again a bluish-white stream jetted into the space over the kerosene lamp. A second later it was Cabbie's turn to breathe, and once again the aaaaahhhh, as smoke streamed from his mouth and nose. I turned to face him as his eyes opened. What I saw was the definition of freaky, an overused term, but perfectly suited. The whites of his eyes, around the brown centers had turned as blood red as burgundy wine. The whites were gone. I looked twice, in disbelief, but they were indeed blood red. The room was deathly quiet. The tattered cloth hanging in place of a front door blew gently inward from the street, the lamp flickered, and over the next few long minutes the only things moving were the beads of sweat that trickled down the cheeks and over the rolls of neck of the great Bubba.

I was pretty much sober by now, and had plenty of

time to wonder: now what? A million thoughts flew threw my brain. How do I get back? Maybe the rain has stopped for the night. I *hope* the rain has stopped for the night. I have to get past Big Face, man with lead pipe, in the dark, probably lurking like a shark in the reeds. Maybe I could rummage for the car keys in Cabbie's pockets and steal the car. I could leave it somewhere and he would probably think he left it there himself. Maybe I could stay for a while, or maybe I can just smack him one and tell him to drive me the hell out of here. Not one good option among the lot.

But youth has a bold face and when you don't know what to be afraid of, you're not afraid of much. I had to convince myself things would end just fine, somehow. I thought back to earlier that day, when I was full of anticipation to explore the island for another day. I was not afraid of anything when I was leaving Lawrence's room. The rum I'd consumed had flushed through my system, and I was seeing clearly. I was in a crack den, on one of the higher points on an island I'd never been to before, inside a house with no doors, little light, at the end of torturous route in the company of three strange characters, who were, incidentally, totally fried by cocaine that had not yet been cut or stepped on by any dealers in Miami.

What should I be worried about? Take a deep breath. Relax. Try to think clearly. Calm down and think clearly. Taking a deep breath in this room was not easy, though, as the air was becoming stagnant. The breeze that had followed the rain had abated, and fresh air no longer blew in the doorway. I had to do something soon. I think I could smell something funky, like cheese, and worried it was Bubba and the cheese was within every fold in her corpulent body. She'd seemed to melt like a chocolate lava cake in the armchair she crushed beneath her and was still not moving, still sat slack-jawed, staring dully into space through red half closed eyes, seeing nothing.

Once that repugnant odor became apparent, whether or not it was cheese or Bubba or mould or just my imagination, it became repulsive. All the smells of this old house were becoming mightily offensive. It might have only been five or six minutes since the rock was blazed, but I was growing more than impatient, I had to move, and perhaps it was the fungus or my impatience, but I had to get out. NOW! I shifted hard to my right, to shoulder check Cabbie. His head wobbled and then dipped. His eyes fluttered so I bumped him again, harder. Once again his eyes fluttered. I turned from my place next to him and got my face in front of his and reached over and grasped his moist arm.

"Hey! Hey!"

He turned toward the sound.

"Hey, come on, let's go. You drive me down that hill."

Slack-jawed, dazed, confused, in a word, stoned, he heard me but did not comprehend. I repeated, this time louder, to take control of the situation. "Hey man, wake up! We gotta go down the hill, into town."

I couldn't be sure he understood, but for some reason he knew how to take an order. I have no idea what he was thinking, or how my voice or manner impressed upon him that *he had to do* as told, but his eyes opened wide and he looked me straight in the face. His white whiskers and stubble contrasted with the redness in his eyes which I could see was beginning to dissipate. They were still red, but not blood red. I had to get him up, if for no other reason than to get him to the car to escort me past a lead pipe. From there I might be able to take the keys and drive myself down the hill. Big Face/Lead Pipe hopefully wouldn't bother me if I had this island elder with me. But the keys were in his pocket and I would have to get him standing to get them. I wriggled laboriously out of the deep recesses of that worn sofa and stood before him.

I looked at Bubba, that mound of flesh draped in a soiled and sweat-stained tent. She was as gone as a human could be gone without being dead. On the long departed midnight train called the Uncut Columbian Express. Melted, done, her body shutting down along with a large part of her brain, or at least the part of her brain that involved consciousness.

"Now this is a scene I will never forget," I said this aloud as I might as well have, as no-one else would hear. Everyone else present was in la-la land and saying it would mean I would remember it forever and be able to recall it one day, some day, when I am safe and far away, if that should happen, and I should be so lucky as to get out of this situation.

I turned back to Cabbie and said, straight into his face, "Come on. Come on! You can do it; stand up with me."

I reached under his arms to lift him to a standing position. This defined disgusting. I cringed at the feel of it. Cold. Clammy. Old-unwashed-stranger's armpits on my hands. I never liked handling fish right out of the lake, Northern Pike covered in slime, and this brought back that old repulsion. He might not have bathed in weeks and reaching under his arms to hoist him to a standing position was like dipping my hands into a barrel of fish guts that had been in the sun for a week. But I had no choice, I had to get him to his feet. I was slightly consoled by the thought that at least I wasn't trying to try hoist the blob that was Bubba. That would be a quantum leap of disgusting beyond this. I lifted him to a standing position, and perhaps my thumbs jamming into his armpits is what roused him, but his body did follow that pain and he did rise to stand on wobbly legs. Once I had stopped his tottering back and forth and his head steadied somewhat, he seemed to revive, and once I had him on even keel I removed my thumbs from his armpits.

I took him by both shoulders to look into his face. "We have to go." Nodding in the direction of the lump formerly known as King, I said, "That guy is not coming. You and I are going down that hill. Understand?"

He didn't understand, and his knees still wanted to buckle. I gripped his bony shoulders and shook him, which seemed to have some effect. I shook him harder, until his head wobbled back and forth like a bobble-head doll. This irritated him, messing with his high, and at the third rattle he looked back at me and said, "Schtop Pit." The 'pit' came with flecks of saliva I had to dodge, but I had him awake, a little, or at least somewhat closer to conscious. I could see the timeline before me: this wouldn't be a fast process, but it was the only process and I had to keep it moving. I put my arm around his shoulder and got him to shuffle his feet, his head downward, mimicking my feet and following my steps – little short steps they were – toward the door. By tilting him forward ever so slightly I got him to take steps, and within a dozen tup, tup, tup, tup, scuffles of well-worn shoes, his feet were once again at the threshold of the curtained entry.

I reached up to pull back the curtain and could not help but look back at the other two, Bubba and King, still immobile and practically melted into the furniture like wax museum artwork on a really hot day. The lamplight flickered across the expressionless face of Bubba; beads of perspiration dotted her forehead and the puffy roll of her neck looked like a pillow for her face. King slouched back, a grin painted on his face with eyes half-open, staring vacantly at the mildewed ceiling. I didn't like him, and felt like slapping him once, real hard, for hijacking my cab. But it would've been like hitting a defenseless child. Had I been a different person I could have relieved whoever now had that famous US fifty but he would have already given it to Bubba, and she might have hidden it in one of her folds of lard, where a million fifties would be as safe as if in Fort Knox. Bubba was out, enjoying something I'd never know, and more than likely she wouldn't remember.

I had to get out of there but if I let go of Cabbie's shoulder he would have dropped like the other two, and that just wouldn't do. I shuffled him under the curtain and to the broken walkway, slowly down each of those four small steps.

Now, getting a stoned person to step down is quite the trick in manipulation of dumb legs. A person needs three hands for that task and, by the way, pushing with your knee doesn't help because they fall forward – hard – as I soon found out. But I learn quickly and once I had him back on his feet and his feet taking enough of his own weight, we began to move. The thump of his forehead on concrete seemed to straighten him out a little, and soon he was looking at me with some semblance of clarity.

Finally, I thought.

Now it would be a matter of a little more time and movement, and no more falling, as concussions would not be helping my cause.

I nudged one foot at a time all the way to the fender of his car. His head snapped back when his backside hit metal and he turned to me as if questioning. I looked into his eyes, and wanted to say sorry for his having fallen like a tree in the forest, but since he probably wouldn't remember I skipped the apology and instead pleaded with him,

"Look... Look at me! OK? Give me your keys."

His head drooped, so I shook him, hard, again.

This time, as if he had woken from a deep sleep his head snapped up.

"Don't start that again," he said.

He didn't like me shaking him, and I wasn't sure if it was the pain my thumbs caused his armpits or the tumble he took, but suddenly, like flipping a switch, he roused to attention. His voice was slurred, but his eyes focused in and out on everything around him and eventually on me.

"What? What? Schtop shakin' me," he said and made a move to step away.

I said, "Wait, we have to drive down the hill. Give me the keys. I can drive. You tell me how to get to town. Understand? Understand me?"

He shook his head. "No, you are not drifin'... drifin' my... car!"

I said, "Listen to me, you can't drive. I can do it."

He was becoming more aware, "No, you... not drivin' my car."

I reached for his arm, but he pulled it away. I stopped, thinking about Big Face, whose presence I could almost feel out there in the darkness. I had to get the hell out of there somehow. Getting into the car with Cabbie in that state was a risky proposition, but stealing his keys and tripping him to allow a getaway, or just pissing him off to so he left me to Big Face was not a good option either.

"OK, you drive, but let's go now!"

"O... K... We go now," he said.

We finally were able to get into the car after he repeatedly stabbed the key at the deceptively tiny hole of the door lock. Behind the wheel he shook his head vigorously, once, twice, then found the shifter and set the car into reverse.

Then, just like I knew it would, as I cringed and stiffened my shoulders, with a fierce thump the car hit something. This did not concern Cabbie at all. He simply, for some mysterious reason, as there wasn't another car for blocks, put his right turn signal on and pulled the shifter to D. I have no idea what we hit – I didn't even want to look – but I was hoping, just a bit, that it was a big ugly man carrying a lead pipe.

We began meandering down the hill on that windy route over the bumpy stone road, and I began to compute the distance. Each second of driving was worth about ten steps in possibly the wrong direction, had I been walking. Each time we made a corner, each parked car we passed without sideswiping it, each tree we passed without a collision, was just that much less walking.

He seemed to know the route well, and we crawled along at five miles per hour or less, barely moving at times.

We made at least five corners on the rough streets, and I knew I wouldn't have chosen these corners, and I also knew I'd made the right choice in forcing him to drive rather than attempting to find the route on foot.

Suddenly he said, "We need gas."

"OK. Is anything open?"

"Yah, mon, my brudder."

He drove on, very slowly, and made a few more turns until we reached a street where a small kiosk about six feet wide with an upturned front outside a clapboard house appeared in the glare of the headlights. Before the little shack stood an antique gas pump listing dangerously northward. We slowed incrementally, barely moving, until finally stopping some 50 feet short of the pump.

"What now?" I asked.

"What?" he said.

I asked, "Why did we stop?"

He looked at me, still glazed over, "We need gas."

He said this with a slur like he'd just had a root canal and his lips were frozen. His eyes were still wandering, watery brown blots in red pits. A man had come out of the house with a kerosene lantern and made his way to the kiosk. He climbed onto a stool behind the counter of the small shed and set the lantern beside him. He was looking at us in the car, stopped, engine off, dim headlights on, at least fifty feet short of the little kiosk he'd set up to sell gas.

I shook my head, and looked at Cabbie, staring forward. After a moment of this his face turned back to me and his eyes rolled about, as if I wasn't there. Then his head slumped against the steering wheel. He had fallen asleep. I was about ready to give up.

"You... wake up. Wake up!"

I took hold of his bony shoulder and pinched hard under the collar bone, right down to the nerve, but this time I couldn't wake him. I let go. It was no use.

I got out of the car, reached into my sock, pulled out

two dollars and tossed them onto the seat.

"There you go, thanks for the ride."

I walked to the kiosk where his brother sat on a stool with his elbows on the plywood counter. There was a kerosene lamp on his left, six bottles of amber gasoline on his right, and the rusted gas pump up front. Moths beat themselves against the glass, their wings fluttering in muffled thumps in the silence of the night. I looked at the man then back at the taxi where Cabbie sat, his dozing head a curly white ball against the top of the steering wheel. His brother didn't seem surprised that the taxi was stopped fifty feet from his clapboard gas station. He didn't even bother to follow my gaze.

I asked, "How do I find the Colonial hotel?"

He lifted an arm, crooked a finger, pointed down the dark road, and said, very slowly, "Yeah, mon. Go down dat way, pass de tree dere on de cornah. Go right, mon. Den go down to de watah. Can't go no furder. Go right again den keep going, mon, all de way."

I looked at him for a long second half expecting more instructions, incredulous that those three simple statements could take two minutes to provide.

No, he wasn't adding anything more; that was it.

I nodded to him, said thanks, and started walking. Before I got 10 steps away, he started again, this time to my back as I walked. I stopped but didn't turn back to him. He said, in that lilting island rhythm,

"When you get to de big church, with a beeeg steeple, you know, and de gate and de graveyard on de side, turn around, mon, you lost and be goin' de wrong way, mon."

"What???

I slowly shook my head and resumed walking. After about fifty steps I had a *did that just happen* moment. I hoped I was now finally out of this strange misadventure but I had to pause and think back to confirm, and cement in my mind, that what had happened over the past two hours had actually happened. I stopped walking and turned full circle to survey the scene and take a portrait of an extremely strange night: white whiskered Cabbie was at the wheel, his head down, the car in the faint light still fifty feet back of the kiosk, headlights dying and now just two faint points of light under the branches of a banyan tree; brother sitting with left side and face illuminated by the dim light of a lamp in his little clapboard box with the front lid propped open, sitting silent on a stool, ignoring the moths, waiting for a customer, or for his brother to awaken and move close enough to get gas from the rusted pump or a bottle or two. The sounds and sights of the tropical night painting a portrait on my consciousness: moths aflutter, toads croaking in the fresh pools of water, remnants of the downpour, crickets chirping and whistling from the shrubs lining the blue cobblestone road. I took in the scene as if absorbing a work of island art, let go a heavy breath, nodded once to confirm in my own mind what I'd seen, then turned to follow his directions to my bed for the night.

It was 3:30 a.m. before I found the house, and passed through the rusty gates, exhausted to the bone from walking for ninety minutes on a route that should have taken twenty had I known the way and not walked astray a number of times. I never did see the church, or the graveyard, that brother of driver was just as sneaky as Driver himself. I placed my feet carefully on each tread as I climbed the front steps leading to the verandah, trying to muffle the sound of my step on the wooden stairs.

At the door I hesitated, praying silently for a moment for the handle to turn under my hand and the door to open. I reached for it and turned it ever so slowly as I whispered, *"Please open."*

Despite the rusted old parts, it turned in my hand. I let out a sigh of relief, looked skyward, and breathed a silent thank you. The door was unlocked. Either Mrs. P. forgot to lock it, left if for me, or this house had such a reputation for being haunted locks were not required. Whatever it was, I was thankful for it.

I stepped inside and eased the door slowly closed behind me, hoping to prevent the loud squeal of the hinges. I turned to face Mr. P's overstuffed armchair, almost expecting to see him there, staring ahead resolutely, somehow keeping his head up and scratching away at the armrest, but in the darkness I couldn't see if he was there, and I was relieved I wouldn't know if he spent his nights as well as his days in that chair. I crossed the room looking only straight ahead, not wanting to know, and reached the staircase in silence.

I trod carefully on each stair, trying to remember where each one squeaked, but I must have remembered the order wrong, because I think I hit every loose board on the way as each footfall brought a high pitched squeal that seemed to rip into the living room and foyer below and the faded portrait of Queen Victoria. I had not snuck home like this since I was a teenager, yet here I was again, sneaking into a house and hoping not to get caught and have to explain where I'd been and what I'd been doing. It would have been a pretty long and hairy explanation, and sleep was beckoning. At the top step, just as I turned toward the bedroom, I heard a distinct metallic click, quite loud, and not unfamiliar, followed by another, slightly louder, again metallic.

What? What was that?

It came from the foyer below, and I realized it was the sound of the deadbolt turning in the front door. So Mrs. P, or someone, -- it couldn't be Mr. P, could it? – had come to lock the front door behind me. I took a step back and looked over the railing to the front room below just in time to see a white-shrouded figure, hunched over due to a curving spine, in her nightgown no less, gray hair hanging down and loose around her face, gliding by on slippered feet below me. It was impossible for her to look up at me, but she didn't need to. She was on her way to the back of the house, and in her right hand, almost as long as she was tall, was an enormous 12 gauge, double-barrel shotgun. The second click would have been her uncocking one of the two barrels.

This was just one more strange event on this long and strange night, this sight of the ancient Mrs. P below me, shotgun in hand. I felt terrible for keeping her up that late before I felt relieved I'd passed the test and her eyes were still good enough to recognize me at 3:30 in the morning. I couldn't help but wonder how close I'd come to being blown through the front door by a 12-gauge shotgun.

"What the hell…. next?" was all I could whisper as I made my way across the hall, to Lawrence's room, to fall upon the single bed, too exhausted to remove my clothes.

I was in a swirling vortex, the prospect of daylight coming again; slim to none. Shapes came out of the dark and I had to duck so they would fly over my head, white zombies and bulbous creatures. I tried to run but my legs wouldn't move. I struggled and was frustrated and then shocked to find that I had both legs in one pants leg. I must have tried to dress too fast and somehow put both legs in one leg. The pants leg not in use was flapping wildly as I tied to shake my legs out of the trap my legs were in. I was being smothered and desperate for air, something choking me. I was sweating, overheated, and the sweat began streaming off my skin. My room was flooding with my sweat, threatening to drown me in rivers of sweat. I wanted to scream but my voice was muted, and my throat could only muster a whisper like the yowl of an old cat. Oh, God. NO! I could not move or scream, or save myself from drowning in a river of my own sweat. I thrashed to get away, until my elbow struck hard against something on my right side, the pain startling me awake. I was in a stifling hot room, full of dust while fully clothed on a bed with a blanket wrapped around my legs.

I realized it was a nightmare. It was not real. I was alive. What a relief.

But my clothes were sticking to my body, I had to get them off. I quickly stripped down and noticed a multitude of welts that could only be attributed to bugs. I looked at each for a long second as if each were a personal assault on my sleeping body, and how long these bites would persist as welts, as they were not at all pretty.

For a long minute I stood beside the bed before realizing where I was. The long walk at the end of a long day of walking, followed by the rum and the 'events' of the previous evening had me thoroughly exhausted and when I fell asleep it was into a very deep sleep. The stifling, or lack of air, the dust, the uncomfortable bed, the lack of proper food, and the overheating had created a major nightmare. After all that had come before on this day and night, even just standing was tiring, so I sat down on the edge of the bed to think. It had been twelve weeks since I'd seen a familiar face, and I had tempted fate on quite a few levels the previous night.

But, just then, I thought I heard someone calling my name.

To have a familiar voice call your name when you are so far from home is, what as known as, a big deal. But again, was there really someone calling my name? Over and over?

My head was pounding, I itched all over, my clothes were wet, it was barely light outside, and my feet still had not forgiven me for walking in bad shoes for ten hours the day and most of the night before. I held my head between my hands, squeezing the temples to stop the pounding of the headache. Your brain will tell you when it needs water by pounding on the inside of your skull to get your attention. I was being told, 'You must drink water, good clean water.' When you are asking brainy to work hard, like find your way home in the dark in some place you've never been before, water is an imperative and not trusting the quality of the water most readily available is not a good thing. "Punish me if you like," I told my brain, "but don't tell me someone is calling me this morning, before the sun has even risen, after a short night of sweaty nightmares."

I lay back down, telling my brain to ignore the voice calling my name. But it sounded like my brother. It really did. I thought, "What is he doing outside my room? How did he find me? Did I tell someone I was staying in this house?" He was calling to me, over and over. What? It sure sounded like a voice was saying,

"Tah… Tah…. Tha…   Tha…. Tha… Tha…."

I couldn't ignore it, could I? I was the last person to ignore someone calling my name who might just leave without finding me. Forever we would end up talking about how we just missed each other that morning in the Bahamas.

I got up, no longer able to doubt what I thought I heard or wait a second longer. I ran to the window and pulled the cord of the blinds. A tornado of dust hit me square in the face, clouding off the slats of those blinds like it had come alive. I unlatched the window and swung it wide open, hmmm, I thought, just like, just like dear old Lawrence might have done so many years ago, calling out to his pals beckoning to him to come play cricket or ride a horse or meet some girls at the beach. Thoughts occurred to me about the spirit of the youth who became man in that room before me and spawned vivid images in my head of him here with me and I here with him in this room. I stuck my head out the window as he would have done so many years before to answer the call of his mates or his brother, or his secret girlfriend being mischievous and wanting in at some dark hour of the night.

The morning air was fresh after the storm the night before, like fragrant steam rising from a tasty bowl of something sweet and hot and wonderful in contrast to the staleness of the room behind me. The scent of the ocean also hit me with almost the power of the rock cocaine hitting the three zombies on the worn sofa the night before. But this high could be topped if I could find that person trying so hard to wake me by calling my name over and over. It was really something that someone would have come this far to find me. Wow! I was blessed. I heard it again, "Tah...Tah... Tah... "

I stuck my head out farther, scanning back and forth across the yard and empty garden as the voice kept calling to me. This was very strange.

"Why is he always calling my name three times?"

Finally I spotted the source of the call: a seagull, a white and gray scavenger of the sky, a flying rat, and it was calling my name - stupid bloody seagull. I thought the seagull was calling my name. I thought the voice of the seagull was that of my brother.

I thought, "Now, what does that mean?" I went back to the bed and sat down realizing it only takes imagining that one seagull is calling your name to make you think you might be spending a little too much time alone. But seagulls really aren't that stupid after all. They *can* call your name if your name is simple enough and your brain is addled enough by lack of sleep and a hangover. Sure, sure, but let's see a seagull call Oscar Philippe Hernandez. Maybe an English/Mexican hybrid seagull could pull it off.

I could conclude nothing else than it might be time to turn around and head home. Yes, time to go home. I would use the last of my funds to begin to find my way back. I would end this trip when my seven-days-served-in-the-community sentence was done. From this point forward the journey would continue, but in the direction of home.

I removed my sweat-damp shirt and put on my other shirt. I lay down calculating that I'd had about 4 hours sleep since first hitting that dusty bed. However, going back to sleep, after the interruption caused by strange thoughts, was not going to happen. I consoled myself with the thought that the benefit of not sleeping is more awake time to experience life. An army programmed to operate 20 hours a day will always win over an army running at 16 hours a day. This idea definitely justified getting out of bed. Then the thought occurred to me that I'd kept Mrs. P. up until at least 3:30 a.m. the night before, sitting shotgun on knee, staring at the front door waiting for my return. I'd better not wake her now. She had to be tired this morning, since she could not indefinitely maintain a vigil against any young punk-come-rapper attempting to make a name for himself by being the one who finally had the nerve to rob the stately old home. I had to wonder, did Mrs. P. sit Mr. P. there facing the front door as a human motion sensor and, if so, how could he alert anyone?

These musings convinced me that I was now fully awake. My brain, regardless of the lack of proper sleep, was working, and I was in traveler mode. Yes! This was the essence and reason why I was travelling: to get to this maximum capacity of thinking and experiencing. All systems go. All cells in the brain being used and new neural pathways being created at a pace outstripping those lost to poisonous substances like alcohol and the fumes created by the three addicts of the night before, Cabbie, King, and Bubba, who exhaled noxious smoke I couldn't avoid inhaling. *Damn drugs, they can sure mess with you.*

My fingernails felt like they were too long. I was carving one against the other in an attempt to shorten them. It was very early in the morning, and I was digging at my fingernails, too nervous to sleep. I couldn't move either, lest I wake Mrs. P. I wanted to let her sleep, but I could hardly bear to sit still. The rock had to have had some effect, or maybe it was just the travelling.

Was travelling just another drug? Did the new brain pathways you had to create go through some area of the brain that releases some chemical like a drug? Endorphin? Was that what I was feeling? I was in full thinking/discovery mode, and from somewhere deep inside I realized I liked it immensely. I really, really liked it. It is tiring, often exhausting, but it is pure fun.

Life is all about ups and downs, and I was fully alive when going through these ups and downs, never knowing how high the highs or how low the lows would be, not knowing what would be the outcome of any day or even of any hour, not knowing if the day was going to be victory or a tragic loss; or how to win until the time, the situation, the challenge to succeed or to escape presented itself. Some do skydiving, some do rock climbing, and some do high risk travelling. Put me in the latter category. Here I was doing it, and the adrenalin rush was releasing endorphins to the point of becoming my personal addiction. It did occur to me also that this is easy to say if you've been successful. It easily could have gone the other way at any stage the night before. Any one of getting robbed, beaten up, or hit with a lead pipe would have made for a bad day to say the least.

I lay in the sagging bed, trying to relax, wondering when I would sleep soundly again, if ever, and decided that even though seagulls were calling my name, I would stay the course, I would experience more, the new brain pathways could not go to waste. That's how I decided that since I was on the way home, that my trip would be ending soon, it made perfect sense to do one last strange thing, so as never to have to wonder, back in the safe confines of my home, what could have been had I taken that trip to some island I'd never heard of before.

Yes!

I would go against the instinct of self-preservation, embark on an adventure as a last hurrah on this trip. Yes, I would accept that crazy invitation to be a pirate for a day on some beautiful island with such an exotic name. Eleuthera it would be! A broad smile crossed my face. This was fun: brain on, sleep off and not important at the moment.

My thoughts turned to the day ahead, as I tried to remember everything about Roddy/Robby/Buddy, or whatever his name, and the plan we'd made to take out a boat. I needed fifty dollars to pay for gas for a trip to Eleuthera for some fun and barbequed flamingo. It didn't seem like a lot, but I guessed it could not have been very far, maybe just the other side of Paradise Island across that toll-bridge. I sorted through my cash, wondering how much I would end up with, and thought again about the cab the night before, and then the two guys on the wall trying to pick a fight, and lead-pipe man, and worst of all - could I even trust this Buddy, a guy I'd had just met in a dark bar, who befriended a semi-drunken stranger. I peeled fifty dollars from the small stack of ones and fives and took an extra thirty, then put back ten. If I got robbed, at least I would have a few extra bucks to come back to, might as well go with just twenty extra.

I thought about what he'd said about flamingoes. I had no idea people ate flamingoes, but why not? They're big enough. They're bigger than pigeons, and people picked specks of meat off those tiny bones. It was probably like pheasant and considered a delicacy. Maybe they had a glass cover for the bird on that boat and I could eat flamingo-under-glass like a Bahamian James Bond.

So, excited by the thought of the new adventure ahead I dressed, forcing the hangover fog from the night before from my head. I packed what I thought I'd need for the day, a towel, my camera, and in case the boat had a sink a few toiletries – there were to be ladies involved and a toothbrush might be needed. I left the remainder of my belongings scattered about, moving quietly, not wanting to make extra noise and wake anyone up, and I silently slipped out of my room, down the stairs, hoping not to encounter Mrs. P.

Chapter Five

BAR-B-QUED FLAMINGO ON ELUSIVE
ELEUTHERA

The sun was shining brightly; it was hot and humid and still early morning, as I began to retrace my steps from the night before. I decided I could still change my mind along the way and find something else to do, or just hang out at the beach. I could still back out by not showing up. I still had miles to go that would give me plenty of time to change my mind. It was crazy after all, the whole idea, but it was not the idea so much as who proposed it and where it was proposed that were probably the craziest.

But the beach was not an attraction that morning, and somehow my feet were still making their way toward the bar. I stopped for breakfast at a small restaurant, and when I left, I again found my steps heading in the direction of that bar. I kept telling myself to not go any farther, that this was foolish, that it was too unknown, too risky. I told myself I didn't like the guy much anyway, so why would I want to spend an entire day with him? He was so full of crap, and all he really wanted was my fifty dollars. He was not my friend. I made a game of it, now deciding that Buddy was the one who wouldn't show up, that he'd probably forgotten all about the plans he'd made, that there probably wasn't a boat at all, and it was just a story he'd made up. Best way for me to prove I was right, that I was so smart, was to show up and wait for him and when he didn't show, do a fist pump in the air, - one more thing that proved I knew how to read BS when I saw it. I had to smile. It really was quite the story, some cockamamie tale of a boat, and a trip with curvy island girls, and barbequed pink birds. What a scam that was. Have to give him credit, though, quite the imagination came along with that ever-present ear to ear grin.

So there I was, torn between two lines of reasoning, do it, or be smart and not do it, and still there I was, making my way back into the hills above town and into residential areas recently traversed, though this time in the light of day and clearly seen for the first time. My innate inability to shirk a commitment, or go back on an agreement had me putting one foot in front of the other up the hill, back to the place where I'd agreed to this crazy plan.

The houses I passed were often decrepit, uneven, and typical for the island, all from varying eras, reflecting differing income levels of the owners or inhabitants, but at least mostly neat and orderly. Each had some distinguishing feature, flowers or hanging baskets, or hand painted number signs, or arrayed pottery shards, or once brightly painted but now rusty tin cans from olive oil or tomato sauce fastened to fence posts or a wall, filled with flowering plants.

Most houses were clad in horizontal pine or wood siding with rusty corrugated metal sheathing for roofing. There were no eaves troughs, but every house had wooden shutters over the windows, some of which had glass and some of which did not, and these shutters and the doors of the houses were painted gay colours to accent the base colours of the walls.

As many of these houses were freshly painted as were faded and blistered, seemingly abandoned or vacant at least, with plots of thick weeds growing just a fence-line away from gaily painted and manicured plots of garden and grass. It seemed a microcosm of society where all varieties of the hard-working and conscientious were cast together into the same neighborhood amongst those who couldn't care less or weren't bothered by the inanity of neatness and order.

The sun beat hard on weathered boards and tropical rain hurried the decomposition of paint so continuous maintenance was an ongoing requirement. A few of the better-kept houses had driveways and carports, a few had gardens, and a few had fences to define the area where goats could graze or be kept out of a neighbor's garden. Most curious to me were the three or four houses that had gates, intricate or ornate, with paint and a latch and a set of hinges, but lacking a fence on either side, as if that was the starting point and the fence would come later, or the gate was the psychological barrier one was required to cross, or go around, and going off the sidewalk around the gate meant you were entering without permission. The sidewalks fronting the uneven rows of houses were never straight, as if laid by individual home builders who were not required to ensure that the sidewalks had to line up to each other to form a straight line. I followed them wherever they went, up and down and side to side, and after only a few wrong turns and minor backtracking, I found my way to where Cabbie had picked me up, and eventually to the bar of the evening before.

I surprised myself by arriving at exactly the time Buddy and I had agreed upon, as if all along there was to be no stopping myself, as if my feet were carrying me unconsciously toward the adventure that was to begin from this starting point. Through all my consternation and telling myself not to step farther down this path, I was actually there at the appointed time. What was I thinking? This was an island, and island people don't believe in watches, or the maniacal ritual observance of time. Why am I here on time? What a dummy, or nothing less than naïve. Oh, the burden of travel and the requirement of experience to properly guide footloose travel. One has to learn, or be found quite foolish if one feels the need to be on time on an island.

"He's *not* going to show," I told myself, already believing this adventure was not going to happen. I sat on an overturned wooden crate near the front door of the closed bar and waited. I decided thirty minutes would be enough to prove that Buddy was a bloody liar and I was a fool and should have known he was a liar. I waited patiently, checking my watch every 30 seconds. After thirty five minutes I said,
"That's it," and got up to leave.

I started walking, then I stopped, then I started walking again, and again I stopped, after the fourth time I decided I was *really* going to keep walking this time and not turn back. I dithered just long enough that just as I began to leave - for sure this time, there he is, here comes my good old Buddy from the night before, and what is this? Not alone but with two island girls as promised, one on each arm? I stared in disbelief as they approached, Buddy grinning from ear to ear.

One girl was round and soft, clad in straining denim shorts and tight red t-shirt top with a photo of Eddie Grant and the words *Rock down to Electric Avenue* on the front. Her bra looked like it was too small because she was bustin' over the top. The t-shirt was also too small and her promising curves were quite appealing, if you liked the softness of curves like on a '48 Pontiac, and the bra was not so much a modesty thing, or a dressing thing, but a necessary thing, confining her ample bust to a relatively upright position above the muffin top created by the belt line of her denim short-shorts.

The other girl was small and thin, perhaps the younger sister, shy and unable to make eye contact or even smile. If her lips did form any semblance of a smile, the smile quivered at the corners under waves of apprehension. She was nervous at the situation and sidled uneasily under the weight of Buddy's arm draped over her shoulder. She shifted back and forth on feet clad in flat white runners without laces and with holes in the toes where the nail of each big toe poked through the thin canvas. She was probably not the first owner of those shoes, and I felt faint compassion for her and then upset with myself because noticing those shoes and the toenails protruding was being indiscreet. Having her notice that I noticed the condition of her shoes had caused a look of embarrassment to cross her features.

It was a fleeting second, and to get past that moment I turned my attention to Buddy and the broad smile plastered on his face. His grin was that of a satisfied man. He had arrived, as promised, with two girls as promised, and I could see he was proud of himself and suspected that for Buddy meeting a commitment was a hitherto unknown occurrence.

The three stood before me and a pause settled. The chubby one, smooth, soft, and rounded at the edges, began to smile coyly with a sideways look, mischievous, as if she knew full well what these two men had in mind, and the little glimmer in her eyes was saying she was fine with it. Little sister, on the other hand, maybe not so much, as she was still nervously shifting from foot to foot.

Buddy said, "Hey boss, you like my girlfriens, dey sweet islan' honey. What you tink? Dey'll do for you?" With that the little one looked up, maybe wondering if I liked what I saw, and in that look I couldn't be certain if I could read,

"Do you approve?" or "Do I really have to do this?" What Buddy had promised as an inducement to come along was surely the motivating factor. A boat ride, pink flamingo, sandy beach, being company for a complete stranger; I doubt if any of that had any bearing on her being there. I could only guess that a fraction of the fifty dollars would be hers, perhaps just enough for a new pair of white canvas runners.

I was at a loss for how to answer. Any one of the four of us not wanting to be there was not what I wanted. I could understand her apprehension. She was likely barely more than seventeen years old or maybe even less, and although I was not much older, I was still older and even a few years age difference at that age is a big deal. Under these circumstances, the boat ride was enough for me. The thought of causing 10 or 12 hours of total anxiety for this poor girl was not a pleasant one, and I had to try to find a way to reassure her.

"Sure, sure, the girls are really…. really something,"

I stammered, and immediately wanted to take it back. I knew it was a stupid thing to say as soon as the words hit the air. The first words I utter, and that's what comes out: "…*really something*'?

I sounded like a foreigner, and not just a foreigner but a dorky one at that. I decided the best thing to do was keep my mouth shut.

Both Buddy's and Chubby Girl's eyes were on me, like they were trying to understand which of Chubby Girl or Little Sister I found more acceptable. To set matters straight, Chubby Girl wound her arms around the waist of Buddy which made it plain she was claiming him for the afternoon. There was to be no confusion as to who would be with whom. Little Sister on the other hand looked even more nervous as Chubby Girl hugged Buddy, and I thought she looked like she wanted to bolt, unlatch Buddy's arm from over her shoulders and run, run, run.

I was in a tough spot. How had this happened? It was

so unnatural and felt so forced that it could never be comfortable. But, it was also late in the morning and if things were going to happen they had to happen soon. I had the feeling Buddy did not want to give up on the idea too quickly, for he let go of the women, perhaps sensing from my tepid response that his plans had suddenly taken a turn for the worse.

In full let's-rescue-this-scheme mode Buddy put his hand on Chubby Girl's shoulder, nudging her toward me. She didn't immediately get it, and shot him a questioning glance. He looked at her and with an almost imperceptible nod of his head in my direction, and a look just short of a wink, gave her the signal, "You gotta go with white boy, cause it looks like Little Sister ain't his ting." Maybe he recalled that I'd said the night before that I wasn't too fussy, that tall, short, fat, skinny didn't matter too much to me, it was attitude that counted and a nice smile was the important thing.

But that was bar talk, rum talk, not real at all.

Daylight shines reality on the night and all that's said and done under the cover of dark and the influence of alcohol.

Here was Little Sister in front of me, who couldn't even muster a smile, never mind a nice smile. As much as I wasn't so wrapped up over perfect looks, there was one thing I couldn't compromise on, if she's not into it, I never could never be into it under any circumstance. I wanted to say to Buddy, "It doesn't feel right, and switching girls isn't going to make it feel right."

That Buddy was about to sacrifice his Girl so readily just to keep his plans intact had not only surprised her but Little Sister and me as well. When Chubby understood that he was offering to make the change, her smooth cheeks, which just seconds before were playfully lifting the corners of her mouth into a wide smile, now tightened into a frown as she realized what he intended. Her smile was gone, and she was obviously hurt. He must have sweet-talked her into coming and bringing Little Sister along to make an even number to keep me happy, and now her plan for some fun on the beach with her man was turning into being handed over to a stranger. It was getting very awkward very fast. Little Sister had started off completely uncomfortable not knowing what I would be expecting over the course of the day, and Chubby Girl, who had now been totally disrespected by being offered to a stranger by the man she thought loved her, or at least liked her, or at least wanted her, looked now to be on the verge of tears. Three out of the four of us there in the sunshine that morning were completely uneasy and uncomfortable. This was not a promising start to the day.

However, Buddy was still driving this bus, and he was not about to let go of the wheel or the prospect of fifty dollars. To salvage the moment before the entire thing collapsed, he reached up and put both hands on my shoulders.

"Hey, mon, come on, mon, sun is shining, mon, we got a day ahead you never gonna forget, mon."

I fidgeted under the weight of his hands. I don't like people touching me in the first place, never mind some creepy guy with big yellow teeth, standing nose to nose with me like I'd asked to check his breath. I leaned back, away from his face, wanting to turn and run like Little Sister. I began to wonder what was happening. Thoughts of the cab experience only some eight hours previously and my complete lack of control of that situation and the narrow escape I'd luckily had from unknown trouble was too close in my memory. It was if I had just narrowly escaped that trouble only to find myself inviting yet more trouble.

But I have this weakness: I'm able to justify almost anything while finding it extremely difficult to say no to anyone, for any reason, whatever they suggest, and this had me nodding affirmatively instead of doing what my left and always smarter brain was telling my head to do, and that was nod side to side, not up and down. No, thank you. Not OK. It's time for me to depart this company and find adventure elsewhere. No, it's not imperative that I pay for this trip and go to the island of Eleuthera.

But, really? Eleuthera?

Sounds very much like *elusive*, and nothing could be more enticing than something with a name like that.

It was an island named and created to challenge the imagination. That did it. The mysterious and elusive island of Eleuthera and my chance to discover it would be on the agenda for the day. A mere five days earlier I had no idea I'd be on New Providence, never mind an island that rhymed with elusive. What were the chances I would ever come this way again or find anything so perfectly aligned with my sense of adventure as an island with a name that rhymed like elusive? Once more, here came rule number one for spontaneous living: when omens speak, you must listen.

I had to ask myself, what exactly are the reasons for saying no to this? I should be saying lead away, my island friend.

But rather than slapping him on the back and saying 'let's go' with enthusiasm I gave a wishy-washy response half way between no and yes,

"Well, OK, we can go. Your girl is looking forward to being with you." Making a point of saying aloud who was with who so there would be no confusion later on.

Buddy and Chubby Girl both broke into wide grins, teeth showing, the sun glistening off his forehead and cheeks, happy as could be. Even Little Sister seemed slightly less reluctant now that she knew she would be getting something from this day. Chubby Girl had regained her smile, and all of us accepted we were confirmed to go, that I was paying and not expecting anything in exchange. So, before I could change my mind, off went Buddy leading the way, the two ladies close behind.

He walked with a confident swagger that required multiple moving parts: shoulders, hips, arms, head – as if following an unheard personal rhythm. His stride placed his feet down at angles to each other and so far apart that if anyone was tracking him in the sand they would be confused about which way he was going. The two girls scurried along to keep up, and I had to step lively as well.

I couldn't help but wonder what we looked like, two scampering girls and one lean white guy with the pied piper of Nassau leading the way.

Ten minutes later we were on the dock, passing conch salad vendors and domino players sitting around rickety tables, with giant speakers thumping island dance music lending rhythm to the hustle and bustle of the pier. On the dock the energy of preparing boats for open water passages was palpable. We passed a series of open-fronted restaurants with wooden stools in front of plywood topped bars, with open back walls behind the kitchen, which hung over the water serving as a dumping place for the pink conch shells tossed out every day. The menu was the same at every joint and the same "Bahamas Best Conch Salad" in hand-brushed strokes was painted at the top of the sandwich-board welcome sign. There were thirty or forty of these small restaurants, each with its own unique colour scheme, but all seemingly painted by the same sloppy painter.

Buddy wound his way down the shifting wooden pier and finally stopped and waited, where he straitened his arm and pointed. I followed his arm and crooked finger, and beheld the boat with an open-mouth and shocked expression. There floated 45 feet of pointy Italian fiberglass with painted flames no less.

On a boat, flames?

Yes, those were actually flames in metalflake paint at the waterline from the bow to the transom. I had to shake my head. Was I the only one who thought flames and a boat were an ungodly mix? Was this not messing with rule number two, that being, 'don't mess with ungodly mixes or mother Karma,' and painting flames on a boat was flaunting both in spades? I was as aghast at the paint as I was at the size of it, and it took a long moment before I was able to come around from the shock of it.

Buddy hopped into the cockpit and with a triumphant flourish turned to me and the girls with an expression that said, "Ta- dah! I told you so!"

So much so, in fact, that it seemed like even he could barely believe it was for real. But it actually was for real. Wow, did I get this one wrong. Somehow, he had the keys to a boat worth more than all the houses he had ever lived in since he was born and would likely ever live in until he died unless his fortunes changed drastically for the better, - and he was allowed to take it out.

His ubiquitous grin broadened even farther until it was the only feature on his face. He had done it and now could say, "I told you so," but in a happy way. I couldn't help but smile in acknowledgment of his victory and roll my eyes skyward in a gesture of 'will wonders never cease.'

He relished his triumph for a moment and danced a Bahamian whine of the sort only one who has seen it would recognize and impossible to describe that involved shoulders, hips, and arms as a soca riff played in his head and drove his moves.

Here was when slap on the back of the head number two should have been administered. Metalflake paint depicting flames on a most unseaworthy-looking fiberglass bullet is not a good combination, but being undoubtedly a drug smuggler's boat on top of it, and me supposedly having a border guard watching my every move, this had trouble written all over it.

This was not good. No, not good at all.

But sun and smiles and the blue water beyond had my internal warning beacons stifled. The gleam of metalflake paint on this missile of a boat, in flames no less, clouded the rational thought area of my brain. This was a beauty of a machine, and I could not help but be dazzled at the finish and the shine and the imitation leather seating. A dash around the open water would be enough for me, and how could I turn down the chance to see what this type of machine could do? Would I ever be invited again on a rocket like this?

But, hold it a second. How far would fifty bucks take this cocaine smuggling bullet? Out of the harbor? No, I'd bet not even out of the harbor.

I felt a moment of unreality, feeling something was up and messing with the world and the way it should be. I waited for the other shoe to drop, for the jig to be up. But then, to my surprise here is good ol' Buddy pulling out a key from his pocket. With dramatic flourish, raising it above his head like a vaudeville magician and his baton he proceeds to insert it into the ignition. And…. Voila, it fits.

To top that trick, he turns face on to me and without looking back to the instrument panel raises his arm then swoohes it down to hit the starter button without looking.

Three chirp chirp chirps from the started somewhere below the rear engine cowling rent the air, then a bang and a pop and then a roar let loose from the exhaust below water.

"Ha haaa ha haa" he exclaimed, and to take it one step

further and to make me fully understand how naïve I was to underestimate him, as an encore, he drew his arm back again and thrust it forward to start a second engine, and then like a conductor leading his orchestra into a crescendo, with a final flourish he pressed his long bony finger onto a third button and, to my astonishment and his glee, a third engine roared to life.

The damn thing had three engines!

It rumbled rather than idled, and the sound that came from the aft section purred in rolling waves, and it felt like a contented tiger was sleeping on my chest. This was a mighty powerful machine, pure and simple, built for pure outright speed, fast enough to outrun the coast guard. Pick up a few bundles of cocaine dropped from a plane and head back to an island with a safe drop point before anyone knew you left the marina.

Three glistening chrome throttles, round gauges of pure Italian style, white leatherette settees, a tiny sink, a long narrow space to lie down, a windscreen all of eight inches high, this was nothing less than a rocket that rested on plastic to keep it afloat before take off. It even had flames, in metallic paint on the side that might just as well have been an SOS sign, as this was as likely to end in catastrophe as anything else.

I asked, "How did you score this... this thing?"

"No mon, dis ting ain't my boat, mon. Dis boat belong to de big boss in Miami. I just gotta watch over it and take it out once in a while to make sure it run good."

"He lets you take it out when you want?"

"No, not when I wan, mon, but enough to make sure it looks like a charter boat and starts when he needs it. US DEA watches dees tings and dees boat gotta move at least once a week to keep dem from going after it every time."

OK, I thought to myself, so we are acting as decoys, I can live with that, as long as Buddy doesn't stop to retrieve a bale or two. I had to ask, "We ain't picking up or dropping off anything, are we?"

"No, mon. I don't do runs. I just make sure it starts when he wants it to start and keep de DEA guessing."

I still could hardly believe someone would leave this machine in the hands of a guy like Buddy. I had some reckoning to do. Had I underestimated him? But, fifty bucks? Where would that take us? I had to ask the question right into his ear to be heard over the rumbling,

"How is fifty bucks going to take us anywhere in this thing?"

"No, mon, dat money is for de groceries and de ladies, mon. Boss pay de gas. He needs dis boat moving and knows I gotta keep it running fas for him."

He looked at me to ensure I understood. "Dis is now a charter, mon. Yank coast guard need to see dis ting moving fast with a white boy chartering it. Dat's you, mon. We legal now. Boss man always wan it runnin' good and full of gas. I don' pay one Bahamian penny, boss got 'count at de pump, mon."

"OK, but there's nothing illegal on board? No dope, no guns, no RPG's? For sure we're not making a pick-up today, right?"

"No, mon. I alrealy tol' you, I don make no runs like dat, mon. I jus boat boy giving it a run now and den. Boss man's big Latino guys do all dat."

I stepped away from him, and looked out to the deep blue beyond the straight.

"Well, OK, how far is it to Eleuthera?"

"Fifty miles, mon, straight east. We skip on de top de waves, mon, all de way, mon. Dis ting do eighty easy, we be dere in no time, mon. You boss for de day; you boss, and you buy de food".

He turned to the two girls, "Yo, girls, go now. Aunty Bev's Conch Shack"

He turned back to me, "We ready to go, girls buy de fish and conch salad. We need de fifty now, mon."

So the moment had arrived. I had to shell out. But, I was on the boat. it was rumbling and gurgling like a growling beast. Buddy came through, now it was my turn. I reached into my pocket and pulled out my crinkled ones and fives. No sooner than they hit air they were snatched from my fingers.

He passed them to Chubby "Go, girl, get some peas and rice and salfish. And a box of cold Kalik." He gave her the money and added,

"Mind de change, girl."

The girls hustled off at his command.

I asked, "Where do you keep the life jackets and safety stuff?"

He looked at me and laughed his barking laugh, "You gotta find dem mon, cause I don't know. Hah!"

OK, so that's how it's going to be? Hmmm…

But at least it gave me an excuse to rummage around. I wanted to see what was on this boat before I went anywhere. I stepped down into the tiny lower cabin and found almost nothing in the way of bins or lockers or storage space. It made me think that this may be why these boats were called cigarette boats: the most you could stow was a cigarette, laying down on its side no less. I lifted a few cushions, opened a few drawers and could find nothing in the way of safety equipment. No lifejackets, no first aid kit, no fire extinguisher, not even a flashlight. I opened every small door and hatch to spaces in the hull, all the while thinking to myself about whether what the Customs guard said was true, that they would be watching me, and right about now someone was winning the bet they'd made that I was indeed a courier just heading out to pick something up.

What if I was just the sucker providing a cover story and this is me in a boat-load of trouble? I thought to myself,

This is not good. This is exactly what those Customs guys thought I was going to do. Better get off this thing right now. But how could anyone know I would be in that bar last night? Could Buddy have been following me all day and into that bar? Is Buddy working for them? Is this a set up? Am I the fall guy who takes the rap? Get off this thing! Get off now!

Just as I moved to step back onto the dock for a quick getaway, the two girls arrived, carrying cloth bags. I wanted to say,

"I'm getting off – gotta use the bathroom on the dock," and I tried, but it was too late. As I stepped onto the rail, Chubby Girl was passing a bag of groceries up. I had to take it from her, then another from Little Sister, which left me no choice but to take them below as there was no flat place to put them down. Buddy was helping them board as I scurried down the three narrow steps to the cabin. As the second of the two girls stepped onto the boat I noticed she had already untied the bow line and had tossed it onto the forward deck. We began to drift slightly away from the pier as Buddy untied the stern line, then with the agility of a true boatman, he got back behind the wheel. All three engines were warmed and ready to go.

So that was it. I was going. No turning back.

All morning long I'd been having doubts, yet here I was, on a drug smuggler's boat heading out to sea. If we were stopped, would the coast guard believe me? Could I even try to tell them I had no idea what I was taking part in until it happened, and I was just a tourist going for a boat ride, that all I had wanted was a little boat ride and to barbeque a flamingo?

The engines revved loudly out of neutral and from that point there would be no conversation. Even at the slowest speed the rumbling prevented voice communication. Within a minute we were sliding out of the marina and into the channel between the two islands. The **brum brum brum brum brum brum brum** of the deep throaty exhausts from three 500 HP engines echoed from either shore. We thrummed along slowly, approaching the channel markers. Then Buddy nudged the throttles a bit and the brum brum brum brum grew into longer notes, and already the sound was resonating in my head. We came abreast of the final channel marker where a clearly defined band of deeper water lay before us, a snake-like S curving into the blue expanse of open water.

Buddy thrust the three throttles forward, and the boat launched itself. The bow went up to 40 degrees, making it impossible to see anything but blue sky. The engines howled as water shot back from the stern into a giant rooster tail, and the boat cleaved a huge depression in the water. As we gained speed the bow began to come down, and within seconds we were on a plane and surging forward, the bow rising and falling in longer and longer cycles as less of the hull cut through water.

I stared ahead and gasped to regain the breath the velocity of the wind had sucked out of me, trying to clench my mouth shut against that force. My hair whipped back and my knuckles whitened as my fists gripped the rail below the windshield. This rocket of a boat bucked liked a slow motion bronco. In mere seconds, with throttles still three quarters forward, we were skimming over the tops of the waves, skipping onto the upslope of every second one. With each skip we came down hard in a crescendo of sound with spray shooting up on each side. Up we'd go with a roar of those powerful engines then we'd crash down into a wave trough, and then almost fly back up again. The engines were at 4000 rpm and already we were doing sixty-five knots. The noise was almost deafening, a rumbling low note reverberated through my chest, and the wind roared as it passed over my ears. Despite all that, an adrenaline fueled grin came easily, a grin as wide as my cheeks could bear, pulling back to the line of my jaw, although I was afraid to open my mouth lest it catch the wind and make my face into a fleshy parachute. Tears sprang from the corners of my eyes and streaked across my temples to find cool places inside my ears. I looked down by moving only my eyes, unable to bring myself to turn my face away from the torrent of wind.

The pace quickened even more as we crested the waves and achieved a level plane, thundering ahead, now reaching ninety knots.

"Ninety! Good God almighty, PLEASE don't flip this thing!"

We were still bouncing, but now it seemed like we skipped to the top of every third or fourth wave, and the lengths of time when we were actually airborne were increasing with each dip and rise.

But then cold fear began to replace the adrenaline high, supplanting my broad grin with a grimace of apprehension until my tightly flexed cheek muscles could not bear either grin or grimace any longer. My stomach welled nervous bile as we now began to bounce higher, stay airborne longer, and come down slower as the open water before us held longer, higher and wider swells.

My mind was screaming and my guts were roiling more and more with each bounce skyward.

"What. The. Hell. Is. He. Doing?? Does this idiot know *what he's doing?*

I wondered if I was the only one who thought this or if anyone else shared this turn from excitement to terror. I bowed down below the windscreen to look back to where the two girls sat. Neither female face was visible, as both had their faces buried in their hands and had drawn their knees up to their chins, and sat with their feet on the edges of the seats. By now all three engines were revving at 5000 rpm. I looked to Buddy and reeled back because his features had transformed into some evil, glassy-eyed, rictus of a grin like he was having a sexual experience.

That's what it was! He wasn't doing this to get to some place; he wasn't doing this to give the boss's boat exercise; he was doing this because HE wanted to, and the two girls and I were terrified passengers on his adrenaline-fueled trip. I was not a timid girl, but this was crazy! I released my right hand from its death-grip on the rail as we bounced upward one more time and turned to face him. I was at the end of my patience.

Buddy was not my buddy.
Buddy was not my friend.
Buddy needs a smack.

I swung my arm as hard as I could and slapped his shoulder with the back of my hand. A faint thwack could be heard over the roar of the engines and the wind. His villainous grin fell when he felt that sharp smack on his shoulder, and he turned to me as if returning to planet earth - and he wasn't happy about it. He instantly got the message. He faced me with a look of seething rage. He apparently did not appreciate being brought back to earth in such a rude manner. His expression was almost murderous and his eyes bugged out. Indignantly, he reached for the throttles and viciously yanked all three back at once resulting in an almost instantaneous deceleration. In a flash the change of speed and loss of forward momentum pushed us all, wherever we stood or sat, from leaning backward to thrust forward. The two girls reached out to keep themselves from sliding onto the cockpit floor as we'd gone from ninety to thirty in three seconds.

Immediately I knew he had no training or skill with this powerful boat. At once, the bow went down and the stern fell into the water, as the sudden decrease in speed caused the boat to wallow into the deep depression it had been carving in the water.

At the same time, the huge wake the boat had been creating washed up behind us to fill the void in the water created by the low transom. Three huge gas engines and hundreds of gallons of gasoline were in the stern of the boat and added to by the weight of the two women clinging to the rear seats. I felt the bucking and the side roll and looked back in time to see a wave swooshing toward us. That white-frothed, churning water washed over the transom and down went the stern and up went the bow as the weight of it pushed the rear of the boat down. That relentless wave was two feet deep and washed over the transom and the two girls completely engulfing them. It rose as high as my knees and flowed beyond me into the passageway to the cabin below. The engines gurgled as the boat fought to maintain buoyancy. The boat wallowed to the right, then to the left, and the bow pointed up like a long finger.

The water that had washed aboard sloshed back and forth over the girls as the boat shifted right and left and back again. They hunched down against the flow of the water as it passed over them. For interminable seconds it was unclear how this was going to end or if we would capsize. The boat wallowed in the trough as it rolled to port until the rail was in water then back over to starboard then back again while the engines gurgled under the onslaught.

Finally, on the third slow shift, the boat won the struggle to stay afloat and the bow began to lower and the water began to wash down the steps into the cabin below and over the side rails. After what seemed like long moments, but was probably only fifteen seconds, the bow was more or less on a level plane. The two women sat with fingers desperately locked around the edges of the cushions they had been sitting on. They both looked so clearly terrified that it was as if their very souls were exposed, as if they'd felt the cold hand of death disguised as a wave had washed over them. Then Chubby came to voice as a shriek rent the air, as high pitched as a schoolyard at recess, and with that Little Sister let loose too with a similar uncontrolled expression of terror.

We tossed about for another long moment, no one able to move or make a sound after that long shriek from the women until at last Buddy turned back and gripped the wheel.

I turned and stared at him, noticing that his brown skin had become tinged green. At first I thought he was going to bend over the side and vomit, but he just slumped over the wheel and looked over the long bow.

At last he stopped staring stupidly ahead at nothing and seemed to realize he needed to push the throttles forward because the boat needed thrust to get out of this rollicking stalemate.

The engines responded with a loud cough, and the boat once again pulled forward out of the low trough it was wallowing in. Buddy stared straight ahead, perhaps concentrating on getting his heart beating again, or maybe not wanting to have to look into the angry faces of the three passengers he'd almost drowned.

The two girls were shaking water off their arms and out of their hair. Little Sister held a thick braid of hair in her hands and was wringing it out like a beach towel. The little bits of girly make-up they'd started the day with was now running like a watercolor in the rain, more or less maintaining the hues it started out with but now diffused unevenly over their cheeks. Chubby Girl had put on mascara that morning, but that was then, and this was now, and the mascara now ringed her eyes like she'd become a large brown raccoon.

We began to move in a sloppy forward direction, still wallowing, but at least moving. I looked down the passage and could see water on the floor of the cabin sloshing about, this too draining slowly away into the bilge. Buddy would not look back, and I could understand that he might be afraid to look at me or the girls. His swagger was gone, his bravado was gone, and perhaps for him, like for me, it had been replaced by the icy sensation that was adrenaline draining from the blood stream. The shock of real fear that he, like the other three of us, felt when the wave tumbled over the stern would take minutes to clear. We had been mere inches from being swamped, and for a long moment it had felt like we were going stern-first to the bottom of the sea.

The boat had exhibited a lack of stability that was incredible, as if the designers weren't aware that a rapid deceleration from ninety knots to twenty would cause a massive amount of previously displaced water to refill that space amazingly quickly, or perhaps they realized this fact and didn't care. This was a boat built for people who never thought of slowing down. After all, anyone willing to climb aboard an overgrown Tupperware dish with three 500 horsepower engines would not be overly concerned about safety and stability. The most important concern was how fast it could get to ninety. Lifejackets? What lifejackets? Hah! We don't need no stinkin' lifejackets!

I could almost read Buddy's thoughts, and he knew I was staring at him with contempt. He was remembering my question about the lifejackets. He had almost sunk big bosses boat out of sight of land without even knowing if there were lifejackets on board. Buddy's hands gripped the wheel hard as he turned and looked back at me. He was steaming mad. I was right and he knew it and didn't appreciate the knowledge. Even worse for him, I didn't speak a word of criticism. However, the near capsize of the boat had not washed away the memory of that backhanded slap on the shoulder I gave him. It was almost as if that slap had caused the near disaster, as if it had been more than a message to slow down, that it had been a deep-rooted insult. He glared at me for another very long moment, ignoring the pitch and roll and tossing of the boat as the water around us leveled and we began to pick up speed. He tipped to his left as the boat rolled to starboard and finally turned his evil stare away from me. It was as if he judged that it was my fault that he had almost sunk the boat since I had smacked him one and made him pull the throttles back too quickly.

I looked up the slanting front deck, wanting to end this somehow, ignoring him. Buddy pushed the throttles forward again gradually, and soon we were rumbling along at the stately speed of thirty knots, not even close to the speed needed to get back on a plane. The bow was still up and being pushed side to side in the water, the boat wallowing painfully in all its immense length, moving forward slowly, Buddy overcompensating and now afraid of the speed this thing could generate. Minutes passed, each of us turning our thoughts inward and reflecting on the last few minutes and how close we'd come to disaster. It had to be worse for the girls than for Buddy and me as they'd been swamped and for a second were actually going down with the boat. It made me shudder just imagining how that would have felt.

This lasted for a while, probably a little too long, mainly because I was filled with a sick feeling at the thought that I had somehow gotten myself into this mess, and I was a long way from getting out of it. I thought about pushing Buddy overboard, I did hate him that much at that moment. But, then I would have to throw the girls over too as they would have been witnesses to murder and mutiny. Triple murder at that, and I liked the girls, and I am not a murderer. This trip was supposed to be pretend-to-be-a-pirate for the day, I wasn't supposed to become a real pirate. Nah, not a good option, triple homicide and mutiny. They would hang me four times.

But the thoughts of him bobbing around in the water, pleading up at me on the boat,

"Please, please throw me a floatie or something. Pleeeease," was pretty enticing, and the water might wash off that stupid grin of his, and clean his pimply face. I had a feeling he wanted to do the same to me. It was a vicious circle and we still had miles to go, and then to get back, so best move on to more pleasant thoughts.

Just then he turned to face me, as if my murderous thoughts had penetrated his brain. He looked at me for a second, and I could see that he recognized what I'd been thinking.

Damn. Busted!

I tried to change my expression to one of,

"Yah, mon, no problem, mon, nice maneuver mon" but he saw through that.

This seemed to wake him from his stupor. He pushed the throttles ahead and the bow came down more. He had got it right about what was in my mind at that moment, but the bad thoughts he felt just as easily could have been coming from the two girls in the back, who were shooting daggers at his back with their eyes.

Buddy now stood looking ridiculously upward at the blue sky beyond the bow. I turned to look at him and noticed that his cheek was twitching. I could see that he was feeling almost sick as if his heart was thumping uncomfortably hard in his chest. That was definitely how I was feeling. I too turned to look forward and hoped he would get over it soon. We needed to get somewhere, to do something to change the atmosphere around us. There was a sensation that God, like that image from the Sistine chapel, had reached down to the four of us, his foolish children, to take us by the scruff of the neck, give us a shake, and make us answer for our sins, our thoughts of sex and killing flamingoes and drinking rum and all things unholy in His eyes. But God hadn't taken us up by the collar, or cast us down into a watery grave; He spared us. I guess he wasn't done messing with us yet.

The rumbling of the engines resembled a deep-throated purr. The exhaust ports gurgled and spat like three drunken tuba players in a marching band on spring break as the boat rose up and down and the exhaust ports were first in and then out of the water. The water shooting from the bilge pump ports began to flutter and finally stopped as the bilges were drained.

Finally, we each exhaled a long breath, first me and then Buddy, as the coolness between us dissipated a bit. My thoughts cleared as I looked skyward into the deep blue overhead. I stared into it for a long moment before looking over to Buddy at the helm.

"OK. Let's go," I said.

He didn't look at me, but apparently understood that the moment had passed; we were still alive, and it was time to move on. We accelerated to only half the speed of before, but at least we could see where we were going. At this speed the ride was much rougher, and as the boat dropped off the crest of a swell onto the face of the next swell a solid thump, thump, thump resounded from the cabin below like the beating of a giant drum. I looked at the compass heading, due east at 90 degrees. We were still on our way to Eleuthera. I was surprised, and more than disappointed that Buddy hadn't decided to turn back. I looked at the two girls who sat shivering on the curved white bench, they looked like two kittens that had been dunked in a bucket of water. Their joviality of just an hour before was a distant memory, as the horror of being submerged was still too fresh.

I turned back to let the wind rip at my hair and eyes. There was something exhilarating about the power of this monstrous thing. It was really something to see the crest of a swell ahead and just obliterate it with pure power. As each long crest rose before the boat, it thumped down to split it in two, just to bounce up and do the same to the next crest. There could be no denying the thrill that came from that much raw power. Suddenly I could relate to the songs written and wars started and lives lost under the spell of uncontrolled power. In a small and insignificant way I had a brush against raw power and felt what it could do, as if the adrenaline and highly oxygenated air blowing in my face had clarified my vision. I could understand why being really close to death could make some feel that much more alive and why that rush could be addictive after just a single shot.

We thundered along for at least another half hour until a long smudge of grey/brown appeared on the horizon. This became a thin line as far as the eye could see in either direction, and it seemed to curve in at each end as if we were entering an immense bay. I watched intently, hoping this was Eleuthera and that our voyage was near an end. A long a strip of white appeared at the base of the grey/brown strip, then the greys and browns became touched with shades of green, and the white brightened. Soon the colours gained definition and the greys and browns shaded fully to green and the water from deep blue to a shimmering turquoise with wavelets reflecting diamonds in the brilliant sun overhead.

We slowed somewhat, and any thought that a slower ride might be a smoother or safer ride was completely false, as with the slower speed we hit the face of each swell with full force instead of skipping from crest to crest.

Thump, the long lean bow would drop, white spray spouting fifty feet to each side, then up it would sail as if reaching for the blue horizon where we would hang suspended for a split second until the bow would drop into the next trough and thump again as it split the next crest into twin fifty foot sprays.

The beach we approached seemed endless, and with almost breathless anticipation I watched it approach. It was beautiful, as if this beach was the definition of the word. Vivid turquoise water dappled with shades of cobalt blue lapped the white sand, creating the quintessentially perfect tropical beach, further enhanced by the sense of relief that at least three of us felt that we'd actually arrived safely after the adventurous – to say the least – passage we'd just experienced.

Closer to shore the water flattened, and our speed increased with the decreased resistance of the smaller swells until Buddy pulled back the throttles to let momentum carry us to the shallow water.

Soon we could see the bottom, patchy and spotted with circles of sand and deep green-grey rocks and sea vegetation. Within 100 feet of shore, and with six feet of water below us, Buddy steered to swing the boat around, set the engines into neutral, and scampered onto the long bow where he opened a hatch, withdrew an anchor, and tossed it over the bow. He eased back around the windscreen into the cockpit and shut the engines down. Silence washed over us so suddenly and completely it was almost startling. The deep quiet was disturbed only by the residual ringing in my ears from listening to the screaming of the engines for the last hour. I shook my head and squeezed my palms over my ears to try to stop the whistling, then gazed about to divert my attention from that ringing in my ears.

The two girls stood up together, stretching to loosen muscles that had been clenched tight from an hour of terror. They looked a mess – smudged makeup, stringy wet hair, sea damp clothes clinging to skin. It had been an especially violent trip where they had sat and swamped, and their appearance was evidence of that. I had to smile. I could see they did not look terrible. Their youth shone through, once again, and adult aspirations had been washed away. I could see what their momma would have seen when they came running to hug her legs after skinning a knee. Neither said a word.

Little Sister was still shivering slightly, forlorn, staring out to sea at where we'd come from, as if she took no solace from having arrived because it surely meant we'd have to do it again to get back. As I watched her, I could see her lower lip trembling slightly and that she was holding back tears. Where she and her sister had been seated at the rear of the boat, the noise would have been much worse than for Buddy and me in the cockpit. Added to that was the fear that the boat was sinking when the water that engulfed her and her sister. It no doubt had taken every ounce of courage she had to get through that experience. She was barely more than a grown child and now seemed very young and very scared.

Her older sister was squeezing water from her shirt, pressing down gently here and there. She turned her smudged eyes on me and Buddy and motioned with her finger that we should turn around. I knew she wanted to take off her top and wring it out, so we did as ordered. "OK," she said a moment later allowing Buddy and me to turn back around, and I could she had removed her bra and replaced her top.

The fun and promise of the morning had been replaced

by the sheer terror that Buddy had produced with this wicked machine, but we had made it. We were here and still alive. Maybe in the grand scheme of things it was just my imagination that we had been at the brink of disaster. However, Buddy would not look at me, as if he wanted me to disappear. He ignored me to the point of ridiculousness as he averted his eyes even when he couldn't possibly have seen anything more than my feet. He was still seething mad and wasn't going to forget about it nor forgive me for being the cause of it. He stepped into the passageway and retrieved the bags of food we'd brought, together with my bag with my towel and dry clothes, which at the time I thought was pretty nice of him. He spoke brusquely to Chubby Girl:

"Take dis to de beach," then motioned for her to jump into the water.

I looked over the side where I could see the bottom as plainly as if looking through a sheet of glass. The sand was marked by small ripples, with thin grasses waving gently on the bottom. Chubby and Little Sister sat on the rear platform, swung their legs over the edge, and slid down into the water.

Within minutes we were all on the beach, and after a long look around, as I savored the silky sand squeezing between my toes I thought, for the first time that day that I was actually happy that I'd decided to take this trip. Suddenly it was worth it. The white sand beach flecked with pink stretched in either direction for what looked like miles, and we were the only humans on it. That outlandish boat now looked beautiful anchored in that bay, and I could see in my mind a *Yachting World* advertisement for Italian smuggling boats, but in this issue I was the man on the beach with bikini clad girls and white sand and waving palms.

How nice that this was not a magazine but reality for

me for the next little while.

That man in the ad was me!!

This was my life for the moment, and I was all it!

I was alllll it!

I walked to a smooth flat stretch of sand and lay flat on my back. It was warm and soft under me, and above me there was nothing but blue, not a cloud, not a contrail, not even a wisp of vaporous cirrus, just calming and caressing and beautiful deep blue. The sun toasted me and a slight breeze caressed me. Not a seabird spoke my name. It was just me under a blue dome of sky, and for a while I lazily dreamed and drifted in and out of a light sleep.

In a while the two girls began to unwrapped the food so I went back to join them. We ate in silence, no mention being made of the infamous flamingo or lack thereof. I knew better than to bring that up. It had been a story made up for my benefit and enticement. We didn't even have a sharp knife, never mind a hibachi or charcoal, and I couldn't even imagine these two girls plucking feathers, even if flamingoes could be found on this island. The fried fish with peas and rice, although cold, were made delicious by my ravenous hunger. Buddy still refused to look at me, or acknowledge my presence, making the atmosphere rather uncomfortable. I ignored it as much as possible, not wanting to let an otherwise beautiful day be further spoiled after what had transpired on the trip to the island.

Once the meal was finished, not wanting to be around Buddy, I walked much farther up the beach to a shady spot under a palm and lay on my back and contemplated that clear blue dome above me and mused about how fortunate I was to have stumbled upon such a living dream that was all mine while I was here. Buddy and Chubby had slipped away and were frolicking in the water, Little Sister was sitting in the shade of a palm some distance away, and I smiled and waved at her and let her enjoy her little section of beach and the peace we'd found on it.

I lay back on the warm sand, breathing deeply and slowly, feeling the weariness of the long walk of the evening before, which was after the longer walk of the day, and followed by the short nightmare-filled tossed and turning hours in Lawrence's sagging bed. I felt sleep wanting to wash over me with images of Cabbie and King and Big Face and Bubba, who sat immobile in that house without a door within the flickering yellow flame of the kerosene lamp that caused images to move on the cracked and faded walls, of the house and the cane-shaped old woman in her diaphanous nightgown hefting an enormous shotgun as she passed through the shafts of white light from the street lamps slanting through the shuttered windows over the threadbare carpet in the parlor.

These images of the past thirty-six hours played in my mind across the deep blue sky above me as if it were a movie screen in a daylight theatre, that screen immense and fitting for so immense the total experience had been.

I was exhausted and hadn't been aware of the extent of that exhaustion until that moment when, completely immobile, I lay flat on my back on warm, silky sand. My eyelids began to flutter. But, was I safe? Would it be wise to fall asleep here? Then my eyes closed again; I was so tired, and this soft white sand so comfortable, so wonderfully relaxing. The movie screen went softly to grey, as if the curtains closed from top to bottom. Again, my eyes fluttered, and I could feel the sun on me. The meager shade the tree had offered was three feet away. I had slept long enough that I was no longer in the shade of the tree, at least an hour, possibly two hours.

Brumpp, brumpp, brumpp, a low rumbling sound came across the sand.

Slowly but steadily the brumpp brumpp brumpp washed over me in my half sleep.

I could imagine it like waves rolling across the sand, brumpp, brumpp brumpp.

Though I was still half asleep and groggy, I traced the waves of sound back in my imagination. I could almost see them coming from the thick exhaust ports of the boat anchored some 100 meters away.

What???

My lips formed the word, as my eyes blinked immediately wide open. The blue sky above me was brilliantly lit, and this light shocked my eyes.

"What the…?"

I exclaimed as I bolted upright to sit in the sand.

The boat! The boat is starting up! The engines are running!

I looked down the beach and sure enough, the boat was running, with Buddy at the wheel and the two girls on the bench in the back, 100 meters of white sand and turquoise water away. Then Buddy moved to the bow, leaned over the anchor line, and began to pull it up.

"What?" I said once again.

I knew at this point what was up, but I had to say it so I shouted,

"Are we going now? We are leaving?"

I'm not sure he heard me, or if he did he didn't show it. The anchor came out of the water and Buddy hoisted it onto the deck, opened the hatch, and dropped it in. He looked in my direction. I stared at him and he stared back at me. Then he started to laugh. Hard. It echoed across the water and sand between us, and I knew instantly and with devastating reality that he intended to leave me behind.

The horror of that thought hit me first in the pit of my stomach like a sharp pain, then it moved into my chest, and then my head, and I started to feel almost dizzy. I started to run to the spot on the beach closest to the boat. On the bow Buddy stood and laughed uproariously, holding his arms across his stomach as he bent over with laughter, almost falling overboard.

I screamed at the boat, some 80 meters away,

"Hey! Hey, you…. You…."

But I stopped before calling him what I wanted to call him. I had to hold in the profanity-laced tirade I really felt like yelling at him in case he was just playing a game and wasn't really going to leave me stranded. I ran into the water. It was a long way, and it would take me a fair bit of time once I had to start swimming, but I ran anyway. When he realized what I was doing, he abruptly stopped laughing and looked at me with a shocked expression, as if for a second he believed I might make up the distance; that I might get to the boat in time. Carefully Buddy crept over the sloping front deck, around the windscreen, and back behind the wheel, where he reached down and pushed each of the throttles forward to engage the engines.

The engines' low growling rumble grew louder, and I

slowed to a stop, frustrated, knowing I wasn't going to get there in time, and worse, that this was not a joke. He was leaving me on the beach. I stopped my useless flailing at the water. This floundering would never be enough to make up the distance. My arms dropped to my sides in resignation, and for a long second I couldn't even think.

Buddy looked at me and now he wasn't laughing, just looking back. Then he hit the throttles hard and the boat lurched upward and forward. The engines roared to life with a sound that seemed to hit me, but I didn't hear it, I didn't hear one bit of it; all I could hear was that,

"hah, hah, hah, hah,"

that laughter of his that seemed to go on and on and on even though he'd stopped laughing. That stupid bark-like-a-dog laughter of his was still ringing in my ears and rattling around inside my skull. He must have thought this was the funniest thing he'd ever done and was having a great big belly laugh because he'd left me on the beach. The boat receded quickly with Buddy at the helm and the two sisters once again seated on the aft benches looking back at me. Neither of the two girls raised an arm to wave. This pained my heart as much as Buddy's laugh.

Then he turned to me, now that they were safely on their way, and his barking laugh started again, and I could hear him yelling something. At first I couldn't tell exactly what it was, but then I made it out.....

"Flamingo...go...get a flamingo...a pink flamingoooooo...hah, hah, hah...."

Ouch! Again!

I stood and stared for a long time. After a while, when the boat was just a speck and waves of sound, now low and muted, were echoing like distant thunder off the trees lining the beach, I turned to survey the situation. Here I was, chest deep in water off this beautiful stretch of sand that was now sadly, tragically, too empty, and I was too alone, and this was driving the beauty out of the scene.

I looked back to where I previously lay and saw my red bag. I had a small towel, I had a t-shirt and shorts, I had some money, and I had my sandals, my toothbrush, and my camera, about half of what I'd been carrying on this trip. I was stranded on a lonely beach on an island I hadn't heard of until the night before.

I clenched my jaw and tightened my lips and slowly nodded my head, trying to stay calm, trying not to scream, trying not to let thoughts like, "How in the hell did I let this happen," enter my head and cloud my thoughts. That could come later, over and over again no doubt, but for now the question was what was I going to do?

But getting that other question out of my head wasn't easy. I supposed I'd have to get it out before my head would clear enough for rational thought. I tried hard to focus, not to dwell on Buddy and thoughts of my fist pounding his face. Think about that later, not now, later, no, don't think about that right now. Finally I gave up and waded back onto the beach, fell to my knees, and started pounding my fists on the sand as if it was his stupid braying face. It would have to do: screaming and calling him every name and every single foul thing I could think of. I called that…Buddy….everything I could think of, him, his brothers, his sisters, his father, his mother, the islands, but especially him, Buddy the Barking DOG.

Then I was next to blame. I began to chastise myself, calling myself and the islands and the sun and the sand and everything around me all the bad names I could imagine, thinking that if I cursed myself enough sooner or later I'd get sick of being called names and I could move on and start thinking about how to get out of this mess.

Eventually I did run out of nasty things to call Buddy, his family, and myself. It occurred to me that this was stupid chasing stupid, and I was wasting energy. No point to it and no good could come of it; except, of course, I did feel a bit better.

So, finally resigned to the situation, I gathered up my things, stepped into my sandals and began to walk inland.

To the north and now, sadly, to the south, what was beautiful beach was now only desolate stretches of miserable sand, and inland from the beach was a low bank upon which grew shrubs and spindly trees. I climbed the short bank and started to make my way between the trees.

After about a hundred meters I came across a narrow strip of rough pavement that ran parallel to the beach. I had to choose north or south and without much inner debate, as it meant nothing either way, I chose north.

I walked steadily for about an hour then decided it would be just as helpful to find some shade and wait for a vehicle to drive by as to continue to bake my hatless head in the sun. I found a suitable tree near the road and sat down and leaned against the trunk to wait. This change from activity to stopping had the unfortunate consequence of giving me more time to think about this possibly dire turn circumstances had taken. At least when I was walking I was doing something to get out of this situation. Sitting still was frustrating, threatening the hard-won, possibly temporary, and fragile confidence that finding the road near the beach had given me.

But common sense kept me seated. The heat of the

late afternoon and the chances of walking to some sort of town or village seemed slim at best. I hadn't even seen a road sign in the hour I walked. I had to control my thoughts, try not to think, and wait. This would be an exercise in patience.

Thankfully I didn't have to wait longer than a half-hour before a vehicle came toward me on the highway from the south, a battered pickup truck. I stepped into the middle of the road and waved it down. The driver eyed me suspiciously, but never asked how it was that I ended up there, too much effort I suppose, and no matter anyway. I turned my hands forward in a gesture of surrender or nothing to hide.

"In de back, mon," he said and motioned with his thumb into the bed of the truck. I climbed in and sat with my back against the tailgate. After a half hour of driving on the poorly-kept road through monotonous scrubland following what seemed to be the beach to the west, we came to a town a collection of rough houses. There were no signs anywhere, no restaurants, no gas station, not even a defined main street.

The truck stopped and I hopped out and stepped over to the driver's window,

"I'd like to find a boat to Nassau, or a room for the night at least."

He pointed toward the water, "No boat today, mon, down dere, mon, go."

Then he drove off as I said thank you to the back of the departing truck.

I shuffled off in the direction of "down dere."

It seemed a basic town on the water's edge, with a curving utilitarian beachfront and a small marina at the northern end where a few sailboats, some rough wooden dinghies and fishing boats were tied up to a single long dock with a right angle at the end in the deeper water.

One short street had two parked vehicles, but no moving cars. A small shop had a penciled sign taped onto the inside of the glass in the door, "Roti Today." I tried the door. Locked. I knocked and after a minute an elderly lady wrapped in an apron came to the door. I looked at her through the glass and said, "I need a room, and I would like a roti or two." She looked at me for a moment then at the sign, and then reached over and pulled it off the window. She said, "Roti done, but I let a room, mon."

Within ten minutes I was in a small room with a single bed of plywood covered by an inch of foam and a thin cotton sheet. One would be kind calling it basic, but it was reasonably clean. By now it was mid evening and became dark quickly, and obviously I was very tired because I barely remember what happened next. A sort of numbness took over.

Sunrise seemed to be the next thing that happened, as I blinked open my eyes and realized night had passed. I was stiff and sore from sleeping apparently without moving much because my hip ached from sustained pressure. Once my limbs would move again I was anxious to get out of the room to survey the town to see if I could find coffee and something to eat. I wondered around, searching without success. It was not a tourist town and had only a few buildings. I made my way back to my rented room and came across a lady washing clothes in a large basin at the back of the building. She was young but had hard features as if she was old and made it obvious she did not want to talk to me in the middle of her chores. I shimmied in front of her for a minutes before she finally looked up. I said, "Hello. Good morning. Can you tell me where I can find coffee, or something to eat?"

She continued grinding a sheet on the washboard,

"No, mon. Roti shop be open later. Maybe today."

"Nothing else, no other place?"

"No, mon, dis no Holiday Inn, and dere be no McDonals."

I had to shrug my shoulders as I walked away, resigning myself to being hungry for a while longer. Being hungry and a smart ass. I had to stay being a smart ass, I suppose, and I said under my breath as I departed, mimicking her accent, "OK, you got no McDonals in dis island, but how about some flamingo? I want some flamingo barbequed by a Bahamian momma. OK, you got dat?" But I said this quietly, not letting her hear. I was in her country and could not afford to be a smartass.

By about 2 p.m. the roti shop was still not open but the scent of frying wafted about the yard. Sitting on a three-legged stool at the front door, listening to the rustlings behind the closed door, I began to salivate in anticipation. I was achingly hungry, and her tardiness only heightened my appetite. I looked through the glass and watched her move about inside, seemingly at half speed. I had to think about something else. Like the watched pot that would never boil, she would never let me in if I watched her through the front window. I looked back at the rough beach of the small town, with rocks, broken coral, bits of conch shell, some smooth stones, and half broken trees at the water's edge. I was losing my love for the islands and had to mentally remove myself for a moment, to change the scene in my mind and wait out the time until the food was prepared. It might have been this mental effort, or it might have been the passage of time, but close to an hour after I expected her shop to open, she finally swung the door open and allowed me in.

She did, at her own pace, cook up some of the most delicious fried plantain and conch salad. By the time I'd eaten three mouthfuls the wait was forgotten, and I was once again in love with the islands. Hot greasy banana, rubbery seafood mixed with little green chilies that were cold but burned my mouth, roti that she said was her mother's recipe from Trinidad with curry and potato, it was delicious. As I finished the plate I knew it was an meal I wouldn't forget.

After, I went back out to find a place to sit, and ponder the sky, and feel sorry for myself, and review my situation. I was alone, very short of money, on an island with no other tourists or travellers, as far as I could tell, with no way of getting back to the main island, nor even an idea about how to go about it. I had to figure out how to get the hell off this island.

But, there was a dock on the small bay and where there's a dock there are boats, boats that go over water and maybe to other islands. I needed to cross water to get back to where I started.

OK, go to the boats.

I walked to the end of the dock and found a rickety shack where a man reclined in a spindly wicker chair. The man filling that small shack was big and looked studier than the shack itself. His feet hung out of the narrow door, and the soles of his sandals looked like slabs of rubber from a racing tire. I had to walk back and forth in front of him to get his attention, as he seemed quite absorbed in his reading material.

I said, "I need a ride to New Providence, any boats going that way?"

He looked at me with a smirk, a real smirk, a crossways smirk that infuriated me and went back to his reading. My patience was thin at best and here was one more man with an attitude, until finally he said,

"Mail boat, mon, mail boat come tomorrow."

I stepped away from those big rubber soles poking out of that rickety shack and left the dock to meander back to the roti shop, back to the three-legged stool to while away a bit more time. The sun was still shining, the clouds were white and puffy, I was alive and well and three meals a day was overeating. All in all, I wasn't doing too badly. I set my mind into meditation mode and prepared to wait for Rhihanna's Roti Shop to open for dinner.

Chapter Six

THE CAPTAIN AND THE LADY BLANCHE

The next morning I woke early. I was not exhausted and couldn't sleep comfortably on the hard bed. I tossed and turned wondering what I was doing in this room where the walls were beginning to close in. I was on an island populated by people shuffling about, doing a lot of nothing. Yes, I was hitting a low. I had nowhere to go nor could I, although I wasn't locked up. It was clear money makes even this small island world go round, and I was short of that. Had I some money to spend, even some of what I'd left under the mattress at Mrs. P's house, I could have arranged transportation, but as it was, I was marooned.

I had to get back for many reasons, but most importantly I wanted to get back so I could find that bar and hang around until Buddy, my pal, my good friend, my brother of the islands appeared and I could smash my fist into his stupid, ugly, braying face, one time for each bark of his hah, hah, hah, and one more for every one of the flamingos I was supposed to eat, skinned, plucked or otherwise. I was boiling inside, yes, especially since I'd discovered flamingoes didn't even live on the island. If he had half an imagination he could have said we would barbeque a pink elephant, and that's probably what he was telling his buddies back in the bar. I wondered what sort rap rhyme was going back and forth in that dark room now, with me the brunt of the joke – if , that is, if they could get the lines out over the laughter. My fingernails were piercing my palms at the thought of it.

But, I had to let that go, and I knew it. I could almost feel the stress dissolving the walls of my empty stomach.

Life flows in waves, high and low, and seldom in my privileged life had the wave dipped as low as at that moment. In reality, it felt so low because so far the lows in my life had been few and I had nothing much to which to reference this new low. To me, at the moment, this trough was deep, and I could only see walls of water around me, But I knew how to paddle. Yup, I could paddle up that wall of water and make my way out of these depths. I rose from the plywood bed and rubbed my face, trying to scrub away these morbid thoughts, to attempt to get back on track. Go, I told myself, try not to scratch welts from unseen bugs, get out that door, and go see the roti queen one more time.

The mail boat was scheduled to arrive at 2 p.m. At 3 p.m. I was starting to wonder if it would show. Just after 4 p.m. as I sat watching the bay beyond the wooden pier, a slight smudge of ascending grey smoke appeared on the horizon. I watched intensely, at first hoping this was my ride, then questioning if this could be the mail boat. I made my way to the dock and sat down to wait on a rail, not wanting to go to the end of the dock if this was not the mail boat.

She docked perfectly, touching the rail to the pier while young crewmen clambered off to tie thick lines to the cleats on the dock.

Old? Yes. Wooden? Yes. Everything wooden? Yes. Ancient? ….. definitely, yes. The crew began unloading boxes, suitcases, striped bags and duct-taped parcels of rough cardboard. Nothing in the way of mail that I could see.

My heart sank. This could not be the mail boat, another night on the plywood bed seemed ahead of me. But, as I had no choice, and nothing better to do, I decided to check with the captain of this vessel as to the whereabouts of the mail boat, as perhaps he would know.

The name M.V. Lady Blanche was painted in black letters on the bow. Blanche: What a name. She was old and she had been a fine boat - maybe fifty years before, from an almost bygone era of wooden boats, and without an ounce of fiberglass anywhere on this stout vessel, probably not even in the galley. She was as proud as a little old lady with a lacy hat and clutch bag tucked under her arm making her way to church on Sunday. She might have been a head-turner at one time but now faded glory and memories with a smile of pleasure and mystery all in one look. I stood on the dock, taking in the details, the blue and white paint over blisters of other paint, noticing the nice way – nice to me in its genuineness – each painter didn't quite cut in the trims perfectly, brush strokes that served as identifiers of each painter. It could be they were sons of sons painting each layer, this grand old lady had been around that long.

As I stood in admiration of her, a face and head protruded from the upper wheelhouse window, and instructions were issued:

"Be prepared to cast off the bowline Mr. Winston. Mr.

Hamilton, prepare the stern line!" This shout was issued in a regal manner but in such a booming baritone that I thought at first he was calling to someone in a house on shore. Official? Yes. Commanding? Completely. Here was the master of this vessel, and clearly very serious about his command.

"Look lively men! We have a schedule to keep!"

The captain's booming yell raised the hairs on the back of my neck, a full ten meters away and the crew moved to their tasks. He turned from watching Mr. Winston, who was moving to the stern line, and looked at me.

"And you," he said, "are you boarding as passenger?"

I looked up at him, and my hesitation caused him to ask again,

"Well, are you boarding, or will you cause our further loss of schedule?"

This too came in a loud voice, wholly impressive. These words uttered in such a voice and bearing gave me to understand exactly what they meant: these islands were barely able to get out of bed in the morning, never mind stay on any kind of schedule, but this man was the captain, and he was a proud professional. One could almost imagine that he was yelling at the entire island, as if he *wanted* to be on schedule, he *wanted* to be a professional, but being master of this boat was his lot, and the islands and the inefficiencies were his burden, but be damned if he wasn't above it all.

I was just about to say. 'Yes, I'm coming aboard as passenger,' but indecision stopped me. I was still not sure this was the mail boat.

"No, sir! I'm not coming aboard. I'm waiting for the mail boat, not a cargo boat."

Despite it being innocent this response caused an immediate reaction. The captain's naturally dark complexion, that had been darkened even more by a lifetime commanding a working boat in year-round sunshine, seemed to be turning to red, as his blood apparently began to boil. He struggled to regain the voice my insult had apparently stolen along with his breath. Eventually, in words uttered in a sibilant hiss, he managed to say:

"This is no cargo boat, my dear man! Have you not seen a mail boat? This is not some common *cargo* boat! This fine vessel and her crew have been charged with delivering the mail. She is the M.V. Lady Blanche, oldest and still finest mail boat in the Bahamas."

His face became even deeper red as he stopped to gather his thoughts, at a loss for further response to the indignation of my calling the Lady Blanche a cargo boat.

Without a word, fearful that he might refuse to grant me passage and wanting to get out of his sight before he bellowed again, I reached for the railing and stepped up the passageway. I could feel him seething with contempt above me, and I knew I had gone too far with that comment. I wanted to take it back, but I stepped on in silence, head down, to not antagonize him further. I moved to the aft of the boat and found a pallet loaded with sacks of something, boxes of tinned foods, and jugs of kerosene – his 'mail?', oddly enough, rather heavy for mail – and sat down out of his line of sight.

I was aboard and out of trouble. 'Keep it that way,' I thought to myself, 'or I'll be sleeping on plywood and bowing to the roti queen for who-knows-how-many more nights.' Let's shove off and head back, hopefully, to New Providence.

Hopefully? Yes, hopefully. It occurred to me that I hadn't inquired as to where this boat was heading. When the man on the dock said, "Mail boat is coming," he did not say where it was going. That information hadn't been offered, and I hadn't asked for clarification. Being off the island was priority number one. Off to where didn't made the list. If ever the expression 'rolling the dice' meant anything to anyone, for me right then, heading to destinations unknown was just a roll of the dice.

Just then the aft line hit the deck behind me, cast off by the crew who then bustled back on board. Apparently being left behind on Eleuthera was no more appealing to the crew than it was for me.

The engine roared, and thick black smoke jetted from a six-inch exhaust stack. A deep drumming beat the deck and rumbled through me as the Lady Blanche slipped away from the. A shuddering coursed through the hull and much to my surprise the Lady B created a serious wake. The captain might have been trying to make a point, or we were seriously behind schedule, but I couldn't imagine this was normal cruising speed. It was likely the captain's reaction to my comment about the Lady B being a cargo boat that made him jam the throttle forward.

Within minutes we were in open water doing about 11 knots, probably top speed, but still a mere fraction of the speed of my passage getting to Eleuthera. But despite that it didn't take long for the island to become just a grey-green smudge on the horizon.

We were away. The flamingoes were safe from day pirates once again, the guests of marauding drug dealers and their dancing girls in tight shorts bouncing at the edge of disaster while clinging onto an Italian plastic bullet. Within a half hour Eleuthera was out of sight and only the line of the horizon halved the blueness of sea and sky. Elusive Eleuthera, would I ever return to that thin pavement I walked, so forlorn and lost that afternoon, to Rhianna's heavenly roti shop? Who knows.

Now I turned back to the open water, to contemplate what lay ahead, which reminded me that I'd now embarked on yet another mystery trip. This three-hour-tour featured no Ginger or Maryann as the last did, and skipper was no friendly man, but I was finally away from the island, away from that misadventure, chapter done and closed, best put it to rest.

I moved to find a place to sit on the forward deck under the pilothouse windows but out of sight of the captain, half in sun, half in shade, with a fresh breeze blowing in my face. I began to feel better. We were on our way, and I congratulated myself on having survived being marooned reasonably well. I had no idea how long a trip back to New Providence would take at this speed, so I made some mental calculations based on the trip to Eleuthera. I remember we were doing 30 knots for about 10 minutes, then 90 for about 30, then about 30 again for the last 10 minutes, at which point we could see Eleuthera six miles or so in the distance. At about half way I'd backhanded Buddy's shoulder and he nearly sank us all. All this meant that it had to be about five hours across to New Providence.

But things felt strange and I could not correlate the timing. It was late afternoon and at this speed those five hours to reach the dock at New Providence meant arriving in the dark. It seemed strange that a mail boat would work in the dark, when hard to see navigational hazards meant certain risk. Veteran captains avoid risk entirely when possible. But we were behind schedule, which might have been why the risk was acceptable.

I closed my eyes and tried to relax, and noticed we were rocking more the further we went. The swells were larger and longer and the wind was becoming very brisk. Off to port, in contrast to the blueness above me, appeared an almost black, very large cloud spanning the horizon to the...south? Was that really south? I noticed the sun, still behind us. It was just after 4 p.m., and the sun was already on its downward slide to the western horizon and yet we appeared to be running away from it. I recalled that Eleuthera was due east of New Providence, which meant we should be going west to get back, but it seemed to me we were going…southeast? Were we really going southeast? In my gut, I almost certainly knew we were not going to New Providence. But I kept denying what my gut was telling me, even to the point of calculating the length of the trip.

Without my being conscious of it, my fingers began to scratch a suddenly itchy spot behind my ear, and I realized I had drawn my knees up to my chest. It was the ten questions at once that masked my thought of doing these two things. It took but an instant for the answer, we were not going west at all, we were not going to New Providence, because we were on a heading away from Nassau. My emotions swung through the range from quick anger, as in "Should I be mad at myself? Should I be upset at Eleuthera, whose residents could barely speak two civil words to me? Or the man on the dock?" to finally, acceptance. "What good will angry do?"

When I was on the island option one was to get on the first boat leaving and option two was to stay in a little town with few amenities and little money to buy them with. In other words, I had no option. This was it. I had had to get on the first boat accepting passengers.

The question became; where are we going and how long before we get there.

The swells were getting longer and higher on each side, diagonally across the course we were following. The flat bottom of the Lady B – made so to navigate sand bars and shallow waters – did not resist the rise and fall but rolled steeply with each wave, very high, and then very low. I was beginning to slide right and left on the deck as each rail rode up and down over the swells. At first I tried to just go with it, but the wind kept building and with it the swells. Very soon I had to pull myself up and ease my way to the railing for something to hang onto. It didn't take much longer for the wind to rise to a howl and the roll to deepen. The large black cloud that had appeared flat and ominous only a short while ago now covered half the sky and was coming fast. This was a squall, common, violent, sudden, and approaching at speed directly off the port side. I could see along the line of the horizon below that cloud that the darkness now reached the surface, meaning substantial rain falling just miles away. The pace of the approach meant we would be very wet, very soon. It was time get into the lee of something, and if not inside a cabin, at least behind one. In a matter of minutes I had gone from enjoying a calm passage to hanging on and seeking shelter.

We were still on the southeast heading as the squall approached, and I wondered how large the swells would have to be before the Captain, this stern and resolute man at the wheel, turned the boat to take them straight on. It would mean going off course and would lengthen our trip and I wondered how long he would still take them on the forward port side. I looked toward the pilothouse window, and could see his wooly head and his intense gaze staring out into the storm, both hands working the spindles of the large wheel. As I clung to the rail I looked back into this stiffening wind that whipped my hair, not in one direction as in the speedboat, but now swirling and blustery. The Lady B was now dipping up and down and rolling from side to side so my feet at the port rail almost touched the water until she rolled up again to a 35 degree angle to dip the starboard rail into the dark blue water putting me high in the air, above it all. We'd dip to port and had I not danced away from the rail, my toes would touch the water. Then up we went until my strength was challenged to keep me clinging firmly to the rail to keep from tumbling to starboard.

The wind was cool, and I knew I couldn't wait to find shelter, which would take some time since I could only move at the apex of the boat's pitch and roll. Taking two tiny steps at a time, I eased my way with groping hands to the starboard side of the wheelhouse. The passageway led aft past two doors and two round portholes through which I could hear the grinding sound of the diesel engine. Near the end of the passageway a door led to a steep set of stairs, and like a drunk I reached for the handrail and pulled myself to the first step against the dip of the starboard swell. Step by step, swell by swell, I made it to the top during the passage of three of those long dips from side to side. I paused at the door, unsure whether I would be allowed entry, then had to take hold of the handle so as not to fall. A flash of lighting compelled me to just go in, and see if I would be allowed to take refuge there.

I stood in the open doorway of the pilothouse just as the first heavy drops of rain tapped against the port side windows. I stood waiting, silently beseeching those inside for an invitation to enter, to close the door behind me. It had to happen soon. The wind was whipping in behind me and the rain rapped on the glass like a demon from inside the cloud that was asking to come in to drench us all.

Five faces turned to me at once. "Close de door, mon! Rain comin' in, mon," one crewman sitting at a rectangular table said.

I obliged him gratefully and latched the door behind me. Through the window in the upper door I could see the black cloud dumping torrents of rain on the cresting waves around us. I looked at that evil-looking cloud, relieved to be indoors, thinking, "No, you can't come in. I'm not answering." The taps were coming in furious succession, until they became the kind of ghostly knocks that make you scared to answer, and the rain was coming in sheets against the glass of the pilothouse and the window in the port side door, running off in the wind as the squall screamed at us. I was shocked at how quickly this rainstorm/squall had closed around us. Just minutes from the cloud appearing to this, wind and rain thrashing, whipping the deep blue seas into white crested peaks.

We raced at full throttle to the southeast until finally the captain turned the boat to face the wind and swells head on. That magnificent old captain stared forward intensely as if willing this proud old vessel through just one more squall, one more time. I moved to brace myself in the doorframe, setting my hands against the top and a foot against each bottom corner to keep stay in place against the new heights of pitch and roll. With the change in direction the boat took on a much more up and down motion, as if climbing a steep hill to teeter momentarily at the top, then a slide down a slope doubling her speed in and for an instant.

The captain spun the wheel furiously to keep the Lady B into the swells, and although he was working hard I could not read any nervousness or anxiety on his face resolutely looking forward. This was my first impression and now that I was in a position to expand that to vivid second and third impressions, I could see that he was probably all of eighty years old but still the proud master of this vessel and its crew and what this meant to him.

He had the thankless responsibility for the lives of the crew and the passengers when necessary, for the bloody Royal mail; for the Lady Blanche herself, in his words the oldest and finest of the mail boats in the whole of the Bahamas islands; and for the cargo he carried for the islanders along the way. They were all under his care, and he had to somehow push through one more squall and get us safely to our destination.

Without asking, I could see that he shouldered that responsibility for the fate of others because that was what it meant to be the master of a vessel on the open sea, in squall-tossed waters famous for taking ships and planes in a moment. Immediately my impression of him as Captain Stern transformed into something much kinder and more profound. I thought then,

"Get me home safely Captain, I'm sorry for my smartass comments, please get us and your Lady Blanche through this storm."

Aft of the wheel the pilothouse was otherwise filled with a table fixed to the floor with one solid round spindle. A padded bench wrapped behind this table, and this is where the crew had assembled. The two crewmen, Hamilton and Winston were there, as well as two others I hadn't seen before. All four had their elbows on the table, and were huddled over a string of dominoes. Each were holding tiles cuddled protectively in cupped hands to keep them secret and to keep them from sliding across the smooth table, and even though we were pitching and rolling violently they barely took heed of the weather as they played the game. Looking at them at this very normal pursuit made me realize that I was the only nervous person in the room, and this calmed me considerably.

Two or three were yammering loudly at all times, which seemed the island fashion, with expressions of great surprise or delight as each would pick a tile from their group and raise it high in the air, waving it about for a dramatic moment before slamming it on the table at the end of the string. SMACK! The tile would hit the table followed by a sharp HAH! or some derivative of 'in your face' by the player. Each in turn would do the same with equal force after adding his tile to the run.

I watched them quietly, observing their detachment from the captain's efforts at the wheel, completely unconcerned for the boat or the conditions outside. This was telling. The captain was truly the captain, and nothing could worry the crew as long as this man was at the wheel.

Rain pelted the windows, the boat was rolling violently from side to side and bow to stern, the wind howled and the only concern these four men had was that this rough weather was causing the dominoes to slide out of line. I realized this vessel had probably seen more than her fair share of squalls, and worse, being based in a hurricane zone and spending her entire career in the heart of the legendary Bermuda Triangle. To have reached this age proved the Lady B could take the conditions.

But then the captain turned and shouted,
"Mr. Hamilton, check the lashings on the aft deliveries."

Mr. Hamilton gave him a "Why me?" look as his raised hand paused from smacking a domino on the table, then CRACK! he smacked the tile down with a vengeance, obviously not happy he had to suspend the game for the bothersome task of doing his job. With mutterings of protest he slowly rose and made his way past me. As he opened the door a fierce gust of wind hit him and he slipped out as the crew patiently put the game on hold until his return.

Another crewman took the pause in the game as an opportunity to pull out a bag of food. He extracted a foil-wrapped bundle then peeled it open to reveal a number of small deep-fried fish. He passed them around, then, deftly moving with obvious practice about the wheelhouse, he set three small fish on a napkin which he then placed on the dash next to the captain. I'd never seen anything look or smell so tasty in my life. If I was hungry before, these little fish, greasy, cold, with barely any flesh on them, made me even more conscious of being achingly hungry. Outside the sky was fully dark, the rain hit the windows with staccato notes, fierce for seconds to then relent, then resume with force. The boat pitched up and down to 40 degrees on each swell, but my only thought was for those eyeless fish, coated with thick breading, island style. Someone's mama fried those little morsels of flavor, minutes after being pulled from the water, like she'd probably fried them for fifty years. I don't think there was anything I wouldn't have given up at that moment to be invited to take one of the remaining fish.

But, I wasn't invited. Passengers should know to bring food along if they wanted to eat, especially unexpected passengers. After the skipper finished his fish I made my way over to stand beside him and to match his swaying with the movement of the boat, hanging on with both hands to the instrument console, temptingly close to the small pile of thin fish backbones and head and little tails.

Speaking slowly, directly at his ear over the din of the rain and the wind and the engine, I asked, "How long before we get to Nassau?"

He didn't turn to face me but I thought I saw a strangely puzzled expression cross his face. I asked again, louder this time in case he hadn't actually heard me the first time, "How many hours before we get to Nassau?"

He continued to stare forward, he didn't turn his weathered features toward me as he said, "Nassau? Young man, we be back in Nassau in one week, not one hour."

Damn! I knew it.

I could take no consolation from having discerned we were going south - or southeast. When I embarked on the Lady B, I knew it was taking a chance, and I could have easily asked the man on the dock, or the captain before I got on, but I didn't really want to know where she was going just as long as I was getting on and going too. That's how badly I wanted to get off Eleuthera. But it was now confirmed, we were not on the way to New Providence.

"OK, so, can you tell me where this boat is going?"

For the first time he turned from the blackness of the windscreen and the compass before him, but his hands shuffled rapidly one over the other, back and forth, to spin the wheel as we dipped and dove up one bank of water over the crest and down another. When he looked at me I could see that his reaction to the question was going to be as strong as the one to the insult to his dignity I'd offered when I first came aboard, and he said slowly, mocking my slow delivery of the question,

"I don't know what you are doing on my boat. But this vessel is in the service of Her Majesty's Royal Mail. We deliver the mail, or any other requirements of the population. We are on a heading to the Exumas."

I noticed he'd deftly avoided the word "cargo."

This response came in precise clipped English, his baritone voice rising in volume and depth like the crescendo of a Venetian opera, words pronounced in distinctly separate syllables, the s's hissed between his teeth. This last, and loudest, of the words was followed by glaring indignation which lasted too long, before he turned his attention back to the compass and the windshield. Ouch. Two tongue lashings in one day, but I suppose I deserved it. Following your nose without thinking can lead to this type of chastising.

I looked at him, quite the spectacle. He could have conquered the planet had circumstances been different and the opportunity to lead a powerful nation come to him. But it hadn't. He was the captain of a mail boat, not the leader of a country. This was the second time his passion erupted, and I stepped back to spare myself one more piercing stare. To ease the tension I asked again, quickly, in an effort to end the sequence of questions,

"Where exactly are we going?"

He glared back at me, "Did I not just say?"

It seemed he needed to make everything a question, and I shouldn't ask him anything unless I wanted him to lose patience and call me an idiot in front of the crew at the table.

I sidled away and the domino players were quiet as I turned to the table. All four crewmen were looking at me, chuckling with amusement. Obviously they knew to leave the captain alone when the boat is rocking and the wind is howling and darkness is upon us and our destination still hours away. The captain had blistered me as I supposed they'd all had been at one time or another. I stepped meekly to the table and nudged my way onto the last bit of bench in an attempt to change the scene in that wheelhouse from four crew, one tyrant, and one wayward traveler into one tyrant and five who did the tyrant's bidding. They understood, smiling as if they knew the feeling all too well. We now had a bond.

Then, with a loud crack on the wooden table, a domino hit down at the end of a line and the game went on. The wind whistled through every crack, the boat rolled up and down and side to side. All four of them were barely sitting, bracing their feet to keep from sliding back and forth on the smooth cushions of the bench. Rain dashed against the glass, the wind thumped at the closed door, thunder occasionally followed a flash of sheet lighting, but regardless of all the commotion, the men played on as if they were in someone's kitchen.

Comments went back and forth for a number of minutes, laughter at a joke, a guffaw over a misplayed tile, swearing at luck, good or bad, cursing at each other for slowness of play, or for winning the string. After several minutes I had to ask, as I had no idea what exactly were 'Exumas' just as I'd had no idea what an Eleuthera was.

In casual tones, I asked the man next to me,

"So we're going to Exumas?"

He turned to me with a broad smile, "What you doin' on dis boat, mon?"

Here we go again, ask a question only to get a question in return. To hell with it, no hiding anything, I decided to confess, to just let it out,

"OK, let's be honest, I'm so stupid, I wanted to go to New Providence, and I thought this boat was going there."

He laughed aloud and rapped the edge of the table with both hands and said to the others,

"I tot dis boat was going dere. I tot dis boat was going

dere."

He repeated it to a laugh from the other three. My temper began to rise but I fought it back. I sat back, not willing to say another thing, as everything I said was mocked. My thoughts turned to how I'd gotten there.

This was free-form travelling in the truest sense of the word. I was going somewhere, unknown, for duration, unknown. My stomach turned.

But, I would be OK. I would make it. Sure I would, it always turned out OK, sure it would, I hope. It was just me looking after me, learning as I went. Laugh all you want. I did something that could have worked out well, or not. I was young and fearless or perhaps young and stupid, but fearless with that fearlessness that comes from lack of understanding about what to be fearful of. I might step into an open pit here and there, but I just had to climb out, and this was me climbing out again.

I smiled at them, acknowledging the humor of the situation.

"Yes, that is pretty dumb, and funny." I said.

They had stopped laughing and one of the men said,

"You mon, you be the mos' honest man I met, mon. But be careful wid dat 'me is stupid' talk. We might jus' believe you, mon. What is your name?"

I told him and offered my hand. We shook hands and then I introduced myself to the other three as well. What followed was a long series of island handshakes, goofy handshakes that involved complex wrist and finger manipulations. I decided I'd better learn this skill. Even before the lingo and the pidgin I had to learn the hand-speak of man-to-man clasping of hands that these islanders had created amongst themselves like a secret dialect, first introduced to me by Buddy, and now these crewmen, surely assembled from throughout these far-flung islands and brought together under the discipline of the captain.

With handshakes done we were now in a different place. I felt I was somewhat accepted, that I'd passed a test, taking the ribbing with humility, especially after the blast from the captain.

Crewman Winston asked, "Hey mon, why you not ask which way de boat goin' wen you got on?"

Not a hard question to answer,

"I had to get off Eleuthera and I didn't have any other options."

He seemed to understand, "Yo, mon, off de islan, on de boat. OK, mon."

I nodded in agreement and turned my palms up in the "What you going do?" expression.

"So, when do we get to Exuma?" I asked.

Again the group chuckled, there seemed no limit to how little I knew.

"Exuma is not an islan, mon, Exumas is a chain, mon, a chain of islands. Dis boat go for one week. We take one week, seven days mon, go to six more islan's then go back."

This came as a revelation, but one I had to accept quickly. I had to run with it, to make a joke somehow. I shook my head and tried to say the words with their accent, I said slowly, "Aye mon, me real lost mon."

At this all four burst into laughter. Winston slapped his knee and the table twice, "Yeah, mon, you real lost. Hah!"

So now I understood. The mail came once a week for the islands and Eleuthera was the first stop, she was late and had at least one more for the day, or evening.

"OK, what's the next stop?"

"Staniel Cay mon, we be dere in two, tree hours."

The dominoes game resumed against the swaying of the boat and the swearing at the tiles for sliding around the table. The dim lantern with a solid shroud around the top cast a narrow circle of yellow light over only the middle of the table, so we sat in darkness, only cupped hands around tiles and the long string of bones in the faint light.

I sat in silence, assessing this last piece of information. It was just past 7 p.m. and we were hours away from our first stop. I had no place to sleep and had not eaten since morning. The boat was pitching about in the blackness of a squall, rain pelted the windshield, and it could have been a worrisome moment, but a table full of crewmen was getting a good laugh at my expense. Sure made the conditions outside an afterthought. I had to just shake my head. I had to ask, thinking I might as well end the suspense and get the answer to my most pressing question,

"So is there a hotel on Staniel?"

A belly laugh was all I heard from the crewmen before Winston looked at his buddies,

"He asks is dere a hotel on Staniel."

He laughed even harder and the rest of the group joined him until all four were rolling with laughter.

"Yeah mon, dere be de big Heel-ton on Staniel. Big high rise mon, wit a beeg swimmin' pool, mon."

He smacked the table with his hands as he laughed. Hamilton took it farther, "Big ho-tel, yeah, wit a disco."

He high-fived the man closest to him, and they did their island handshake with thumbs wagging and finger yanking. After they stopped Winston turned to me, trying to not laugh again, "A hotel on Staniel? Dats good, mon, but dere ain't no hotel."

Now, finally an answer, there was no hotel on Staniel Cay. I wasn't sure if I should be pleased that I got an answer, considering what the answer meant. The four kept chuckling. I wasn't quite so happy, desperate, almost ready to crack. I didn't know how much longer I could take this without breaking down completely. I stepped back to the captain who hadn't said a word since putting me in my place. He was still spinning the wheel back and forth, staring from the compass to the window to the compass to the window.

I didn't care if he blasted me again. I had to know.

"So no hotel, I got that, but is there a place to stay on Staniel?"

He didn't turn his head, but had heard the conversation at the table behind him,

"No hotel on Staniel. But Hattie has a cottage she be rentin' now and den."

OK, I was getting somewhere.

"Do you think I would I be able to stay in Hattie's cottage?"

He looked at me now and seemed less irate.

"Hattie run de islan, I radio her and ask if her cottage is not all booked up." He looked at the ship's clock.

"Power shut on de islan at 9 p.m. so we be dropping you in de dark. She have to come show you de way."

He paused, and then reached for a mic on a cradle. He spoke into the mic for about five minutes, in fast Bahamian language. He spoke to others differently than he spoke to Hattie. He clipped the mic back on the cradle and turned to me,

"She can take a boarder in de cottage, $20 per night."

Twenty? That was what I was paying for Lawrence's room in Nassau. That was almost what I was paying at the Shelbourne in South Beach. But I had no choice, and for that price it might be a nice cottage, maybe even really nice. It would have to be if she could charge twenty dollars a night for it. My mind conjured images of a feather bed in an island cottage overlooking the sea with a hammock hanging on the front verandah and rum in a coconut with a little umbrella on top.

"OK, great! I will stay there, thanks. How will I find her place?"

He said, "We not be stopping long dere. Dat liddle

dock, no way in dis wind we be staying long. I will get alongside de dock so we can off-load de mail. You stay out de way. Hattie will come. When I get close you step off."

He looked me hard in the eye to ensure I understood. I looked back at him respectfully and his expression softened slightly at my slow nod. He knew that I knew what he wanted from me: stay out of the way and do not get hurt getting off. Accidents would not be tolerated even though the wind and rough waters would allow for at best a risky unloading of whatever mail was destined for that island, and now a passenger.

A light misting of perspiration had appeared on his forehead that might have been there awhile without me noticing and was beginning to show as one bead of sweat and then another. This man with the steely exterior, who might have been pilot of a 747 had circumstances been different, was the master of this vessel, without auto pilot, with a bare minimum of navigational instruments, almost completely without navigational aids around outcroppings and shifting sandbars, without weather charts or even radar to see in the dark, working daily in waters famous for unpredictable and violent squalls and for making ships, boats, planes and all else disappear.

He caught me studying him, and I looked away, but I understood him better and realized that he was making quite an impression on me. Weathered and wise he was.

I turned away to leave him to his task and find a dark corner to hide in until I would disembark, understanding his concern for the upcoming approach under these conditions. The flat bottom of the Lady B exacerbated the roll and pitch and sideways crabbing across the water caused by the force of the wind. The pilothouse acted like a sail in the strong winds, and at times The Lady B slid in the water to starboard even as her bow pointed to port. I settled into the farthest corner of the wheelhouse with the crew who had now put away the dominoes to completely darken the interior of the wheelhouse. The crew fell silent within the driving beat of the of the pelting rain, the rattling of the door in its frame, the high pitched whistle then low moan, then high pitched whistle of the wind forced in around the closed door. With feet splayed wide on the floor I held rigid to stay in place against the rolling swells as Captain Roland Grey, epaulet festooned and regal, spun the spokes of the wheel furiously in the dull green half-light that shone from beneath the rose of the gimbaled compass before him.

After an hour or so of wind and engine howling, of pitch and roll, the captain pulled back on the throttles and the engine noise dropped. We were nearing the island. The crew began to muster reluctantly, now resigned to the reality of having work to do in the rain began collecting their gear from lockers in the rear wall.

Through the windshield a single point of light appeared in the distance. It was faint, perhaps nothing more than a lantern, and the only light to be seen as it dipped up and down in the distance describing jagged lines on the rain sheeting the windscreen. I had to shake my head at the thought that we were compelled to approach an almost invisible dock on a completely black island in this wind and driving rain and amazed that this man, this Captain could approach this island, without radar, virtually blind, in this wind and rain. Nothing beyond that single faint light could be seen in either direction over the length of the shadow that was the island we approached, this being the only slight differing hue than the clouds above, still a roiling purplish black pulsing with lightning from within and illuminated just enough to describe the craggy outline of the island.

We approached gradually, making small advances toward the dock, rolling from side to side while the captain manipulated the wheel and the throttle. At times we were sideways to island, at times bow-on. We still pitched up and down, and I felt the boat go up and to port on a wave to shore, then it crested to slide away.

It seemed the waves formed a barrier to had to cross before reaching the flatter water nearer the dock. The crew had assembled on either side of the captain, watching silently, jokes and comments put aside, awaiting the approach and a command. We rose up and slid down, the engine raced then slowed. The captain rocked the throttle back and forth as he spun the wheel into a blur of wooden spokes and palm-polished handles. Then with a thrust to full throttle we powered ahead and slid over the top of a wave to cross the barrier and slide toward the dock. To stop this movement and to steady the boat, the captain spun the wheel hard to port and pointed the bow toward the middle of the dock then pulled the throttle fully back. The engine roared, we surged toward the dock on the swell of the wave while the engine pulled in reverse. The captain barked commands, looking straight through the windscreen,

"Mr. Hamilton, Mr. Winston, prepare to offload. Mr. Benjamin, Mr. Carpenter, prepare the aft and forward lines. Look lively. We have only a moment in the lee, and we're not doin' dis twice."

The wave on the stern pushed us forward, and we were running toward the wooden dock even against the reverse thrust of the prop as the crew disappeared. The next command was directed at me. The captain's eyes burned into mine, and he told me in no uncertain terms exactly what I should do,

"Return to main deck, wait at de passage. When goods begin to offload, step down to de dock. Do not jump and do not, I repeat, do not fall between the boat and the dock."

He paused then said, "You understand me?"

This question came forcefully into my ear so as to be

heard over the noise of the wind, the rain on the windshield, the drone of the diesel engine, so loudly that it hurt my ear.

"Yes!" I said, then turned and left the wheelhouse.

As I reached the bottom step, the boat, previously racing bow-on to the dock, spun to port. The engine raced as the captain worked the prop against the water to swing the stern toward the dock. His magic, at having us at the precise speed required had our momentum sliding the boat sideways, ever so gently, contrary to all I thought would happen in these conditions, nearer the barely visible dock. The crew began unlashing lines and straps holding the bundles of goods to be moved over the rail.

Then it was up to me. Perhaps it was the stern instructions, the look he gave me which ripped my confidence, as now I felt the good captain and crew were not the only ones facing a challenge, and at that moment it became a daunting challenge. From a simple step off a moving boat onto a barely visible dock to this, me questioning my very coordination and ability to *not* screw this up. I too was involved in this approach and had to not fall, now that the dock was within stepping distance. I only had to step down from the pitching boat. Sure, no problem. Considering two crewmen would have to precede me onto the dock to catch the lines fore and aft, I just had to do what they did to gauge the distance and drop and time it just right. Sure, what could possibly go wrong?

In the faint light I could see the outline of what appeared to be a woman, standing, waiting. The wind was whipping her loose gown around her. The kerosene lamp she held lit a moving pool of light around her feet. This was the only light but at least something to use as a reference point to gauge my simple step down.

The boat rocked away from the dock once more and a gust of wind came with a fresh sheet of rain. The woman stood still against it, the rain pelting her back. We rose slightly and fell on the remnants of another wave, and the captain steered to port, then starboard, to keep nursing the port rail toward the dock. I could see my stepping-off point would be where the woman with the lamp stood. Near the bow and at the stern, the two crewmen stood on the outside of rail, ready to step to the dock with me. As we came within six feet both crewmen tossed the thick lines they held into the darkness.

The lines landed, and when the boat was within three feet of the dock I could just make out the leaping figure of the forward crewman. I heard his feet thump on the dock immediately followed by the thump of the crewman at the stern. Each gathered up the loose end of the line like he was catching a runaway horse. The distance closed and I lowered the cable at the passageway then shouted to her,

"Move, please."

I wanted her to step lack as we approached. She looked up against the rain for a second then stepped away. The pitching and rolling, the strong wind, and the driving rain made stepping onto that dock and not jumping a struggle against my instinct.

Finally, I could see wooden planks in the light of the lantern and I reached out my foot into the darkness. The boat surged sideways, nestling up against the dock as I stretched out further then let go of the railing. Slightly misjudging how low the dock was I stumbled forward before regaining my balance just before falling off the far side of the dock. The two men still on the boat began passing bundles of goods over the side to the two crewmen on the dock below.

The woman looked to me and gestured without speaking, 'We go'. A kerchief stuck to her hair matched her dress and was tied at the back of her neck. She turned to walk in long strides away from me, down the dock and around the corner toward the shore. She was moving away, and suddenly my interest in how the crew planned to somehow land the cargo had waned. I am not selfish, but that was not my job. I had been considered a bother from the moment I stepped aboard the Lady B, the best thing I could do now was to stay out of the way and not lose track of my island escort and my lodging for the night.

"Wait, wait for me," I said in what seemed barely a whisper against the wind and noise of the engine. I followed the faint pool of yellow light illuminating her feet and round backside to where the dock ended and the sand began, quick-stepping to not lose sight of her.

However, that possibility didn't stop me from turning to look back, as if compelled, as if I was missing something.

The captain, deeply concerned about losing his sorely tested night vision, essential in the darkness, had not allowed lights during the unloading of goods, so the crew was working furiously offloading boxes in the faint reddish glow of the port running light. The white sides below the band of blue at the rail of the Lady Blanche were faintly visible moving against the lines that were first slackened then stretched taut as she slid away from the dock on an outgoing wave. The next wave coming in swung the Lady Blanche back in to hit the dock hard. His head was now hanging out the window just fore of the port light and looking like a burgundy ball in the glow of the port light, and he bellowed to hurry the crew,

"Get those goods ashore, Mr. Carpenter. We're not waiting for another wave."

Mr. Carpenter, like Mr. Hamilton, and the other two didn't move faster, they were at top speed already, not needing encouragement, concentrating on handing down all manner of goods needed by these islanders for the week or until the Lady B's next visit.

But, not fast enough, and the boat rocked once more against the dock, and again the sound of creaking wood could be heard. It was a spindly dock, it's thin legs set into the sandy bottom, and this tested its strength to the maximum. Finally the last of the parcels was passed down and the crew could let the lines loose. They scrambled for the opening in the rail to climb hastily aboard as the boat closed the space once more, then just as she moved away again, the second of the two crewmen who'd been on the dock made it through the passage and back on deck.

With the crew back aboard the captain looked for a thumbs-up. He turned toward me and extended his left arm, visible in the red glowing light as he flicked a brief wave to me, just a quick movement made in the short pause he could take from the work required to keep 40 tons of mail boat from crushing the little dock the residents of Staniel Cay had built for themselves. This was his duty, and I never respected a man more than I respected that man at that moment, especially given that he still took a second to wave farewell. I swung my arm up over my head and waved back to him. I said something like, "Safe passage to you," but the wind and clatter of the palms thrashing about the island over my head prevented anything from been heard beyond a few meters. His arm disappeared into the cabin and the engine roared back up to full throttle and on the receding water of the most recent wave, the Lady Blanche's bow was turned into the incoming waves and within seconds was out of sight except for the green of the Starboard light as she turned to the north. Then, after only a few moments more the sound of her engine was gone too behind the howl of the wind and the thrashing of the palm fronds.

The woman, Hattie, was further up the path at the end of the dock, and was waiting impatiently. She yelled to me, "Waves don' come dis way, nevah before," over the noise, then turned and began to walk through the heavy vegetation.

I could hardly believe I was back on shore. Those six hours on the water had felt like sixteen. We'd hit a thousand waves and rocked a thousand times in that six hours, and I felt drained but utterly happy, almost goofy happy, that I was ashore. I wanted to raise my arms to the heavens, to kneel and kiss the sand. What a relief it was not to have to further endure the rocking, back and forth and up and down, in the pitch blackness to the sound of the rain, the wind, and the engine while it and the Captain both worked so hard to keep us bow-on to the waves for those hours.

At the same time, regret swept over me. The captain had made quite an impression. I had just come through an experience that I thought significant, and would be with me for a while, and I was now on solid ground. He on the other hand had to head back out for more in that still violent storm. This little dock was no refuge for the mail boat. They could not tie her to that small pier in these conditions, so the captain had no choice but to take her back out into those swells, and carry on in that dark and miserable night, and I was sure he had done so without a thought even crossing his mind to protest the necessity of doing so.

Chapter Seven

HATTIE'S AND THE NIGHT OF THE COCKROACH

I **turned away from** where the boat had departed and let out a sigh of relief. That was done, the captain had done it, the dock was intact, the 'mail' delivered, and a passenger disembarked without drowning or being crushed between the boat and the dock. For his sake, I wished for the wind to die down. When I turned back to the path, it was black again, and the lamp and Hattie were not in sight. She'd left me behind. I called out,

"Hello! Hey! Hello, I am still down here. Wait!"

I took two long strides in the direction she'd gone and just as I started the third stride the front of my sandal and protruding toe cracked into a thick root crossing the path.

I tripped and fell to my hands and knees, my bag rolling into the darkness before me, intense pain shooting up my leg.

I turned and sat down on the path grasping my ankle tightly to relieve the pain shooting from my toe. The light and Hattie reappeared. She called out.

"Don't be just sitting in dis rain. Come now, keep up."

"Sorry, I lost sight of the lamp," I said as I grimaced in pain, groaning out the words through gritted teeth, hoping my toe wasn't broken.

"Well, don' be losin' no sight of de lamp, or you be sleepin' in dis road."

I wanted to say, "Yes, ma'am. Sorry, ma'am, for breaking my foot, ma'am," but I just looked up at her as the rain hit my face.

She turned away, and I got to my feet and began hobbling after her, trying to stay as close as possible, matching her footsteps to avoid hazards. The long gown she wore was drenched and clinging to her back, her legs, and her round buttocks. I stepped carefully, trying to keep from tripping on other roots crossing the rutted path she called a road. Some twenty meters farther we came to a more defined path six feet of broken concrete wide and I did see in the pale lamplight a painted yellow line. If what we'd been on was a road, this must be a highway.

We walked another fifty meters or so then turned again to the right to follow another sandy path. After further 20 meters we turned onto a narrower path so completely overgrown we had to push back the vegetation to get through. Within ten steps on this path we came to a rough wooden shack with a rickety and poorly fitting clapboard door. She reached for the latch and it was at this point I realized that this was my room for the night. My heart sank to my sandals and my throbbing toe.

Cottage by the sea?

Hammock?

Rum with umbrellas??

Mysteries lie at many of the turns that a person's life may take, and each mystery ends with a good or a bad or a happy or a sad, but the mystery of where I would be staying that night was not ending near the good or happy end of the scale. She pulled back the crude slat door until it stopped on a branch growing near the edge. She reached out, grabbed hold of the branch and twisted it until it broke free, allowing the door to fully open.

"Whoa," was all I could whisper, partly in awe of her strength, but more at the fact that a branch of the size she'd managed to wrench off the tree meant that this so-called cottage had not been occupied for a while. Either that or the trees around here grew with atomic speed. She stepped back and held the light so I could pass through the door she held open. A gracious gesture, indeed, but, no, I could not. I swung my arm out with a wave,

"No, please, after you," I said, with a small bow.

I followed her into the shack. Without my being aware it happened, my hand gripped my jaw to keep it from dropping open. Seeing what the feeble lamplight revealed in that shack had me holding my jaw shut lest something found its way in. The shack – that is what it was, in any language or any country and nothing better could be said of it or describe it, other than a shack – had interior walls limned with greenish, or gold/green plaster, that at one time may have been either of those colours. Now it was hard to say, and the cracks in the plaster revealed the original colour of its earthen base which was almost red or brown in places and winding in cracks here and there on the walls like the surface of a blistered desert.

But it wasn't the colour, the cracks, the contrast between the two revealed by the weak flickering yellow light of the quarter-inch flame of the kerosene lamp that had my jaw dropping open. It was what moved on these walls – what moved ALL OVER these cracked walls. Hundreds of huge-looking, shiny-winged cockroaches crawled in every direction on the walls, the ceiling, and sadly, tragically, all over the cot in the corner covered with a grey army blanket and an army of cockroaches.

I stood still in disbelief, shocked, as I had no idea bugs could grow that big.

That cot in the corner, rusted metal with striped mattress, would sadly, unfortunately, for at least this night, this windy, rainy, bone weary night, be my bed.

But, only if, only could be, *my bed*, after I displaced the current inhabitants, these foul, shiny, greasy, monstrous, waxy-winged cockroaches.

Prospects were not improving for this weary traveler.

Hattie looked quietly about the room, and followed the course of a few of the larger ones on the wall nearest her. She knew what I was thinking and knew what she had to do. She set the lamp down in the middle of the floor and reached into the corner to grasp a homemade corn broom. Taking it into both hands, she assumed the position of a baseball player at the plate and swung the broom against a cockroach on the wall.

Ssswwwishhhh, went the bristles of the broom slicing the air, then *crack*, as it hit the wall and a cockroach.

The broom fell away, but there on the wall still perched the cockroach, using sticky feet and flexible legs to absorb the blow. He flexed his long pincer-like antennae, and then each of his wings, then scuttled across the vertical surface no worse for wear after being hit by the broom.

Hattie looked sideways at it with a puzzled expression, then looked at the broom like it had disappointed her. She swung once more, this time harder and faster.

Swissssh... the broom smacked the wall again.

This time rough bristles flew off the outer edges of the broom. Once again the broom fell away, and again the cockroach flexed and resumed his wall crossing. But, he did stumble, the blow had at least dazed him because when he came across a larger crack in the plaster he couldn't hang on and fell in a spin to the floor. He landed on his back, his ugly, gristly legs exposed on his underside, six or eight or ten of the damn things – who's counting? – and then, with a deft flick of some part of his body he flipped back over onto his feet.

Hattie was apparently not as stunned by these

impressive acrobatics as I was because, rapier-swift, her foot shot out to seize the opportunity, and like a wolf pouncing on rabbit, she stomped her rubber-soled sandal directly onto the cockroach. A sickening crunch followed, like the sound of a walnut cracking.

She held her foot down for a long second, twisting it, causing further crunching noises, then slowly raised it to survey the damage.

Oh, my God! It was still wiggling, and even though a third or more of its body parts and a good portion of its innards were left behind, it was trying to drag itself to safety. Hattie would have none of this, no chance, she had already spent more energy than she wanted to and with a vengeance she stepped once more onto the pile of disconnected cockroach parts. This time she spared no energy and leaned all her weight onto that foot and twisted right and left and right and left like she was following a Chubby Checker *Learn the Twist* tutorial, and more crunching and even squeaking could be heard from under her sandal. This time when she lifted her foot to survey the results of her efforts, the cockroach was in at least a dozen pieces and the grease spot was four inches across.

She breathed heavily, her chest rising and falling under her wet gown of patterned cotton. Only the sound of her rasping wheeze as she tried to catch her breath filled the space. Finally, when she could speak, she looked up at me as if nothing had happened, and said,

"Dere you go. Is just a little cockroach. No problem, mon."

Just a little cockroach? A *little* cockroach?

These had to be descendants of the ones that survived Los Alamos. I could not believe it. But it made me mad. It made me really mad. It was just a little cockroach after all. She was right. Who was the master species here? I wasn't going to take it anymore. I was mad as hell and wanted to kill one myself. I seized the broom from her hand and started smacking every cockroach I could, left and right and against the ceiling, in a fury as if possessed. I swept them and smacked them and did uppercuts and backhands and curl and drag moves. Soon the floor was crawling with cockroaches. I danced like a cheerleader on crack, hopping onto one then another, sometimes landing on two at a time, sometimes getting one under each foot. I twisted my feet on top of every fresh victim until I heard the crunching and even the squealing of cockroach legs on concrete. Hattie caught my enthusiasm and joined me, and started hopping on and off the ones still moving. Some were making it back to the walls and were trying to climb up to get out of reach. Hattie seized the broom and swatted them back down to the floor, and I hopped onto them as they landed.

I can only imagine what we looked like if someone could have seen us from above. Here we were, two grown adults, rain-soaked like drowned rats, hair mussed and flailing around our faces, one large and brown and one skinny and whitish dancing crazily, hopping from one foot to the other, sporting demented grins on our faces as we concentrated on crushing cockroaches.

After no less than a good five minutes, we pretty well had them all. We stopped and I set my hands on my knees, bent at the waist, trying to catch my breath. Cockroach parts littered the floor conjuring a memory of a painting I'd seen of the battle of Gettysburg. We both breathed heavily, the sweat on our clothing replacing the rain of the evening. I looked at her and in three long breaths, with one word between each, I said,

"It's…just…a little…cockroach."

I let out long sigh of relief as I caught my breath.

Hattie was much more winded than I, having had to expend twice the energy considering her size. Her breath was raspy, but with an effort she got out the words,

"OK, we got dem all. We done. You sleep here. I go."

I looked back at her in silence for a long moment. Yes,

she was going to leave now. Of course, this was now my cottage, my bungalow-by-the-sea. She stooped to pick up the kerosene lamp.

Huh?

I had to say something. I could not let her leave with the lamp. I said,

"OK, but let's take one last look and at least sweep up the dead ones."

She looked at the floor and nodded, then set the lamp back down to use both hands on the broom. With the lamp out of her hand, I stooped over to pick it up under the pretext of directing the light as she swept. Before long she had arranged a neat pile of broken wings, bodies and innumerable legs, then tugged open the door and with three sharp blasts with the bedraggled broom sent them out of the shack.

"OK. I go now," she said.

But I had the lamp in hand. She looked at the lamp, then at me. Then I asked her to stay a little longer. Maybe a premonition, maybe I didn't want her to leave, but I said,

"Can we take one more look? Maybe a few are hiding?"

She said, "It's just the wind. It's this wind, the storm from the east. No problem now, we keel enough of de bugs, no more now."

To reassure me she extended the broom under the bed, and to her surprise two cockroaches scurried out. We hadn't got them all, it seemed. I pounced on one, then the other in rapid succession. They crunched and I stepped away for Hattie to sweep these out the door with the others. I looked back at the cot, and I knew we would have to move it aside to ensure we had them all.

I slid it away from the wall and at first glance, it was not so bad. There was very little movement, even though I expected a lot of it, and was relieved, until I saw him in the corner.

The biggest, ugliest cockroach of them all, Big Daddy Cockroach, was backed into the corner, apparently ready and willing to do battle.

Bring. It. On.

I could almost read the message in his tiny mind, all one-sixteenth of an inch of it. His body was at least three inches long, with legs so large the spikes on the undersides were clearly visible. His antennae made him look like a miniature Texas longhorn, three inches from curving point to curving point, suitable for mounting on the hood of a 65 Cadillac Eldorado. This one, the King, was at least half again as long as any we had crushed before.

Cockroach King, His Ugliness, caused me to shiver, and he was looking right at me.

It was obvious I didn't like him and he didn't like me, and we would have to have it out before I could sleep in his domain, there simply wasn't room for two of us in this lopsided shack. He'd found a safe place to hide, but was found out, and now with him witnessing the slaughter of his entire flock of subjects I knew I would not sleep a second knowing he was alive, possibly seeking revenge.

I stared him down, not taking an eye off him as I reached to take the broom from Hattie. I brandished it toward him, its bedraggled straw looking more like a bad hairdo than a broom, planning to jam it in his face, using his horns as aiming guides to zero in on and pin him in the corner with the last of the strength of broom's bristles long enough for Hattie to pounce on his glossy back.

Just as I was beginning my lunge forward he darted straight up the wall, then along the ceiling line, in a dash to the louvered glass window. I whirled around, twisting the broom like a baton to change the angle and thrust it forward with a tennis-player grunt. He was within six inches of escaping before I knocked him off the wall and back to the floor. He landed on his back but immediately sprung over onto his multiple legs, then deked left, then darted right at full speed to the wall once again, causing me to draw the broom up. But, at my move he pulled a full left and sped across the floor toward the crack under the door. My shoulders dropped as I understood he was going for the door and the window move was a fake. But I got it – busted ol' boy – and took two quick steps to block this escape. I had him now and brought the broom down hard on his entire body.

By this time my weapon was only half the broom it used to be and this crunch on the floor caused a half-dozen more straws to fly free. But there were some pretty tough bristles left and I had him trapped, and forced my weight down the handle of the broom. Just as I was about to stomp down on the bundle of bristles he appeared, first his head, sans horns, then his forward set of arms, pulling and crawling his way through the straws looking like Stanley searching for Livingston slashing through jungle. Once his head was free the two long antennae flexed forward to become rearranged like horns again, then his spiky legs crawled out, one sinister set at a time, and finally his bullet-shaped body and glossy wings. Apparently, he hadn't liked being pinned under those bristles, because he as he emerged he made a hissing sound and emitted a strong odor. Now he was really making me mad, stinking up my cottage-by-the-sea. But just as I was about to stamp my foot on his head he darted up the broom handle directly toward my right hand. I jumped back and tossed the broom toward Hattie.

"Here, you take it,"

I said, as the broom flew in her direction.

The broom bounced off the unprepared Hattie and fell to the floor, shaking the King loose. Once again he went straight for the crack under the door. This time, when he was mere inches from his salvation under the door, the flat rubber sole of Hattie's sandal came down, very hard, on his head. She too must have hated the King, as she twisted and turned and twisted her foot some more, for five full seconds on the back and head of that giant bug. She stood still for a moment longer. Then very slowly she lifted her foot.

The King had been dethroned.

His head was next to his fart-producing ass end – perfect place for it.

His wings were inches away from where they'd started and his legs were skittering around every which way like they had minds of their own and twitched spasmodically as if unwilling to give up the fight. Hattie and I observed this new arrangement of the body parts of the largest of them all, the last of them all, the ugliest of them all, the one that actually stunk up the place before being crushed, and I had to smile. Hurray! We'd won! We got the biggest of them all. This room was now a lot more like a cottage and now no longer a storm refuge for cockroaches. I felt we'd accomplished something, and the thought that this shack was going to be my room for the night and possibly for the next seven days was now just a little less sickening.

Hattie swept for longer than necessary, scrubbing the floor with the remaining bristles of the broom, and I could almost believe that she might be having second thoughts about having been so blasé about the presence of the cockroaches, working hard to make up for the condition of the room, which she was renting for an exorbitant amount to a traveler without any other option and without having kept it up during months of non-use.

She swept the same spot for ten or twenty passes, and it was getting almost silly, as if she could remove the parts, the sheen of the guts, and even the memory of what we'd just done by incessant sweeping. I started to feel she was doing this to avoid facing me because she knew the conditions were unacceptable.

But this was just making the best of it, and it was still better than being out on the sea in the storm. Palm branches on the trees were still whipping in the wind, the lower vegetation, ground palms, ferns, and shrubs all thrashed and clattered, hard broad leaves against hard broad leaves. The sound was a chorus of low whistling, hissing, and clashing rising and falling like a crazy orchestra using plastic cymbals. The wind gusted in through the openings in the louvered glass window with its broken crank and forced the wooden door to shake against its restraining latch and doorjamb. Suddenly the meager room in Eleuthera seemed like the Beeg Heel-ton the crewman on the Lady B had joked about. How could I have gone down from that?

Step into *this* new reality.

Hattie slid the cot back against the wall, and picked up the crude grey blanket. It looked like the ones I'd seen in old western movies used by cowboys or soldiers. It had been lying in a heap for some time apparently, as when she began to fold it a number of things fell to the floor – not sure what they were, but for sure not wanting to find out. Some things better left unknown. A musty smell assailed my nostrils with an almost overwhelming aroma of potato sack. All it needed was a good watering to make it spring to life, that's how organic the blanket was. She folded, or more accurately, bent it as neatly as possible, and placed it on the end of the bed. Stuffing was escaping from a number of holes in the mattress, and she placed the blanket over as many as she could as if to make them go away, then nodded in approval, satisfied she'd done what was needed to make this shack habitable. She reached out her hand palm upward, looked up at the ceiling, and then at her hand, and then at me, and I knew what she was getting at. Her gesture said, "See? Dry. No leaks. You're out of the rain, young man, try to get some sleep."

That's when she picked up the kerosene lamp.

I hadn't said anything about this room to this point, and I'd joined in to help rid the place of the giant cockroaches, but at this, I had to protest.

"You can't take the lamp, there's no light." I said, my voice cracking at the word 'lamp'.

She said, "I go back to my house."

"OK. How far?" I asked.

She said, "Not far, 20 meters."

I said, "But I need the lantern. What if the big cockroach sent a signal with that smell and his clan is coming to rescue him?"

She lifted the lamp and shook it slightly. The flame rose then flickered lower. She watched it then nodded,

"Okay, you can have it, but I go back to my house wid it first," and went through the door.

We made our way up a sandy path. The wind still thrashed the palms overhead but the rain had stopped and we soon came to her house, a small bungalow set off the road. She went to a side door and opened it to a dark room then turned and passed me the lantern.

Back inside the shack I set the lantern in the middle of the floor and sat down on the bed with my back to the wall, suddenly feeling very alone. The wind rattled the tin roof and rustled under the door and through the louvered window. With Hattie now gone and after the drama of the cockroaches it was almost too quiet, even with the music of the wind playing plastic cymbals outside. I became conscious of throbbing pain in the toe I'd stubbed, and I drew both feet up to the edge of the steel cot to gauge the damage. The nail had been forced up by swelling, and throbbing coursed up my leg in slow waves. Stomping the roaches had not helped it at all. I hugged my knees to my chest and stared down at the flickering lamp, listening to the sound of the wind in the trees above.

It was a sobering moment. I was suffering miles deep angst.

Now, I was really alone.

I pondered mistakes and foolishness and forcing adventure and having no fear and being caught in a cycle of misadventures I was having trouble breaking out of.

I again started thinking about the ebb and flow of life

like waves, wondering about where the flow was taking me and questioning where the bottom of the trough was going to be and how would I get out of it when I got there if this wasn't it already. What had been so bad about the safe confines of home? Why was I in this interminable trap, and what could I possibly do to change it?

After a seemingly long time, when I realized I'd gone over the same thoughts three times and came to the same conclusion, or lack of, three times, I forced myself to stop thinking about it. An exercise in diversion was required; negativity was bringing me down. I stared without blinking until my eyes became blurry and images crossed, and the patterns on the floor began to move. The fractures in the concrete floor began to look like little rivers on a map, and a place I had only dreamed of, a place of exotic mysteries appeared before me, a map of central Africa, flowing water and all. My mind wandered and I imagine the lines were rivers with moving water. I could almost imagine the entire continent. The fragments of broken legs missed by the broom were the shrubs, and bare spaces were the plains, and the rivers brought water to feed the plains, and fish lived in the streams. I was hallucinating or something was wrong with my blurry eyes because suddenly across the plains came water buffalo or perhaps elephants in twos and threes. They were coming for water in the little rivers that were the cracks that moved in the flickering light.

Wait.

This was not a map of the plains of Africa but the floor of a shack in the Exumas.

Those aren't water buffalo or elephants invading the flood plain after a rain in the mountain highlands, these were cockroaches!

The damn things were coming back!

Cockroaches were coming under the door.

I wanted to swear or scream and shout at them to go away.

"Did you not see the pile of your dead comrades at that door? Do you want to die too, you stupid cockroaches?"

"Leave me alone!"

I willed the light to remain bright, but it would not. The map of Africa, with its rivers and plains was darkening as the light was dimming. The outside corners of this map of the entire continent was now crawling with water buffalo in the form of cockroaches and were now in almost total darkness. The sun was setting on the entire world beneath me – the kerosene lamp was flickering low – it was almost out of fuel.

In painfully slow increments the corners of the room darkened and the faint circle of light around the base of the lamp retracted until it was just a tiny flame less than that of a match, "So that was why Hattie shook the lantern." It was almost out of fuel and she had to have known it would only be minutes before it went out. I watched the map, and before long the corners were in darkness as were the rivers over the edge of the horizon. Then the small circle of yellow light at the base of the lantern was just a point of light reflecting off the base, and the flame was just a speck on part of the wick, and then even this gave up the effort and the tiny flame died.

Now I sat alone with my knees to my chest on a striped mattress on a bamboo cot with a Buffalo Soldier blanket at my feet in a shack in the Bahamas in the pitch darkness surrounded by a marauding mob of vengeful cockroaches. I shook my head at these thoughts.

I'm cracking up! I'm totally losing it!

Maybe they don't even bite, who knows? I'm sure no man has ever died from being eaten by giant cockroaches. But what do I know? Maybe cockroaches have eaten thousands of men but I never heard about it. Maybe mothers are mourning the loss of babies that had been carried away by cockroaches. Maybe I was going nuts and making this up in my head to confirm my lunacy.

Over the sound of the wind in the trees beyond the simple wooden door and the louvered window, I could swear I could hear the footsteps of fresh troops in the cockroach army. Battle group Alpha, 101st Airborne, equipped with night vision, transparent wings.

Yahhh!! I am **losing** *it.*

But I did read somewhere these things would inherit the earth if there were a nuclear holocaust, being twenty times more resistant to radiation than humans, and they could survive being submerged in water for an hour. They might just multiply on all the garbage we've created and take over the world by force. I might be the first victim in the war to take over the world and rid the earth of human beings, and they were coming to dismantle me bit by bit like I had their compatriots just hours before.

I grabbed the blanket and shook it hard, then wrapped part of it around my legs. I pressed my back into the corner and pulled the rest of the blanket over my shoulders and head, tucking it around my head, closing off any openings until I was cocooned. I tried to take the shallowest possible breaths to avoid inhaling the fumes of the blanket, as I tried close my mind to everything around me, to concentrate on a happy memory like being eight years old, and it's Christmas and Santa Claus will be delivering gifts and everyone is happy. The fire is warm, and special Christmas bread has been baking and the aroma is intoxicating from the oven because the door is open. Are those reindeer hoof beats I hear over the house? Reindeer are on the roof, and Santa is coming.

But reality reared its ugly head through these visions, and in despair I realized it was not reindeer hoof beats, and I am not near a fireplace wrapped in a lamb's wool quilt, I'm inside a cocoon of musty old army blanket and those are cockroaches crawling on the blanket!

Nooooo! Get off me!

I was sweating profusely, practically suffocating. I was having some life-like nightmare vision.

I'd actually managed to fall asleep under the blanket, but I was trapped in a cocoon and the giant cockroach had come back to life. I could see him reach around with the one leg still attached to his body and retrieve his head from where it lay beside his butt and put it back on the proper end of his body. Then one by one he gathered his legs and wings and set them back together again. But somehow during the repair process he'd become thousands of times bigger and was now ten feet across. I was hiding in my cocoon and I would be no more than one bite for his horrifying mandibles. My way-too-vivid imagination made sure every ugly detail of his head and jaws was perfectly defined and only feet away from me halfway under the door and squeezing through slowly because my dripping sweat was driving him mad with hunger. I was suffocating, not sure if the stifling heat or lack of oxygen under the blanket was causing it, but I was going into some strange non-reality. The nightmare was so vivid. I shuddered at the vision of this giant cockroach and the phalanx of troops that were with him, searching for an opening in my cocoon.

I struggled against the blanket, trying to breathe, trying

to flail my arms to fight them off, and shout – if only my voice would work – to wake Hattie and have her come back with her big foot and crush that bug one more time, but my voice wouldn't work and my arms wouldn't swing and my feet were slow and numb. I gasped for a choking breath, as I shook the blanket free and suddenly there was not only darkness in front of my face but darkness and cool air.

I took a few deep breaths of semi-fresh air, trying to rid my mind of the the still-fresh vision of the sinister giant bug. In the blackness I could feel the vibration of movement of other real cockroaches on the blanket so I went back under, pulling it over my face again.

Now I felt the movement on the blanket near my face, so I flicked my finger on the spot and bounced the nasty thing off. I congratulated myself as I heard him clatter to the floor. Three more followed their fallen comrade and three more times I flicked them off the blanket. At that the procession seemed to stop and I hoped they'd given up. Maybe they didn't like getting flicked on the underside all that much, and they had a way of telling their buddies this route was not safe because once those three hit the floor no others crossed the blanket near my face. I opened my cocoon again to get some air and was amazed at how much cooler and fresher it was outside the blanket. I was afraid now to close the opening again, in case I had a reoccurrence of the vision of the colossal cockroach.

I took six or seven deep breaths like a pearl diver preparing to descend and began to wrap the blanket cocoon around me again. But just as I started to pull the blanket over my head, I noticed something very strange, but wonderful. I could see in the darkness something that looked like a thin blue line, faint and almost invisible. I was confused; I was oxygen deprived and probably hallucinating, so I had a tough time understanding what I was seeing. I tried to figure out how I was positioned in the room and realized I was facing the door, more or less, and that the blue band was most likely light showing under the door.

What? Could that be daylight?

Have I actually made it through to morning?

Is that the sun – the glorious, life giving, cockroach chasing, demon exorcising gift from all gods – actually rising?

I pulled the blanket down and stared at the crack under the door. My eyes hurt with the strain of peering at what I hoped was slowly brightening daylight.

It was! Daylight was coming.

The long night of cockroach wrassling would be over. The nightmare of the giant cockroach creeping under the door was just that: a nightmare caused by being short of air under the musty blanket. I had been about to go crazy if it hadn't ended soon and proof of that near miss was the fact that 'cockroach wrassling' had become part of my vernacular. So I wasn't quite completely crazy, but it had been a close one.

Oh, glorious day! Oh, happy day!

I was hungry, unrested, thirsty beyond belief, sore from trying to sleep in a cramped position, and my toe was throbbing.

Oh, glorious day.

Never in my relatively short life and limited experience had a morning meant so much as that one. I listened for the rain, gone. I listened for the wind, and all I got was a blue ringing in my ears from silence completely different from the roar of the wind beating the Lady Blanche and the rain pelting her wheelhouse as she valiantly weathered the squall. The silence was almost painful, a whistling in my ears from their having been accosted by so many waves of sound, from clacking dominoes, to thrashing palms, to a diesel engine straining at maximum RPMs, to the baritone shouts of the captain at close range, to roaring waves and howling wind – wind that can tear things down and tear things up. Fear of what the darkness hides can sound like ringing in the ears; fear of the sound of footsteps of innumerable enemies preparing a sneak attack, even fear of the sounds of one's own thoughts, and the reflections they bring, the confusion they bring, the indecision and poor decisions they bring.

I paused for a long moment but then threw the rough blanket to the head of the bed and stretched my stiff legs. I heard the cracks of stiff ankles and knees and ignored them but could not ignore the pain that shot through my head. I was dehydrated. Neither the crew nor captain had offered, and I never thought I'd need to ask for it, having a cottage for the night arranged by the captain. If only I had known what this cottage was going to be.

But these all became minor discomforts and could easily be forgotten as long as the sun was rising. An attitude of what doesn't kill you makes you stronger was needed here because once enough time passes after discomfort, simply having it in the past makes everything that much sweeter. I was still in a little shack full of dust and cobwebs and cockroach parts, but the sun was shining and an adventurous life was still ahead of me, and even if it was just a glimmer of light under the door, the sun was shining, it was a new day and I was excited to face it.

I opened the door and looked at my surroundings for the first time in this half-light of early sunrise. The sky, visible through the palms, was clear, and a faint lighter blue tinged the horizon to the east. It was a deep cobalt blue, as rich as any colour I'd seen, almost phosphorescent, and the stars, still visible in the leftover blackness of the night, twinkled in the sky as it transitioned from black to blue. On the ground, broken branches and wind-strewn fronds were lying about, and the air was calm during this time before sunrise.

Palm trees were spaced unevenly, but the dominant shrub was some leafy variety I didn't recognize. It was a very deep green in this light and beautiful in its coarseness. This was not a place of neat and orderly, or manicured or landscaped. This was an island that provided at best a tough existence for those who lived here and stayed on, scratching to get by on very little income, with a supply line consisting of a weekly visit from the mail boat, no more a tropical paradise of the tourist variety than the shack was a cottage by the sea.

As I gazed about, I saw a water pump in the middle of a small clearing in Hattie's front yard. Thirst rasped my throat at the sight of that pump, and I went directly to it and began desperately pumping the handle until beautiful clear water poured from the spout. I drank until pain tore at my side then fell back against the pump to allow the wave of unexpected discomfort to dissipate. After long minutes the torment subsided and I was able to stand upright only to feel deep weariness wash over me. I was not rested at all, and it was only my thirst that had forced me off that cot in that sorry little shack. With the unsteady steps of a rummy on a Sunday morning I wandered crookedly back to the shack. In this light the cockroaches were hiding, apparently they were more nocturnal than I had realized, and I felt like it would be all good if I tried to get some more sleep.

I laid down using the rough blanket as a pillow and fell asleep.

I slept until mid-morning, awakened by the heat, the corrugated metal roof acting like a solar panel. Thank goodness the cockroaches of the previous night were now just a memory, and except for the pile of crushed parts, wings, legs and waxy torsos that lay in a tumbled display near the door I could almost think I had imagined it all. I looked at the broken parts and had to shake my head at the resilience of the bodies on those things. Stomping wasn't good enough, as they seemed to absorb into the sole of a rubber sandal, so one had to twist while pressing down to get the wings and legs to detach and the hard shell of the body to crack. Having to stomp once or twice was bad enough, but to have to add that twisting squish was disgusting.

Uggghh. I shivered at the thought of it.

As I swung my legs over the edge of the bed for my second attempt at rising for the day I could smell, floating on a breeze, the mouth-watering scent of frying onions, fish, or deep fried something, maybe conch, which caused a Pavlovian reaction to the point where I was helpless to resist moving with my nose raised like one of his dogs to locate the source of that delicious aroma. My nose led me to Hattie's front yard, where I discovered her in front of a lean-to shed with shelves stocked with supplies for existence on this island. I stood still, unseen, salivating, watching her as she stood before a propane stove. It was clear she was the town merchant, and while I had slept she or a helper had brought up the boxes dropped off by the boat the night before. I made a noise, perhaps it was the sound of human drooling, and she became aware of me behind her.

She said, "Good morning. I make fish. You want?"

My eyes glazed over at the sound of those words. I said, "Yes, I want, thank you very much."

I ate the fish so completely that the bones she warned me about didn't stand a chance, then paid her for the meal and purchased additional supplies to feed my continued hunger: tomatoes from her garden, a loaf of homemade bread, two large cucumbers, a jar of mayonnaise and two tins of corned beef. I returned to the shack almost giddy with this prize, as the bony little fish had made barely a dent in my hunger. I made myself a thick sandwich and ate it in a series of four very large bites, chewing not required.

Forty minutes later, feeling much better, I stepped back out the door and set out on the road for a walk to explore the island that was to be my home for the next few days. I came to a path leading to a narrow beach where I came across a number of school children of varying ages. One had distinctive orange hair, and he was cute with a smile that could melt your heart and make you dearly wish you could be that young and happy again. His smile lit up his face and his complexion almost glowed against his orange hair. I could only wonder how that gene got tossed into the pool. Rumrunners, pirates, privateers, slaves, plantation owners, here was proof at least one of them had red hair. A little luck of the Irish, I suppose.

I stopped to talk to two young boys who had crude sticks with thin nylon fishing line attached to one end and a rusty bent nail tied to the line. The line was tangled and undoubtedly as hopeless at catching fish as the rusty nail would be at hooking them, but they had their hand crafted fishing poles in hand and were smilingly optimistic.

I wished for their sakes that they would catch something, recalling my youthful visits to a pond with similar apparatus only to come home dejected and deciding that catching fish was almost impossible. I had faint hope that these two would not be so disappointed.

Leaving them to their fishing venture, I continued on a windy path until I had found the far side of the island. I came across a passageway through some rough shrubs to a stretch of wave-washed beach about 400 metres in length, bracketed at each end by high outcroppings of extremely coarse black rock. I smiled at the pure serendipity of finding this thing of beauty. The waves reached almost as high as the shrubs that formed a line in the sand that had been drawn by countless thousands of years of waves, and the two ends would require laborious climbing to get over the rock walls. The perfect combination of the few local's lack of desire to sit in the sun on the sand and the extra work they'd be put to in order to enjoy such folly meant this beach could be mine and mine alone. Two rock promontories to guard the north and south, a wall of shrubs and other restrictive vegetation on the island side, a curving beach of deep soft sand that was an entire 400 metres long were my reward for my exploration. Yes, perfect.

I sat down at the high water line of the largest wave, thirst quenched, hunger satisfied for the first time in three days and set my eyes and mind completely on nothing, nothing at all.

I closed my eyes and, for an exercise in imagination, conjured an image to match the roar coming toward me from the ocean. In my imagination it could be the low rumbling of a train in a tunnel, steel wheels grinding under immense weight and pounding on joints in metal tracks, sending shuddering low sound waves that built as the train neared the end of the tunnel. It would quiet for a second then, sounding like low rumbling thunder, the wave would rush to shore until with a booming crash it would break into a hissing froth to run up the beach stopping near my feet, to then slowly depart with another separate but distinct hissing.

Things were looking up. This is what I'd wanted to do all along, sit on a beach and count waves. My immediate goal became to understand the pattern of the waves. I thought I'd try to discover whether what Henri Charriere said about every seventh wave being bigger than the six previous when he told the story of being carried from Devils Island to the mainland on a sack of coconuts, having being liberated by catching one of those seventh waves that had washed him out to sea. I thought that understanding the waves that mirror the rises and falls of the course of life could somehow help prepare me for or adjust to those rises and falls. According to Charriere the largest wave was always followed by the shortest, and they would build until the seventh was the highest again. If they were coming in sets of seven, and whether or not this was the rule or not would have to be determined by visiting a series of beaches over a series of days.

My imagination took wing. Couldn't an entire study be made on this subject? I might be just the person to do it. I could handle that and make sure it was scientific, for sure, take notes and all that, and look at external conditions and time and place and phases of the moon and tides and wind conditions. Yes, this sounded like an interesting challenge. Naturally, the first step to completing that study would be to find someone to finance it. There were government grants for research projects. How could I get some of that? I supposed I could find out the name of a local politician and start sucking up by helping out in his campaign office making nuisance cold calls or maybe take out his daughter or something, that might help find out who doled out the public cash for almost useless studies into nonsense. And this could be one, sure, why not, the study of waves and their relation to life sure seemed a noble calling to me at that moment, and probably a hell of a lot more meaningful than ninety percent of the other useless studies done by FOP's, the friends of politicians.

I drew a line in the sand at the level of the highest of several waves, and over the next hour only once did it get washed away, so I concluded the largest in each series had to be at least an hour apart, but this was confusing, too, and it became apparent that this was going to take some serious research.

I sat and began the first stages of my wave study, and I watched semi-transparent sand crabs and ants cross the sand. One ant even crawled over my foot, and out of petulance I buried him in sand, only to see him crawl out a minute or so later. I buried him again, in a footprint-sized hole but sure enough a few minutes later he popped out of the sand, so, I dug a deep hole, so deep water was starting to collect, then I tossed him in and filled the hole with sand. I waited and waited as a full four more sets of seven waves came and went, and finally, after a good half hour, the ant popped his head through the sand, uncovered himself completely then resumed his zig-zag course across the beach as if nothing had happened. Let him explain that one to his mates. Hell of a morning for that ant. Maybe it would be ants and cockroaches who inherit the earth. They are both tough and persistent and sure enough there would be one monumental battle at some point down the road. I'd be betting on the ants if they could uncover themselves from a foot of wet beach sand and just go on as before. I saluted him as he zigged and zagged his way down the beach away from the tomb I'd built over him, plucky bastard.

As the afternoon wore on I watched the waves wash a series of items onto the beach. First it was the typical plastic bottles, then a few items of floating cloth, then small, then larger pieces of blackened wood. I picked up a few and examined them closely. The wood was fire-charred. Soon a life ring from a sailboat washed up among the flotsam and this too was charred by fire, so much so that the name of the boat of its origin was not visible. It was orange, black and some white from the interior foam of the life ring. I sat back down in an area where the waves were washing this all onto the beach and waited until one large wave brought an entire group of items: parts of a partially melted backpack, foam plates, plastic garbage bags, all of them showing signs of having been burned. Then I saw two poignant things. One was a child's doll, without its usual clothing, and when I picked it up and turned it over, I found the front side to be melted – scorched by flames, obviously. The last item that washed ashore, like a message to me, was an empty rum bottle, bobbing along without a cork, and even this had signs of fire on the label. I mused reflectively about what this could possibly mean.

By the time an hour had passed from when the first piece washed ashore I had, around my feet on the beach, a collection of forensic evidence that something very serious had happened. I wondered about the little girl who owned that doll and the pieces of burned wood that were likely from a dinghy and, worse, the scorched life ring, something that you would not easily let go of. Considering the storm of the night before, and that I was fairly certain nothing else could have been on the water except for the sturdiest of mail boats under expert and experienced command, these items were perhaps what remained of a sailboat that had had a fire on board. The evidence was unequivocal and quite frightening. I held the melted doll – the plastic hair burned off, the face melted, the bottom half fused into one mess of now hardened rubber – and a sickening feeling came over me. I could not look at it, as the disaster played out in my imagination. Why would charred pieces of sailboat, then dinghy, then life preserver, all wash onto shore burned up, unless some shipboard disaster had occurred?

I looked out at the still surging waves, crashing and rolling and still seething from the storm the night before, and put my hands down and squeezed fistfuls of sand, happy to be on shore. In my mind I could still see the captain and hear his booming voice and remembered his incredible sense of the gravity of the storm we were involved in, all of which was juxtaposed against the charred pieces of wood and what they likely meant. One situation ended as best one could hope in a storm, landing a passenger and freight, and the other ended with a fire on board, and who knew or would ever know what else happened to that sailboat and that crew and passengers. Recalling that man, the captain, I almost missed him and felt renewed appreciation for him and his commitment to getting his beloved Lady Blanche safely through rough seas. He truly demonstrated how one should command a vessel. He certainly commanded my respect.

I continued to sit listening to the roar of the waves. Each new wave struck the two limestone promontories on either side of me, sending white walls of foam over them, spraying upward and then trickling back down to the sand below, until another wave crashed and shot up a great curtain of white spray. On the sand around me sand crabs scurried about, hiding when I moved, rushing over my feet when I sat perfectly still. Their little black eyes on almost clear exoskeleton heads were their only contrasting feature. Multitudes of fast and agile sea birds ran on the sand almost as fast as they could fly, running ahead of the waves as they washed ashore. I have no idea what they fed on out there on the sand, probably some small creature that washed ashore, but they had to be almighty patient, as I never saw one eat anything, and they were not scavengers waiting for something to die, like turkey buzzards in Arizona. These little birds had to run like sprinters. I went into the waves once or twice, but just to get my knees wet, as the water depth varied from ankle deep to three feet over my head in a single wave which seemed willing to pull me in to join the family on the sailboat.

Finally, when the sun was getting low over the shrubs guarding my back, I made my way back onto the path and returned to the shack, relieved when I got there that a family of big, ugly, hard-to-kill, crawly things had not come back to their former home, now known as my bed. I used the remaining bread and other ingredients I'd purchased from Hattie earlier in the day to make two more sandwiches and sat on a rock outside the shack to eat them. I was in Hattie's yard and could see that she had made dinner for a large number of people, young and old. I didn't want to impose so I sat quietly in the shadows and ate in silence, watching the windows of the house, without intent of any kind, interested in the interplay between the people and longing to have something – a family, warts and all – to think about. They laughed, they argued, some were scolded, some were rebellious and talked back, but they all ate together under a single bulb hanging over the table in the lean-to off the house. To me in that moment it was the definition of family, with all its foibles and beauty, in all its good and bad that contained what every family contained, the balance of good and bad that got families through somehow. I sat there eating my sandwiches, chewing slowly. The family was foreign and yet so familiar, and here I was watching them from an unseen position, missing family, missing being part of whatever it is that makes up a family.

Soon the lights went down, the kerosene lamps fired up, and the family dispersed. I used the matches Hattie provided, lit the refilled lamp, went back into the shack and lay down on the cot. Overloaded with sensory input for the day my brain shut down. It was dark, and it was fairly early but once the generator shut down, the island and I would have to shut down as well. I was not looking forward to it, but at least I knew, based on the shortage of sleep I'd gotten the night before, I would not have any trouble falling asleep.

Morning came much the same as the morning before, appearing as a band of light under the door. Once again I imagined it well before it actually appeared I was so desperately waiting for it. I was anything but refreshed, almost shaky with nerves, but six hours sleep was so normal for me that six hours was all I could lay still for.

While I slept, a good number of red welts had appeared on my arms and legs, particularly on the thin skin of my wrists and ankles as if whatever was biting me could tell I was out for the count and they could take their time to find the easiest spot to bite. I was probably snoring up a storm of carbon dioxide as a fragrant invitation to every biting insect within 100 metres of my bed in that shack. I had to resist scratching them as I knew bites that became welts took much longer to heal, but I couldn't resist at least brushing them lightly. It wasn't enough and they were driving me crazy, so I decided salt water was needed for these welts. I stumbled out of the shack and dragged my heavy feet to the beach, my beach, where I went into the water and rubbed the welts gently with the palm of my hand, trying to massage out any allergic venom. Despite that, as I walked back to the yard, the itching returned, so I stepped over to Hattie's water supply, the pump in her front yard. After a good rinsing at the pump the swellings were only half as bad.

The donkey-bray screeching of the pump must have awakened Hattie because she appeared at her door, disheveled and sleepy-eyed, in a costume similar to that of the day before but more wrinkled, and squinted at me standing there in the yard. She rubbed her eyes then waved me over. Apparently she understood the reason for me being there at the pump because she gave me a green paste to apply to the welted insect bites, which helped nicely. As I applied the balm, Hattie moved away and a minute later came back with a few hard pancakes which I ate so heartily she offered more.

I looked at her with new appreciation – at that moment she was like a soft, round goddess. Hunger appeased, itching arrested, happy, I was smiling at her, until she caught my admiring look.

She blushed thoroughly, her cheeks pressed up against her eyes by her return smile, flattered by my unabashed appreciation of her at that moment. I could see that complimenting her so completely without saying anything made her self-conscious. To spare her further embarrassment my heart-felt thank you was spoken to the floor as I pretended to contemplate the patina of that foot-worn surface.

Within a half hour I was back in the shack trying to review my agenda for the day which took but a second since I really had no agenda. There was really only one thing to do, which was to sit on the beach and continue my study of wave patterns.

I walked the path to the beach once again, and again I noticed a fork in the road. Taking the left fork meant the beach and my previous destination, the other path was a fresh unknown. I stood at this turning point for a moment. I was in a strange state of mind where a simple fork in the road had profound meaning. The events of this past week had me really wondering what could possibly happen next. I was on this little sandy path, and it was a simple fork in the road, but somehow, on this adventure it seemed there could be nothing simple about it. So after a pause, and without really choosing to do it, I allowed the mystery of the moment to lead me along as if by magical enchantment that I was powerless to stop, and I stepped onto the right-hand fork in the road.

Chapter Eight

CAVE, CAVE, CAVE

I strolled off in this new direction, and within a hundred metres the path led to another beach, which put it on the far side of the large outcropping which bordered the south end of the beach I'd visited the previous day. At the end of the path I entered a small clearing that was hacked out of the shrubs and in the middle, in the midst of a collection of refuse – bits of rope, orange floats, some fishing net, a hammock, tin cans – there sat a crooked little shack, like the one I was staying in but bereft of paint and even more crudely constructed. I crossed the sand to approach to within twenty meters of this shack when an elderly man brandishing a long curving stick appeared in an opening in the weatherworn wall. He was wearing a rag of thin cotton over his shoulders and ragged short pants and looked as rough and unkempt as any castaway. I stopped walking, not sure where the boundaries of his space were among the debris lying about. A grizzled face encircled sparkling brown eyes that looked me over from head to toe. I'm sure we were equally foreign to each other. His eyes were small in his crumpled brown face and his white whiskers were sparsely scattered about his jaw. I had to guess that years of self-administered haircuts, probably without the use of a mirror, were the reason for the hair clipped in gangly groupings about his head.

I thought I saw something that hinted at friendliness in his eyes, as above his round cheeks, bracketed by wrinkles pointing arrow-like toward his little eyes, something mirth-like appeared, and I realized he was harmless.

The curving stick he brandished was only his standard reaction to unexpected strangers.

The stick dropped, "I am George," he said suddenly with a strong accent.

This three-word introduction was warm and inviting, and I smiled at him at which his face broke into a wide grin. I waited for a second then approached him with my hand extended.

"Hello." I said.

I stopped within a meter and he just looked at my hand, so I withdrew it.

He said, "You come – go diving?"

With the sound of the waves washing up behind us on the beach I could not quite understand what he'd asked. Driving? Had I come to go driving? I looked back at the path I had just walked in on and thought maybe he was asking if I drove to his beach. I hadn't seen a car on the island, except for a derelict Jeep in the shrubbery near Hattie's. I looked back at him and said, "No, I came by the mail boat."

He nodded as if to say, "Yes, yes, ha ha," then repeated, "You come – go diving?"

Then I understood. His accent was so strong that it seemed different than the ones I'd been listening to since arriving, as if since being sequestered on this beach on this little island his own dialect had developed. It was the dialect of Uncle George. He'd said diving not driving, and when I realized this I laughed, which seemed to confuse him as much as I'd been before. But that didn't matter. I was laughing and he was started laughing, becoming quite small as he curled up in the middle, his wizened face cackling with laughter, at nothing really, because he had no idea what I was laughing about. But it didn't matter, it wasn't important. This made me laugh harder, and a warm feeling washed over me at the laughter we shared.

He looked toward a log at one side of his clearing and gestured to me to follow. He sat down, folding thin legs at his bony knees, still chuckling. Diving, not driving. Hah! No, I just came walking. Walk, walk, walk. I used two fingers pointing down to indicate walking and pantomimed following a winding route, then pausing and scratching my head when my walking fingers reached the fork in the path, then continuing until – surprise, surprise, the fingers jumped – I came to this beach, to meet Uncle George.

The fingers continued the pantomime, bending to signify sitting, then walking again, back to Hattie's to lie down and wait for the mail boat to come back. He watched my finger-legs moving and followed the path I described, and it came to him all at once, causing him to laugh harder, as the step by step path I described became clear to him even to the point of my sitting on the log with him. He laughed for a long minute until finally stopping to wipe tears from his eyes with the back of his hand.

"Why you come if not diving?" he asked.

Again I had to explain this seemingly strange occurrence. I retold a short version of being marooned on Eleuthera and getting on the mail boat to Staniel and when I started to feel embarrassed at this folly I raised both my palms skyward in a sign of surrender to the mishaps I could not seem to get out of the way of. Something about my gesture started him laughing again and again the laughter doubled him over. He seemed to think I was doing something comical. Truth was, I thought *he* looked pretty funny with his grey stubble, little short grey hairs all over his head, deeply creased cheeks and little marbles for eyes. He was all of five feet tall including the upturned clump of hair at the top of his head, and maybe 120 pounds after a big meal. His clothes were the best part, as if his wardrobe was comprised of hand-me-downs from those who slept in the foc'sle of Blackbeard's *Queen Anne's Revenge*. Not that unlikely, considering that pirate had been know to spend at least some time on these islands.

He was laughing and this got me started again and, again, I had no idea why he laughed. I started to wonder what he was in his diet, and how do I get some of whatever it was that made everything so funny.

Eventually he stopped, falling silent for a second, then in all seriousness turning to look at me, asking,

"Why you get on de mail boat?"

I stopped and squinted at him, playing up the role, trying to make him laugh again. I rolled my eyes back then scratched my chin. I said, "Because the mail boat had a nice name."

But this time, my first attempt to actually say something funny and make him laugh, he stopped and pondered then slowly nodded his head.

"Yes, the mail boat does have a nice name."

I looked around at his rough encampment and asked, "You live here?"

He looked around as well, as if seeing it for the first time. "Here? I live here?" he asked me back.

"Yes, is this your home?"

He began to nod, then told a winding story that I lost a few times along the way, until I finally understood that he was expanding on: "Yes, but only since I left home when I was young."

He went on a while longer, something about how he'd lived on the island since he was born, and in that shack since he left his parent's house on the other side of the island, which had to be quite a spell as he was probably in his seventies. I gleaned from his gestures and the story I barely understood that he lived on this beach where he was the unofficial guide and send off for dive tourists to the caves which lay just off the island. Where he pointed appeared to be nothing more than outcroppings of limestone, but apparently these outcroppings concealed fresh water caves. How many years he'd being doing this I could only guess, but I could not get that question across, nor how many years since his last visitor. I could barely comprehend how he could possibly have existed in that little hut waiting for me and others like me to arrive, travelers and adventurers and treasure-seekers alike, to say hello and then maybe even goodbye before visiting the caves. I could only shake my head in amazement.

However, my destination today was not this unknown island, or caves or whatever they were, and the mystery of what there was in the craggy, seabird-and-mangrove-clustered rock across the water had not piqued my interest in the least. Coming across this wizened old man was interesting enough and made this quite an entertaining interlude during my exploration in the sand and the sun which had still not reached its midday peak. I guess I too needed someone to talk to, like he did, but whatever the reason, the laughter and the sun and the sound of the waves washing up gently onto his pinkish white beach was comforting, and I was at ease. I settled into the sand and leaned back against the fallen log and took in this funny little man and his surroundings.

Old George was frail and thin as an old cat stricken with arthritis, moving with creaky joints. He grinned like a mischievous leprechaun at everything I said; almost anything I did had him animated practically to the point of breaking into a dance like a castaway Mr. Bojangles. I enjoyed his audience, and recited the folly of my adventures, embellishing scenes with sweeping arm and hand gestures. Where it was funny I would laugh, and he would cackle with giggling laughter, and when my story was sad and I was alone and not feeling well, he would console me by putting his withered hand on my shoulder and looking me the eye with an expression of compassion. His brown irises in their little pools of watery yellow would entreat me to continue with my tale, as if he wished to grant me strength and encouragement that things would get better, silently saying, "I feel your pain." Perhaps being half deaf and only half understanding what I was saying was his greatest attribute because he seemed to be as sensitive a soul as could be. It was as if my story was his story and he lived and cried and was happy or sad in sympathy with what I had gone through, and he conveyed this through simple expression alone. He understood little of what I was saying, I'm sure, but his sensitivity to my emotion seemed to be stronger than his understanding of my words.

The story I told was not really all that special – it was not Jason and the Argonauts or Sinbad and his sailors – it was a pretty basic solo trip made over the course of a few months. Despite that he seemed to see it as if it was some great adventure, and this made me relive even the most trivial details. I was feeling lonely, and it was strangely comforting, though surprising, that I could have made a friend in such a strange place, and even more surprising because he was at least fifty years my senior. Here was a soul untouched by my world, more aptly, my polluted world. It was hard to imagine he'd never seen a television or a television commercial or a politician's speech or the aftermath of a rigged election or been exposed to sensationalizing or hidden agenda media. The thought of the randomness of this chance meeting was nothing less than amazing, and I was thankful for having been in the right place at the right time to have found a man, old and almost crippled, from my world but who lived a strange-beautiful distant sort of life.

We talked and laughed for a couple of hours in a one-sided conversation infused with comical expressions and gesticulations. I kept going mostly for his sake since he hung on every word, and though I doubted he understood very much of my story, he seemed to hear me as clearly as anyone ever had in my life. I had to stop him from almost crying when I described the episode where Buddy left me on the beach, with me pounding my fists in the sand as I screamed after him in the departing boat. He was also deeply affected by my depiction of Mrs. P and her tears at Lawrence's door and her wistful voice as she explained that her son had departed so long ago for a short trip and that she was still, and would never stop, waiting for his return, and how her heart ached every day since his disappearance, and of the poor aching soul of his father, inheritor of a once grand sugar cane plantation and owner and sole occupier of an overstuffed red velvet armchair that perhaps had been his father's before him. Here was Old George feeling for the father of the long lost son as if it was his own son who'd disappeared, and for their shattered lives because their prodigal son had not returned to take them and the plantation into the future. I knew he didn't really hear everything properly and probably understood less, but somehow he could read my expressions, and it was difficult to break away from his rapt gaze.

What I did understand is that he was alone and longed for conversation so my presence was a gift he couldn't let go of. It probably didn't matter at all what I was telling him, it was how I was telling it and the very fact that I was telling it. I felt this, and felt for him, and it was tough ending our conversation, but I had to break it off. Time was ticking I had miles to go and a life to live and had to somehow wind this down. As I reached back to the log to

raise myself, consternation shadowed George's features as
he realized that time was up and I was about to leave. To
stop me from leaving, he looked out to sea and pointed to
a low outcropping of limestone a short distance away
across the water and said, "People come dive dat islan'.
Some pirate hid treasure in de cave, many peeble try fine
de treasure."

He stood up and walked to the edge of the surf, and
stood looking at the island for a long moment.

It was nothing more than a craggy lump of limestone
with mangroves at the edge and seabirds circling above.

"I never go now." He said.

"Dere be cave with fresh watah dat rises from a spring
inside de islan."

I looked at this island with new interest. Pirates?
Treasure? It was not far for a strong swimmer, but too far
across open water for me.

I said, "It's far, there may be a current and I'll be a
shark bait half way across."

The little man looked at me sideways for a long minute
without speaking. This pause was unnerving. I thought he
was reconsidering what he'd previously thought of me, as
if he couldn't understand how I could have come all this
way if not to go to that island. Why else would I be there?
I might have been off base with this assumption, but as he
looked at me I began to think he was questioning if I had
come for that reason but was now backing out of it. He
looked at me and said,

"Yah, mon, too far. Other men swim, but too far for
you, even in da boat."

I shook my head. What was that supposed to mean? I
thought I could feel a change in him. The mirth, the
giggles were gone. Instead he seemed to be judging me,
challenging me.

Then he said, "You take my boat. Many people come
to see caves, you too."

Now this simple offer was more of a gauntlet tossed than an offer, as if I'd made an excuse for not wanting to go. But this was crazy – no, this was more like insane. Did I have to wrestle with the thought that this man was challenging me to prove myself by accepting his offer of his boat to visit a limestone outcropping? But, did I have a choice? Could I decline? Was this not what this entire trip was all about, and been so fantastic because I accepted challenges, learning and growing while conquering fears?

Had I not just extolled the virtues of travel and adventure for two hours, and lapped up his attention and praise like some sort of paper hero? Were the stories I told the last chapter of this trip? I had committed to myself turning back and heading home after my seven days in the Bahamas, so was today going to be the end of the adventures?

I let the pause settle on the space between us only as long as his sideways glance had settled on me just moments before. I considered that perhaps I'd misunderstood. After all, I was still guessing at the meaning of at least half of his words. My head said no, no way, nada, not a chance, not for me, adios, I'm not that crazy, but in the end I decided to do it, go at least part way, maybe paddle around a bit out his sight, see what his beach looked like from over there, and come back to say, "OK. There. I did it."

So I nodded, yes, I would love to use that little wooden boat to cross to that lump of limestone without a name to discover what the attraction was, that which brought divers and treasure hunters all this way, and perhaps become rich by finding pieces of eight and bars of silver just lying on the sand. Then I remembered picking up that book in Lawrence's room, something about treasure and islands and faded handwritten notes and underlined passages. No, there can't be a connection. No. I shook my head to get rid of these thoughts and to come back to the present. I nodded a second time in acceptance of the offer to use his boat, unable to say yes aloud, still not really wanting to do it.

He got up walked away, and I had to follow. At the water's edge, beyond a few leaning mangroves, was his boat, nine feet of tortured wood in the shape of a dory. George explained that it had been a tender for a sailing boat at one time but one Christmas morning it had washed ashore like a gift from Santa Claus. It was apparent that to him it was a treasure. It lay keel up among the grass, and its rough wood could be seen through three or four layers of peeling paint. It was an antique, but a working antique and his pride and joy. He scrabbled sideways against the seized-up side of his body and hustled ahead of me, shuffling and dragging his left foot through the sand, the excitement of his return to being a tour guide almost overwhelming him.

We arrived at his boat and I, with growing trepidation, half-heartedly assisted him to turn it over. Sand crabs scurried from beneath, barely escaping being crushed, and old George, with surprising strength dragged it into the water until it was afloat.

"Hold it," he said to me and scurried back to collect two oars and tossed them into the boat.

We spoke no more. I knew what was expected and again felt I had no choice. I stepped over the rail, and he pushed the boat into the deeper water over the first small wave. I looked at him with resignation and set the oars into the locks. His face was alight with a priceless grin, and, what the heck, maybe I would be the one to find the treasure, or something. His bent body, leaning left, his wizened features and almost toothless grin sent me on my way.

"OK," I thought, "Do this. Go for a little paddle. What the heck, it might be fun." The wind was calm, unlike the past few days, and the waves were small, no more than ripples – no major pounding on the coral. The small island across the way did not look inviting, but it was an island to explore, and would be mine alone while I was there. I began to row, watching him standing at the edge of the surf, a funny little man with tattered clothes. Soon I was out of the waves, and still George did not leave my departure point but stayed still until I was almost across and he was just a tiny figure on his beach and his tiny shack behind him.

Near the island, I turned the boat around so I could see the island he'd convinced me to explore, really starting to wonder what I was doing going to this little rocky island where a few spindly trees and mangroves grew. I thought, "What's the big deal? Nothing here but a scruffy bit of mangroves and limestone." Not even a landing spot for a boat. A few mottled seagulls drifted overhead and a few bobbed about at the edge of the mangroves, where bits of plastic and assorted flotsam were trapped in the bare roots completing the scavenger look of the place. The island appeared to be mainly black limestone, sharp, and lumpy in varying degrees. The old man had indicated some type of diving under or into a circle with a fresh water spring in the center, so I rowed in long pulls each way, back and forth, trying to see if I could find what he had been so excited about. I surveyed the shrubs and could not see a way through the branches that formed a barrier around this side of the island.

There had to be some way through, or something to be found, or this was nothing more than an outcropping of limestone and no one would ever come visit this lump that looked like nothing more than a navigational hazard without a light. There had to be more, something had warranted the visits by divers and sailboats and the excitement of the old man and his insistence that I see it. The fact that it was so well hidden now enticed me, and the thought of this being a secret only a few people and Uncle George knew about made it more interesting, so I kept rowing, although I almost gave up once and then twice and seriously thought about turning the boat back to George's beach. Then I noticed, under an arch of mangrove roots, barely visible, a short stretch of sand. This had to be the landing point. I gave three hard pulls with the oars then lay flat in the boat as it skimmed under the arch of branches. The dory glided just under the roots and came to a stop against the sand of that small beach.

I hopped out immediately to tie the painter to a thick branch then looked around at this little beach. It was just a little patch of sand at the bottom of a limestone wall, a few meters long and half that wide. Then I noticed a small stream of water flowing onto the beach from the base of the black wall of limestone. This had to flow from the interior of the island. So this is what old George was talking about. I lay down on the sand and shimmied to the stream of water to look through a small void in the limestone wall. The water flowing out was cool, and I dipped my palm to taste the water. It was fresh water, to my surprise, fresh water that could only be from a spring. Under that space in the limestone wall I could see sunlight on water, and knew I had found the entrance to the interior of this little island.

I parted the soft sand and crawled my way through against the steady flow of water. Within a meter or two I was off the sand and into deeper cooler water, in a roughly round pool. At the perimeter were limestone walls, rough-hewn, a jagged gray/black. Rain had worn this limestone into random patterns. The water in this pool was cool and invigorating, and I explored as I went, looking through the clear water to the bottom about two metres below. This was a dazzling display in the sunlight that shone through the water, casting ripples of light on the coarse bottom dotted with bright colors of sea life. As I moved across the surface, I watched my shadow undulating on the bottom, and behind my feet a wake churned a trail of shadow bubbles. I wished I had goggles and fins as this was truly breathtaking and I understood what the attraction was. The little guy had been right; he had seen this, and he was right to think I needed to see it too. I rolled over onto my back to float and catch my breath, then lay still, the sun beaming fully onto my chest and face. This was so nice, so very nice. I gazed straight up to the clear blue sky and stopped moving completely, feeling about as close as it was possible to floating on a cloud. Bliss, hard won, well deserved. I earned this. I was here. I was as alone as on a desert island, away from the world, in complete solitude.

The physical sensation was unreal, being heated on top and cool on the bottom. It was like baking under a broiler while lying on a snow bank. I had to smile to myself which grew into a huge grin, then a chuckle, then finally a solid fit of laughter. "Oh, that shack, oh, that storm, oh, those bugs." The past few days were behind me now, and I was floating on a cloud of pleasure. I rolled back over to warm my back and resume my fuzzy gaze of the bottom below me. I made three long circuits of the small pool, and began to notice a marker which I drew my bearings on. On each of my three circuits I saw below me a dark opening slide past. Was this the entrance to the cave Uncle George was describing? I remembered his excitement and his gesturing hands flapping around his head as he tried to impress upon me how much there was to be discovered. At times his dialect made his speech indiscernible and prevented my fully understanding him, but I could still get the gist of what he was saying, and knew it had to be good if it could elicit that much excitement from the old man.

I had no idea what to expect. None. Everything I was doing was ad-lib, and I knew I was already taking a chance, rowing across to an island away from another island I hardly knew. At this point I was not about to take this any farther and prepared to take a long last look around at the walls of this little fresh water lake, walls festooned with hanging vines and ringed by hardy trees growing impossibly from cracks in inhospitable limestone. That would be good enough, time to slither back under the mangroves and row that little boat back to its owner. I took it all in once more and tried to absorb it all took a long deep breath and prepared to leave. I would go back now. But wait a minute. I'm here. I had come all this way, and I would be talking to George very soon, and he'd wanted me to see the cave, so how would it be to say, yes, I paddled over, but no I didn't see the cave because….

I tossed this around in my mind. I had come through being marooned, a storm on a tippy boat, a rough night with some big bugs, and I'd fared well enough. A sensible person might have reasoned that the way things were going, it might be best not to tempt fate, to be careful for a while. But, like a gambler weighing the odds, what are the chances the dealer has another blackjack coming? Maybe I'd been through enough misfortune. Maybe I was due for a little good fortune now. Was there not a saying about things coming in threes? Was this the third, or was it the mail boat, or was the third the shack? Then I decided, all at once, that it was a stupid debate about luck, good or bad, coming in threes. I thought, "Yikes man, you're thinking a little too hard. Let it go." I came to a distinct conclusion: I would swim a little longer in this cool clear lake then go back. Just a little more of this, then put an end to it, delaying the inevitable task of facing Uncle George and having to face him with the thought that, "Yes, I found the pond, but no, I did not summon the courage to take it one step further and swim into the cave. No treasure for me."

I swam on my back, feigning disinterest, ignoring that I'd noticed two additional areas of shadow, so different than the colors of the bottom, that were surely passages through the limestone, separate entrances to those damn caves. I looked down on each pass over an entrance, and the more I wanted to ignore them the more they beckoned to me. Now things had changed. The peace and contentment I found in the incredible privacy I had, the solitude and the beauty that was all mine to enjoy did not seem all that important now. Rather than seeing feeling the beauty I had ruined the perfection as I fought with myself, thoughts going through my mind like,

"No, yes, no, yes. Pirates' treasure? No, maybe. Danger? Maybe, probably. But maybe just a short dive in and back out again. Pirates' treasure? Can't be, can it?? No. Maybe."

Finally, yes.

I took three deep breaths, turned into the water and dove straight down, promising myself I would just go in a short distance, maybe a meter, then turn around, so that is what I did. I made it part way, then turned and swam back into the small lake. It took five good hard strokes before I could turn up and into fresh air again. It seemed the tunnel into the mystery cave the old man was so excited about was a bit longer and more challenging than I'd expected. I was almost through when I turned and swam back to the lake. I had to stop and think. I would be able to say to George that, "Yes, I found the entrance to the cave," and "Yes, I did swim into the entrance," but "No, I was not so crazy as to keep swimming.

No, I'm not a lunatic to swim on and on into a tunnel when I don't know where it ends. No, not me. No, I'm way too smart to do something so foolish. Hidden treasure is just a myth and it's not there. I know. I did swim in, even though only part way, but I'm pretty sure it's not there."

Satisfied and proud of myself for having done it, for having gone alone into and come safely back out of a hidden tunnel in an island, I floated on my back once more, and again the sun shone upon me where I floated in my perfectly silent, perfectly private lake inside a limestone island that was mine alone for as long as I wanted it to be.

But the perfection was being disturbed by not having completely lived up to a challenge that could just maybe lead to learning something, even if only about myself and maybe testing the boundaries of my comfort zone, searching for a new outer limit, the line, the maximum.

Would my not challenging myself with the utmost experience be the thought that would haunt me?

Was there really something there to find?

Why didn't I try a little harder?

Maybe it was there?

One more, only one more stroke, I told myself.

If I don't reach the opening by the fourth stroke, I'll turn back, and with confidence I could say, I did all I could.

I took three deep breaths and went back down for a second exploratory dive.

I turned back once again, this time after only two strokes. Frustration with myself now made the beauty of the private lake a mockery. I'd said I would do four stokes into the tunnel but this time I only did two before I turned around. Suddenly I'd created an issue for myself. How did that happen? It was eating at me. I wanted to shout at the walls and the blue sky in the opening above. This would not do. No, I was going back. I took three deep breaths and went back in for a third time. This time I did four hard breaststrokes, and I knew I was much deeper into the passage as it turned upward. I took one final hard stroke, and immediately came into an absolutely amazing, breathtaking, blue grotto, where a small craggy opening a meter across some five meters above the dark water allowed sunshine to cast a single brilliant beam like a light sabre onto the water. The passage into this grotto had taken my breath and I had to ease over to the wall and reach for a handhold so I could stop and rest. This was challenging because the walls were formed of sharp ridges of limestone, and I had to grasp gingerly or risk tearing my skin open.

After a minute I let go of the edge to turn and float on my back, looking up at the beauty of this cave. The upper reaches of the cave were dripped with stalactites and were dappled in the reflected sunlight with hues of blue, green, opaque whitish greens and even orange and pinks. This incredible beauty was all mine! I'd earned it. I did it! I had been about to give up but I didn't. It was so, so special because of what it meant to me. The beauty of this cave was the reward for my perseverance. I lay on my back in this cool, clear, fresh water for a few long minutes, taking in the beauty, tracing the beam of sunshine reflecting on the walls, tiny flying insects and floating particles dancing and glowing in the searing light. But even hard-won prizes are short lived after all, and soon I'd had enough of reveling in it. The beauty and the sense of personal accomplishment was waning, and I turned back to find the passage from which I'd entered.

I paddled around looking down and unease shook me when I couldn't immediately find the cave entrance. This cave had much less light than the lake, so the entrance to the passage was much harder to find. I tried to ignore the feeling and keep looking. I stopped against the wall to rest, once, then again, and went around the pool again, becoming disoriented because I was beginning to get nervous. I couldn't recall what it was that I first saw, or the angle of the sun to use as my bearing. Was it to the left or to the right? Or was that after I stopped and really noticed it? I just wasn't sure. After my third circuit of the pool I spotted an opening. "Hah!" I said to myself, "There it is. Take a short rest, then three deep breaths and through the passage into the pool just inside the island, out of this cave. Four hard strokes and back to the little lake." I plunged down, entered the passage, stroked once, twice, three times, and began to reach up toward where the opening to the lake was supposed to be. My hand hit hard against the rough upper surface of the passage. I stroked hard once more, then again, and reached again, and once again my hand hit a hard surface, the limestone tearing at my knuckles and finger tips. This is getting serious. I was running out of air and was sure I'd gone double the distance I'd gone getting into the grotto. I would have to turn and go back right now, or risk running out of air. I turned and stroked five hard breaststrokes and to my great relief came up into fresh air.

But I was in total blackness. I had air, but the sun had gone out. I had surfaced, yes, to gasp in rasping breaths, but somehow I was now in a second, deeper cave. I did not find my way out. I had inadvertently made my way deeper in. "Oh, Uncle George, why did you not tell me there were caves, plural, not one cave, but some caves and these were interconnected? Why did you challenge me to see these caves? Did you say the word 'treasure' just to tease me?" I knew immediately what this meant. I understood completely and felt sick to my stomach. What was I doing in here when I knew nothing about these caves? I wasted time and valuable energy chastising myself. Every move I'd made to this point was a bad one. Saying I was beyond foolish was being too kind. This was beyond stupid. This was Darwinian 'get the hell out of the gene pool, the human race doesn't need you' stupid. If I didn't need both hands to cling desperately onto something, some limestone or coral or whatever made up these sharp walls in the darkness, I would have given myself a smack on the head to the point of pain.

Despite the lack of decent handholds, I had to rest and found a just bearable finger-hold on the edge of the pool, but it was so small and so sharp I could only hang on for a moment. The sharp limestone was almost razor edged and in the total darkness holding on to these sharp stones to rest had its price. But this long and intense self-berating was serving no purpose; I had to try to figure out how to move forward to find a way out of this. This could be very serious. But before I could do anything, I would have to overcome the feeling of growing despair sickening my stomach as my gut told my head something it knew but could not accept: I was becoming tired but it was imperative that I make another swim very soon. Time was passing, and there was no time to waste, no time to second-guess. I took three deep breaths before going back down to search for the passage to this cave.

I reached for the opening and found it, then stroked hard to make as much distance as possible while clawing up to try to find an opening but only smacking my knuckles on the ceiling of the passageway time after time. But finally, I reached into an open space and pulled myself through the surface with a great gasp. But not into light! Into complete, all encompassing, total blackness, darkness so complete it was like being under a black velvet blanket. Disorienting blackness, numbing, making me desperately open my eyes wider and wider which didn't help at all because there just was no light. The first minute was spent catching my breath; relieved to have air to breathe. I was gulping it down but even before catching my breath my brain recognized a horrible fact and I wanted to scream, having realized I was likely now even deeper in the cave system. How could I have done this? How could it have gone this far?

The 'no-fear, go for the adventure, go where your nose leads you' attitude had really gone too far this time. The 'closer to death brings you closer to life' concept is not so hot when you're faced with the closer to death part of it. In this case it wasn't an extreme base jumper who dies instantly, this is where a person can die slowly in sorrow and shame above all because foolishness – no, stupidity – was at the root of this dangerous situation. Every step of the past week had been leading to this. Here I was, totally lost in a cave system where there was absolutely no chance that anyone could save me. It was one step after the other after the other: the bar, Buddy and his girls and the promise of flamingo, the elusive Eleuthera, and the island in the exotic Exumas. Nonsense! All that was after the fact. How did I get on this journey in the first place? Could this be just a case of every step after the first one you take is a step taking you to your death? No!! This is crazy thinking and I am NOT going to die in these caves. No! I got into this; I will get out of this. Think! Think how to save yourself!

OK. First thing: energy is going to be needed. The caves had a way in, the way in will be the way out. Air is available. Good. Fresh water is plentiful. Good. Two days could pass before there would be imminent danger to the body unless, of course, hypothermia sets in. OK, forget about two days, maybe ten or twelve hours. Water temperature is probably 82 or 83, body temperature is 98, heat loss is 17 times greater in water than in air, so OK, you've got about three hours. Forget starvation or thirst, it will be cold, which will disorientate your brain and numb your arms and legs. So you've got to think fast, real fast and real good, as the race between losing sense and losing coordination will be an ongoing and decisive battle. It will almost be a more of a mental test than a physical test. Yes! I congratulated myself on this a big revelation. Even small victories are still victories. This would be a mental test.

How long could I sustain the mental strength to keep away despair, panic, claustrophobia, and whatever else might come as the hours wore on? Days? No, it would not be days. I was not about to spend days in this blackness. This is nothing. Nothing! I can conquer this. I must conquer this. I will conquer this. With that I readied myself for another attempt. Find the passage in the water below, find that tunnel. But wait: first ensure it's the right passage. What? How do I do that? Sounds good in theory, but each attempt to find a passage expends precious energy, so don't be frivolous with the attempts. What? No, come on now. There will be no need for numerous attempts. I could make four or five tries, and then rest as long as necessary to catch my enough breath to try again if necessary. I had to be systematic about it. I had to find out how many ways in and out there were before I took any, so if I did fail to find the way out in one passage I could try again in another and eliminate them one by one.

But then, like a kick in my stomach, another thought hit me: what if I go farther in? What if I ended up deeper in this cave system? I don't know anything about it. I might....

No! I am NOT GOING TO DIE HERE!

No, I am not!

I cried this out loud into the black dome above me, and it came back to me as quickly as I got it out. I was screaming at myself, but I needed it. I needed to be screamed at. I needed to scream at myself, so I did, and I called myself every name I could think of. I was a lot of bad things and when I got tired of that and of hearing that other voice saying it from the roof of the cave, I stopped again, realizing that if I was so stupid as to waste my last few breaths yelling at myself to no purpose, then perhaps I deserved to be in that cave and the planet was a better off without me. I fell silent as I clung to the rocky surface as best I could. I realized I would not be able to last indefinitely. I was expending energy even just staying afloat treading water, which would drain me as fast as the temperature of the water. These realizations were proof that this was not going to be just a mental struggle that I would not be able just to figure out how to beat this challenge mentally because there was a time limit. Like any great competition, this had a deadline. I could only stop to rest so long. Almost without thinking, I dove down into the pool. Impulsively, without considering timing or resting, I dove down deep and searched with my hands in the darkness for signs of passages out of the cave. I did find one and started to swim into it but then stopped, realizing I had to sort out how many openings there were, in case this led deeper into the cave system so I turned and went back. I reached out for the coarse surface of the cave wall which stung the tips of my fingers, by now I they would be cut and bleeding. As I hung, treading water, my foot hit the wall shooting pain up my leg when my blue-nailed, swollen toe struck the rough surface. I reached out carefully with my good foot, hoping I could feel a flat section where I could get a toe grip and not have to tread water continually. There were mostly sharp edges, and it was not easy, but finally I found a minor toehold and a couple of small crevasses for my fingers, so I was able to hang on. The relief didn't last long, though, because the immediate strain on my wrist and hands assured me I wouldn't be able to hold on for long, and oozing warmth around my fingers could only indicate blood was now coming through.

Despite this, I knew had to think carefully about how to go about finding my way out. I had to do whatever I could to make note of the features of the walls around me and dive back down to look for any openings other than the one I had located which now was just off my left foot. I dove down and swam hard but carefully to my left, reaching tentatively so as not to do more damage to my fingers and knuckles.

I stopped once and tried to relax to clear my head then continued until I had made it about half way around then I retreated to my previous location, just above the one passage I'd found and returned my hands and toes to their precarious grip on the sharp-stoned wall and desperately sucked in fresh air, trying to reduce my heart rate. Once the clamoring in my chest abated somewhat I dove again, this time going clockwise around the chamber, feeling for an opening. I discovered that this was not a round cave at all, even though that's how I wanted it to be. The thought that it was jagged and winding was too much to consider, as the chances of finding the openings were much slimmer in that case.

Frustration was setting in. I didn't want to lose my bearings, but realized I'd made a wrong assumption about the shape of this pool. But I'd made the assumption so I would have a starting point. If I'd said to myself, "This cave is long, twisting, windy, with no clear defined pattern," I might not even have tried to find a way out, just given up and be done with it. But I knew it wouldn't be that easy. First, it was not possible to give up, and second, it was not possible to give up. Even if I wanted to, I couldn't because that meant death, and that was not an option. Now it seemed maybe the idea of surveying this pool and determining openings might have been a bad one. My next that was, "What if I really did come in on the opening I'd located?" If that were the case, I could swim down that tunnel and come out in the blue pool I started in. The risk of trying every tunnel I happened to come across was that if I was wrong, I could end up deeper in the system. I started to panic again as I realized I was losing my grip on my wits. I also realized that I'd already come to that conclusion and now I was coming to that same conclusion again! I was making no sense at all. Then reality slapped me on the back of the head: I could die in this cave just as easily as any other one. On the other hand, I might just get lucky and I'd find some inkling about a way out, or it might even open to the outside. I concluded that I had to find my way through the darkness to the first cave and then call that home base then from there find the passage out, back to the lake. No problem. Sure, as unconvinced as ever.

I took six deep breaths then dove down and reached for and found the tunnel. I thrust as hard as I could with my arms, scratching the walls on either side and bumping my head on the top of the passage with every stroke. My head began to feel warm, and I feared I had now cut my scalp on the sharp rocks. I pulled harder, hoping I'd reach the end of the passage soon. I had only a few seconds more to make a decision to turn around or to find the end of the tunnel. Finally my hand splashed up into only air. I stuck my face out of the water and gulped fresh air with huge gasps. I rolled over on my back, trying to stay afloat without reaching with my tortured fingers for something to hold onto.

I was so happy just to find air that an awful truth didn't immediately dawn on me. It took only seconds for it to hit, and I realized that once again I was in another cave, that I hadn't found the blue grotto. It even seemed very possible that I was deeper inside the cave system, and worse, the passage back to where I had been, if that was the only option, would be very difficult. I'd barely made it through the passage to where I was now and would have to do at least that again. A second level of frustration and more seriously, desperation, washed over me. I wanted to cry, and my face, which I'd held up as I swam on my back, dipped into the water. a quantity of which I sucked in, torturing my lungs and throat with searing pain.

NOOOO!!! DROWNING IS NOT AN OPTION.

The body's natural reaction is to cough water out of the lungs, and it really hurt when it had to do so, but I didn't want to die. I didn't want to drown, so I coughed.

I had to be strong and figure this out somehow. So this was a new cave, away from the blue grotto by at least two pools: the dark one I'd just left and this one. Again I came to the conclusion that the way out was to keep my head straight because panic would lead to poor decisions, and there were important decisions to be made. If a number of attempts had to be made, if for no other reason than as part of the process of elimination, then at least I had to maximize the number of attempts. OK, then, if a person was to fail at this, what would be the reason? It could be blood loss, and weakness due to cuts on the head, the hands, the feet. OK. It's important not to worsen the cuts on the hands, head, or feet, so the attempts have to be controlled and careful. I couldn't go thrashing about, smashing into things in the dark. All right, the first step has to be to rest to prepare for another attempt. Breaking down would make the challenge easier. Thinking about nothing but getting out was too high a goal, so set a smaller, more achievable goal. A good one would be finding a place to rest without having to grip like a spider on the walls of the caves. Another would be to conserve energy for heat and strength. Maybe find an area where the water was shallower so it might be possible to float on the back and breathe upward. That would change the focus from mentally mapping the entrances and passages to finding a place to rest. It was a big decision because not searching for the passageway means not finding a way out, but without proper rest a thorough mapping would not happen. Searching required rest, rest made refocusing priorities easier.

I was about to dive again to make another search then stopped, deciding once again to try to visualize where I was, if that was even possible. My head told me it wasn't, but not even trying was giving up. I reached around and felt the walls and screamed out loud at myself at the pure ridiculousness of what I was doing. I yelled, and my voice echoed back at me like a second presence,

"You can't see your hand in front of your face, how in the hell are you going to tell where you are just by feeling some jagged rock? That is stupid, man!"

I had an answer for that stupid voice,

"Well, you got any better ideas smart ass! You tell me what to do. If you're so smart, what the hell are you doing in this cave?"

The echo stopped eventually but I couldn't stop myself from shouting at the echo like it were indeed another person,

"We're both in this dum dum, you and I. We got ourselves into this mess, now we, you and I, have to get us out."

Then, of course, I had to answer,

"Well screaming doesn't help, and neither is calling me

a dum dum, so shut up with that!"

The cave eventually fell silent, and when it did I felt even more alone. The ringing echo faded slowly like a departing friend hanging out the window of a train as it left the station.

However, some small consolation lay in my discovery of a resting place for the back of my head on a bit of smooth rock. It was an incredible contrast to the rest of the jagged limestone feeling like a pillow in comparison. It was positioned perfectly so I could place the nape of my neck into the smoothest part and actually allow my arms to float beside me and my legs out and stay still and rest. The relief was incredible. I breathed in the fresh air, and actually sipped a little water to ease the burning in my throat from screaming. A lot of good that had done. So much for mental strength.

But it was, pure and simple, blind luck that I'd found this smooth rock. Just a minute before I was considering having to change strategies and start searching for a resting place rather than an entrance, and now I had one – and in just the right position, too. What a fluke, but thank God for that smooth rock. At this point something as simple as having found a spot on those rocks that did not tear my skin every time I happened to brush against it made me feel happy. I closed my eyes to give them a rest, hopefully to at least partially relieve the random yellow circle floating in my vision caused by straining to see something in the complete blackness. My eyes were aching like my throat. And I could feel torn, jagged flesh on the tips of my fingers. They weren't painful, and I understood this to be a consequence of the cold, because they, too, like my toes, were numb. I was a mess, suffering sensory deprivation. Feeling nothing but cool water around me was torturing me.

My ears were ringing with a sound like a barely audible dog whistle which seemed to be growing louder, and I was getting sick of it. It was making me want to lash out, but there was nothing I could kill or crush or mutilate in this damn cave, nothing but jagged limestone.

Stupid limestone, what was it even good for?

I visualized crushing those crusty cockroaches using a chunk of this rough limestone, which seemed to help.

That would have saved the life of Hattie's broom at least and added a nice finality to the life of the King Cockroach that'd the nerve to try to get me by climbing up the broom handle and then haunted my dreams where he'd put his ugly alien head back on after we'd stuck it on his even uglier ass and come back ten times larger to try to get at me through that little space under the door.

"I should have killed you twice when I had the chance," I said to the darkness above me.

Suddenly, because I wasn't paying attention, I slipped off the smooth rock. My face went under the water, which again went down my throat, and again I had to cough it back up causing great rolling pain and burning in the lungs.

Oww! Ouch, Ouch, ooooohh, that hurt.

I waved my arms and found the smooth rock again and nestled my neck back on it once more. I wanted and needed to rest longer, just to stay easy a little more. I felt more than heard the thump, thump, thumping of my heart and the recognition of that sound, that beautiful sound of life gave me something to listen to other than the ringing that wouldn't stop. It was a sound that had started before I was born and continued even now, a harbinger of life and promise and happiness and sadness and gifts and disappointment and all things good and bad. It was my heart and had been beating one beat after another after another faithfully without thanks or recognition. The heart gives something you have no right to squander; you have to give back something; you have to go on for it to go on. It will thump over and over and will not quit on you, so you can't quit on it. My head said to me,

"It is telling you, man, it is telling you. Try again,

NOW!"

With that I took one deep breath, then another, then slid off the smooth rock and dove into the black pool once more, swimming down and around the bottom, until I found a passage. I went back up for air, took four more deep breaths, and went down again. I took two, three, four strokes, then a fifth, until I almost panicked as my lungs burned and screamed at me. Finally, I felt the surface again. I came up and again pulled in gulps of air.

"I hear you, I hear you,"

I gasped aloud between gulps. I felt for ledges or handholds and had to tread water because there was nothing in this cave to cling to. I realized that not only had I not found the way out, but I'd found another cave. I actually went deeper into the cave system! I'd done what I said I would not do! I let go a grunt of anguish. My heart had told me to move and I had, but I hadn't found the passage out and, more sickeningly, I was six hard strokes deeper in. How could a little lump of limestone on the water hide such an elaborate cave system? Damn it. Damn it all to hell.

But I knew through my cursing that before I went crazy I had to at least get back to my smooth stone – the one providing simple respite, six hard strokes back. The memory of the pain in my lungs from the swim into this cave was fresh but I was treading water and I knew I could not think for long. I had to suck in some air and get back to my smooth rock and not dilly-dally about it. My home base was now a smooth place in a forest of spikes and from here I would have to find my home base. If I stayed too long the cold and numbness would get me, but if I tried again too soon I might lose breath before making it out.

But there was that thought again,

"What if I go deeper again instead of getting back out?"

I had no choice though. The smooth stone would have to be referece point and home base and cave number one would be half way – home as it were, a resting place that I needed to call back into service. Sadly now my goal had diminished so tragically that right now my goal was not finding my way out, but just finding my way back to the one smooth stone that gave me respite. My expectations were dropping in quantum leaps.

But without further delay I pulled in several deep breaths of air, as hard as I could and, just as I was getting dizzy, dove back down into the water to find the passage back to smooth rock. I went down into a passage, hoping this one brought me back and was not another taking me deeper. I counted one, two, three, four, five and, finally, the sixth stroke and, again with lungs wanting to burst, reached up into only air.

Yes!

But was this the same cave I'd just left?

I reached around frantically for the familiar smooth rock, searching for that familiar feel. I touched something smooth, something that was not limestone. I reached higher, it was smooth, it was the smooth rock. I wanted to scream for joy that I would now be able to turn over, hook the nape of my neck back on the smooth rock and rest. I sighed with relief as I lay back and let my body float free and relax fully, my arms floating at my sides, like the body parts of that sad plastic doll that had washed up on my beach – was it only the day before? Just floating and letting the muscles calm and the breathing slow down, saying to my heart,

"Sorry. I tried my best. I'll rest here on this smooth rock and then try again."

I lay there, balancing carefully for a long time on this lifesaver of a rock, yes, balancing on my neck that was starting to protest at having to do all the work.

Then I noticed a change in the blackness above. It seemed not to be pure blackness anymore. It was now blue, an almost purplish blue. But within that color was another feature, the recognition of which made me realize I was beginning to lose the mental battle because above me in the blackness a mirror image of myself had formed, slowly, as if I was to lay witness to my own colossal mistake. I shook my head to make it disappear. But with it gone I was alone again and, foolishly, I missed it and willed it back. Concentrating on the memory of what it looked like, I was able to conjure it up again.

It was me, right down to the blue toe, and I could even see the new scrapes and cuts on the ends of the fingers.

This image even mirrored my movements and floated in air as I floated in water, and if I tried really hard to concentrate on the features I could see the mournful expression on my face, desperate and scared. This thought sent a shudder down my back. My face in the reflection realized the seriousness of the situation. There I was, laying still and balancing on the nape of my neck on some miraculous smooth round rock.

How fortunate I was in this fortress of razor sharp limestone to have found this smooth rock. What were the chances that I would find my salvation in the only smooth item in a mountain of razor blades?

Luck, I suppose.

My body floated and I could see myself as if in a mirror, and I smiled and my image smiled, and I visualized my rock.

Then a thought occurred to me, my mind being a pragmatic and calculating one, that this couldn't be the only smooth thing in this cave. It would be too strange that in a series of caves, with walls of impenetrable limestone, that I could find the one and only smooth thing.

I had to believe that this could not be the only smooth

item in this entire island. If it were, it would be the same as being pricked by the only needle in a giant haystack. Possible yes, but more probable that there was more than one needle, or, in this case more than one smooth rock. This gave me hope to be reasoning for a change, reasoning that provided some relief from the desperation I had been feeling. To confirm my slight change of attitude I searched the darkness and once more conjured the image of myself floating above me. Yes, that face had changed, too, the desperation and defeat were not as distinct.

It was a minor victory, but something that might indicate a change of fortune. With new hope I sought to expand on this small victory by trying to remember how I'd achieved it and try to create another, perhaps more significant. So I looked up, into the face of the face above, and said aloud,

"You didn't find the only needle in the haystack, you found something in a limestone cave, now try to find the next something."

I reached out my hands, only to be rewarded by more slicing of the tips of my fingers, regardless how nimbly I tried to avoid brushing hard on the limestone. No matter. I had to reach out. I had to try for some sort of victory, even an insignificant one. I had to find something. Finally, I touched something smooth when I turned face down into the water, but I needed air, so I set my neck back on the smooth stone and stopped to rest and savor my tiny but so significant a victory.

This was victory number two.

The first was finding the smooth stone then actually reasoning that it could not be the only one; the second was that I would find another, and sure enough I had been right, there actually was another.

I searched the blackness over my face for floating me, just so I could see the smug smile of a tiny victory, just so I could say "I told you so."

There was more than one smooth rock in this cave,

although this second one was just below the water line and just below the one smooth rock that was my salvation. I smiled up at my image. I smiled for once and for a change, but within the smile my lips trembled, as I saw myself in a cave, and I could still reason, I was still thinking. The next thought was that it was a shame that all this power, all this life I contained, all this that I was blessed to be born with, could end and be ended on some solitary smooth rock in an otherwise jagged limestone cave. I shook my head to chase these thoughts away.

I turned from the floating image of myself, ashamed to face myself, having been blessed with life and good fortune and the power of reason and now on the verge of squandering it all.

I became disgusted with myself, and to quit this morbid train of thought I slid off the rock, back under the surface, and reached up to massage the back of my neck to relieve the pain. It brought some satisfaction, yes, but the effort of treading water was even more tiring with ever numbing limbs. I had to build on the positive of finding that second smooth shape, and use it for all it was worth. I turned my body to feel for the other smooth rock. It was there as before, but now that I was paying closer attention I could feel that it was curved. Yes, it had a curving shape. I ran my fingers over and over the smooth curving shape, thinking… slightly curved and tapered….

What?
I felt farther along the curve.
Holy Mother of God! Am I feeling a ribcage?
Are these smooth rocks a skeleton?

If so, that would mean the smooth rock I'd been resting on is a skull embedded in limestone!

I'd found the remains of the last person who got lost in here!

I'd been laying on top a dead man!

My thoughts exploded and all the thoughts of the week merged. I screamed out,

"Lawrence!! Is that you? Did fate bring me to this island, to sleep in your bed, to retrace your steps, so I could find you???"

I screamed, "I am not Lawrence!!!" at the cave at the top of my lungs.

I thrashed and splashed, wasting a great deal of energy, shouting again and again,

"I am not Lawrence, I am not."

But I was going crazy. Yes. I was.

Regardless, the thrashing soon made me tired, and I had to stop and rest on my dear friend, whoever he was. Why can't it be Lawrence? It might be Lawrence.

He saved me by letting me rest on him and would have to again. I was close to drowning and out of breath. Beating the water and screaming at nothing, incoherent, in a blind fury thinking too many, too many, too many thoughts took my last breaths and my last bit of energy, and now I was flailing again, but this time flailing to stay alive to catch my breath and stay above the surface. I was going under for that dreaded third time, and I couldn't get a grip on anything, until the tips of my ragged fingers touched once and then again before finally getting hold of the smooth shape – my salvation – that I now realized was a human skull.

I gripped what would have been eye sockets and forehead and fought to roll over in the water and onto my back so I could accomplish the distasteful task of setting the nape of my neck back onto the perch that was the top of the skull of… of… *Lawrence?*

The heavy rasping of my breath returning echoed back to me as I rested atop my new best friend, my savior, my resting place and refuge against the fatigue of staying afloat. The exultation I felt at this respite from drowning at that moment was fleeting, as in a second the ugly thought came to me – oh, horror of horrors – am I to be just the next layer of bones? Would I be the resting place for the next person so foolish as to swim into this cave? Is there another layer of bones beneath Lawrence? Aaaaahhhh.

"Save me again, Lawrence," I screamed.

The sound came back to me in near-deafening waves.

Listening to the silence for so long and straining for sound so long, my ears wanted to replace the absolute silence with that sort of high-pitched whine that's usually described as ringing, but that had nothing at all to do with ringing. Nothing is as poorly described in all of nature as that sound that's nothing at all like ringing but is constant and real and whining and deafening as it grows relentlessly from a steady blue tone to one higher and higher pitched, until near madness ensues. In this near madness, my most urgent need besides rescue was to scream out as loudly as my painfully raspy throat would allow at the blackness above me and at my faithful friend, Lawrence, giving me solace and rest,

"Noooo! Nooo! This. Is. Not. Happening!"

I screamed this until the words came echoing back:

Toooo meeee… Toooo meeee…

The ringing whine in my ears came back with a

vengeance together with the pain in my throat as payment for my screams and my eyes screamed in pain as they searched for light where there was none, pupils opening past whatever they'd previously been capable of opening and still trying to open more.   Over the high-pitched whine in my ears the echoed words came back to me from the ceiling of the cave, seeming to concentrate and focus on a point in my skull.   It was like the sound of a thousand bagpipes playing in my head.

Bagpipes??

Bagpipes are haunting me!? Someone in this cave with me was playing bagpipes?

Bagpipes are not a musical instrument!!

What?

Was someone, in a voice part mine and part my brother and part my father, all three voices melding in chorus, trying to tell me something and doing it in voices that sounded like bagpipes?
Surely death has more meaning.

Please!

This is so stupid that bagpipes are adding to my torture, playing some twisted, wretched, horrible version of Amazing Grace in that inconceivably deafening, screeching sound that is bagpipes. What had I done to deserve this… this… torture, at this hour of my death?

NOOOOO!

I HATE BAGPIPES!

LEAVE ME ALONE!!

BAGPIPES AREN'T SUPPOSED TO BE INSIDE MY HEAD

MAKING THAT AWFUL NOISE!!
LEAVE ME ALONE!!!

I wanted to cry out loud at how insanely stupid this was, at how meaningless, how trivial, how incomprehensibly insignificant my life apparently was! At this moment it seemed like I was nothing and never would be if I could have no more meaningful or profound thought at the time of my imminent death than something ridiculous like that bagpipes are not a musical instrument.

Oh, life is so cruel! When it sends bagpipes to haunt my end, to make the last sound I hear the I sound of bagpipes.

This thought alone made me want to cry out loud. I blew out a breath of exasperation at the walls of the cave above me, crying out again,

"Aaahhh, you loser! You stupid, stupid loser. Loser of love, loser of life itself!!"

My throat burned and my ears rang as I screamed and the screams echoed back to me in that confined space.

With the sensations of pain in my chest and ears, I stopped thinking, but that didn't stop the intense shivering brought on by the cold water and fear.

I vibrated with the intensity of the shivering, but when it passed, I knew... I knew... I was getting really cold.

But I also realized I was losing the mental battle that I thought at first it would be. The bagpipes proved I was losing it.

However, it came to me, this also meant that I was still

thinking, even if just a little, and if I could think then I could realize I was losing it, then, maybe... I could get it back.

Like dozing off, when you only know you've fallen asleep after you wake up and the time has changed, sanity can slip away as well. But, tenuous as it was, like toes on limestone or my neck on a skull, I still had a grip on reality, because I knew this was still a mental battle, a mental battle that I meant to and would win.

Bagpipes?

Yes, those misshapen udder-like sacks of tartan that have tortured a million ears, if I get to swim out of this black hole of hell – and I bloody well will – I'll have a mission to let the world know that bagpipes are not a musical instrument, no, they are an instrument of torture!!

Not only that, I had to live for my heart, so faithful to me, for my family, and to tell his mother and father where dear Lawrence had ended up, to bring closure to the poor tormented soul of Mr. and Mrs. P, so Mr. P could stop that incessant digging at the arm of the old red chair and un-haunt that beautiful plantation house, and for the sake of Lawrence himself.

Yes!

This was needed. Convince myself the world still needed me, I still needed me.

I could not die in this blackness so that my disappearance would make my mother the next Mrs. P.

I could not.

Through force and effort, I calmed down. The rings in my vision from the constant searching for light persisted, and when I looked closer I could see that the reflection of me was still there in the middle of a circle. It hurt my eyes, but there I was, me, looking down at me, looking up at me, but that made me almost sick. I was there, looking sad but triumphant that I'd found some purpose to save the world, but I still couldn't find my way home.

I was lost.

It was frustrating to watch my body in the image above try to find its way from this dark pit one more time. I was learning a plain and simple lesson that rational thought and reason are blinded by panic. Finding a solution to a serious problem takes clear thinking, but in a state of extreme anxiety rational thought is clouded by panic. At times, even when things are going well, rational thought can be fleeting and it was deserting me in this desperate time. The fight now was not only to stay alive or find the way out or to breathe or float or swim, but to desperately hang on to that slippery virtue, rational thought, which is sanity.

What am I thinking? What am I thinking? Confusion was making my head hurt. I had to get out, but I was not thinking clearly. I gave my head a serious shake to clear the nonsense. The vision of me floating above the me in the water shook its head too, and had a smirk on its face as if to say, "I know. I know, and you have to figure it out," and all I could hear in my head was floating me saying, "You went the wrong way. You didn't come in that passage, how could you get out through that passage?" and then it let out a big laugh and was gone. It was laughing at me, taunting me then it was not there. It was part of my imagination and was back where it belonged.

But it couldn't stay away. In the total blackness in the

cave my eyes continued to conjure floating me and it would not be restrained and was free to do as it pleased, to float about, and apparently, it pleased to do so. I watched it wavering above me, detached but still mimicking my every move. Again I realized that I felt very cold. My teeth were chattering and I couldn't stop them. They and my toe both throbbed intensely and the pain concentrated itself in a spot just behind my ears.

I wanted to cry like a baby, a miserable baby. I could feel a slight warmth at the back of my neck, which was surely my blood painting the top of the skull under my neck and the fullest realization of the seriousness of my predicament hit me again. It was more than possible that I could die here, and telling myself I was not going to wouldn't be good enough. I was losing the ability to convince myself that I would not die here. Now I was really losing the mental battle and saying that in an effort to regain control of the thought was no help at all.

I could die, and it might be sooner than I expected because my shaking would not stop which meant I was becoming hypothermic. My tears of pity for myself would contribute salt to that fresh water which was less fresh now that it had some of my blood and sweat from anxiety. These beautiful pools were being spoiled and would be for a long time if I were to add my bones to those I was resting on. My body would lay here and slowly rot away and become food for something or maybe nothing at all and then even that part of me would be a waste due to this incredible folly. For a second I thought maybe I should reach down to find out if there was another skeleton below the one that supported me, but then I thought, "Why?" What purpose would that do other than to prove that I and smooth-skull-and-ribcage man I lay upon were not the only two stupidest people on earth because some other person had made the same mistake. Maybe there's a pirate or something down there as well, one who had planned on using the cave as a hiding place for a few thousand pounds of gold.

Then the chattering stopped and I felt less tired as a wave of something warm washed over me – adrenaline or what I couldn't tell and thought I might never know, because how would I know if I was about to die? It seemed I would never learn another thing or see another thing, which brought a new wave of sadness which renewed the shivering and chattering teeth. I was close to total despair as I shook all over and slipped off my perch on Lawrence's skull and dove back into the black, cold water. My eyes strained to see in the darkness to no avail. I reached for the walls under the water line, searching, thrusting my arms, smashing my hands against the coarse walls over and over and not caring at all because why should I care if my corpse slowly decayed with nice intact skin or with terribly skinned knuckles. Who cares?

My thrashing was useless, and I gave it up and settled back with resignation to my familiar position to reflect on time and decomposition and how long would I be rotting away before I was a twin structure to my silent friend. If he was breathing he would be breathing down my neck, but he wasn't; only I was, for a while longer at least. Not much longer though. I was cold and tired and now even getting too tired to chatter my teeth. My thoughts wandered. I couldn't feel the pain in my toe anymore, and the bleeding in the various damaged spots may have stopped but I was not conscious of it. I thought about home and that I don't have anyone to love here; they're all as gone as I am gone as my hands and feet are numb. But numbness is peace, which is good in a tormented body. I just had to close my eyes now because they hurt badly, with the yellow rings from searching blackness. It might be best to rest them, take a little nap and wake up refreshed and ready to think about how to get out.

Despairing thoughts returned:

"Yeah. Sure. Like I'm getting out.

Hah!"

Maybe I should say goodbye to myself by saying goodbye to the floating me above me, that mirror that hung above me hadn't changed in all the time it was there. It mimicked my thrashing about, but it never changed, just hung there, now with the same dull stare that it had when it first appeared. I frowned just to make the floating body frown too and then I said goodbye to floating me, and cocked my head slightly to the side so I could say goodbye to dead Lawrence, my good friend, who granted me a resting space.

Good old Lawrence may have died just so I could come along and have a place to rest in this cave.

"Goodbye, Lawrence," I said.

I said, "Goodbye, Uncle George," who told me to come in here – or not. He might have been trying to warn me. I don't know. Perhaps I'd misunderstood him. The weariness was returning, and I wanted to sleep, or at least close my eyes so the yellow rings would disappear. But I also wanted to pay Hattie for her room, and I should have said goodbye to the captain of the Lady Blanche and the crew.

And Mrs. P... Oh no, not Mrs. P. Not again for that sad lady, to have to clean up clothes and belongings left behind and to lose another one to that room now that I was gone too for a mysteriously interminable length of time. And my mother back home would have to clean up my room or leave my room and my scant ribbons of minor glory and wonder what she'd done so badly in life that I would leave her to die without knowing what happened to her son who never came home....

My heart said, "No, no, I can't leave all those goodbyes unsaid!"

But my despairing brain was thinking I had no choice, no choice at all. I couldn't say goodbye to Mrs. P or my dear Mother because I could not find my way out of this stupid cave system. I only had myself alone to say goodbye to. I opened my eyes and floating me was above me again as if waiting for instructions. I said to floating me,

"Yeah. You waiting for instructions? Huh? Do me a favor, OK? Since you can fly and I can only swim, why not fly out of here and tell Mrs. P what happened. I don't want her waiting for me, or Lawrence, to come home. Let her sleep now. Tell her Lawrence and I are in a good place and she and Mr. P can rest now. OK?"

I said this clearly to floating me in the blackness to make sure floating me understood.

I knew I was done because I could hear my voice like some madman speaking to no-one but himself or even more damning, an image of himself floating above himself.

Was this confirmation of madness?
My desperation?
No confirmation needed – way past that.

Surrender?

Not just yet, but then I closed my eyes and waited, half asleep despite the anger at myself and my own stupidity for getting myself into this.

Maybe I really had slept, but when I did open my eyes again floating me was still there.

"Why are you still here?" I asked and closed my eyes again.

"This time," I told floating me, "I will not open my eyes again because I don't want to see you there."

But that made me think that maybe floating me wouldn't disappear unless I kept my eyes closed permanently.

Maybe floating me was my spirit and wouldn't be released until I was dead and laying for eternity with Lawrence. Regardless, I kept my eyes closed for a very long time, or so it seemed. I wasn't really sure because it seemed I had lost everything now that I'd lost track of time. I'd lived by time – time spent at this and at that, time accomplishing this and that – and now I felt like I'd lost it and without time my mind was truly foggy and confused.

I was feeling that I'd lost everything if I lost time and if I'd lost time then I'd lost hope. True despair is born from lost hope. Before very much longer, though, I imagined I could see floating me move. I was watching through my eyelids because I still wouldn't open my eyes, but I sensed that the image was there, and I knew I would never be rid of it. Eventually I would let the numbness in my hands, arms, and legs expand to encompass my body, too, and my feigned sleep would become real, permanent sleep. I would sleep and decompose and my bones would add another level to the bones I now rested on. The skull that was my savior really only provided me the time to consider what I had done, and the mistake I'd made.

These dreadful thoughts made me open my eyes to see if floating me was still there. Yes, he was, but his expression was dull and his stare was blank. But then it changed, and floating me seemed to shiver, and began floating back and forth above me, above me and the bones of Lawrence. It circled just like a spirit should, flying like in a cartoon, like it was Halloween, and I had a vaporous spirit flying above me. How weird. My mind was obviously playing tricks on me. Maybe this was going to be the one last comical thing I would experience. Indeed, it would be a sad moment when it was finally gone, but it had to go.

Suddenly I imagined I could see my ghostly vapor dive down just below my feet through the water at the far end of this cold, black pool, and down some more, swimming under a protruding rock into a tunnel to take three long hard strokes, making a sharp left and a sharp right then two more ups and one more down and then up, up, and up some more into the blue grotto, the first cave, the cave with the sunlight streaming in through the top fissure in the rock. I followed in my mind, not wanting to say goodbye to floating me. I chased the trail of bubbles in the water that floating me created as he flew through the water until he emerged into light, warm and yellow, illuminating the beautiful colors of the first grotto. How wonderful it was that floating me could see color, beautiful blues. Colors!

I opened my eyes to see the color, but the color wasn't there.

I was still in the blackness of the cave with the bones of Lawrence.

Damn! Damn! Damn! That lucky floating me found his way out!

"Damn you!"

I screamed, now enraged that floating me was in the light when I was still in this darkness. I turned and, with my numb and bleeding hand, slapped the smooth skull of Lawrence a stinging blow, as I screeched despite my hoarse throat,

"Lawrence, I can't take this anymore! I gotta go!"

Heedless of the risk, I dove down into the water, across

the pool to the far end, retracing the route floating me had taken into the depths. I found the protrusion of rock hiding the entrance to a passage, swam down three strokes just as floating me had done, continuing hard, face first, into a left turn and then smacking my face again making a sharp right. I took more hard strokes, hands pulling hard on water and knocking hard on sharp limestone, lungs searing hot and wanting to burst, arms thrashing, eyes stinging with the force of the water as I stared into the darkness.

Pull, pull…hard…up…lungs burning…up…one, two, and finally a third, and then dizzy and wavering until at last…the beautiful light!

I had found the blues and greens of the grotto.

Floating me swam out and showed me the way.

He knew all along, he remembered the way!

YES! I was out. But no! Could it be??

Please let it not be that floating me was just messing with me again.

Was I, or wasn't I?

My tortured eyes searched the light as I gasped huge gulps of fresh air that never hurt so good, recognizing rocks that never looked so good, with tears of joy that never felt so good. I wanted to shout,

"I'm out!"

I did shout, "I'm out. I. Am. Out, out, out!!!"

I couldn't believe it.

I could…not…believe it. Was it really possible that I could be out? No, I couldn't have found my way out. But, really it hadn't been me at all. No, it was the floating me that had wanted so badly to quit the place that he'd made a dash for it. Lucky for him, but more lucky for me I'd had someone to follow out. Good thing he'd chosen correctly and found his way out.

But then my thoughts turned to Lawrence. How could I leave him there?

I have to go back for him.

Yes, I could do it. I know the way now. It's down and right then left and up and around that outcropping and up again. I have to go back and get Lawrence. I spilled my blood on him, and he saved me. I'd hit him for some unknown reason and he'll never forgive me. I love him for saving me and he is there and I have to get him back to him mother. He should be back with his mother.

But he's dead. Yes, he's dead, and part of the cave.

These confused thought made me wonder,
"Did I leave my sanity in there? Do I have to go back to get Lawrence and my sanity too??"
I told myself to be calm,
"Calm…. Breathe, breathe. Come on now, take a few deep breaths, and think… I suppose it would be best to let him be. But why did I hit him?"
These thoughts were hurting my head.
"Why did I hit him?"

I had to breathe and calm myself. I shook my head and shivered. I shivered so hard my teeth chattered and for a minute, a long minute, I began to worry the shivering wouldn't stop. I turned on my back to rest, with arms and legs so sluggish I could barely tread water. I had to warm up soon or I would drown, here in the blue grotto. What a waste that would be to me and to dear Lawrence who saved me and gave me respite.

Still I felt I was close to drowning right there on the brink of saving myself. That seemed an even more lonely prospect than dying with Lawrence would've been.

I paddled about with arms that felt like wooden oars and searched for the passage that led through the short tunnel to the small lake within the limestone island. As I moved slowly around of the pool I gazed at the colourful blues and greens reflecting onto the ceiling of the cave from the sunlight coming through the small opening to the sky. I made it fully around twice before I found the passage then dipped below the surface and with a shudder at the feeling of having to go once more down and through a passage. I pulled the three strokes and up into the brightness of the small lake. This water was much warmer, and the feeling of it made me anxious to get all the way out. I found the passage under the hanging mangroves and thrashed my way against the roots and over the few feet of sand and flowing water. As I touched the sand I felt the sting of my fingers sifting the coarse grit and for the first time I knew the extent of how damaged my fingers were.

Out in the open again, the light hurt my eyes, but I had to look around and there she was, Uncle George's little boat. I rammed my head against her, and willed a numb arm to reach up as I tried to throw it shoulder first over the gunwale. That arm was not just dumb, but plain stupid, and deaf to my pleas.

"Reach over you stupid thing."

The thick stump of arm and hand, pale, almost blue, was like a foreign object that struck the side twice, three times before finally making it to the top of the rail, which was only a pitiful six inches above the water line, but six inches higher than that blue arm wanted to reach. Then, using the right arm as inspiration, the left arm had to be convinced to swing out of the cold water and get to that rail. Thus, inch by painful inch, over long minutes, befuddled head, half frozen arms and shoulders and hips dropped into the bottom of the boat. My teeth were starting to chatter harder as my clumsy fingers on numb hands struggled to untie the line wrapped on the mangrove. After much fumbling and more swearing, the boat floated free as I fell into the bottom of the boat.

At this point, I felt an enormous relief that I'd made it into the boat as I realized that I'd not been numb just of hands and body, but numb of mind and spirit and as close to losing my life to the cold and the dark as I had been to giving up and losing my sanity as well.

The boat drifted, with me as a human lump of passenger.

It drifted some thirty feet until it reached sunshine, beyond the shadow of the island, and the sun hit me like a warm bath, caressing my skin. I lay there for a long while, floating in that boat on water so blue and so calm and only a few feet deep not even rocking me or causing the boat to drift much. I lay there, just numb.

After a while, when my dull mind realized I was slowly drifting out to sea, away from the Island and Uncle George, I began to flex my hands. They curled at first, then didn't want to uncurl. I held them up to the sun and told them to loosen and, to my great amazement, they listened. Each finger straightened.

Even though it was a tiny victory, the sense of that victory hit me like a thunderclap. It was a blessing from an unknown heaven that I could convince these cold fingers and hands to do as I willed. I muttered a simple thank you and pressed my wrinkled palms into my eyes, realizing I was going to make it. My limbs were listening to me again. A lump rose in my throat, and my heart swelled at the recognition of my victory over the cold and darkness, but I had no time to cry tears of joy. Even though I just wanted to warm my face in the sun I had to stop the drift away from Uncle George. I bent at the waist, fighting dizziness, then found the oars and set them into the locks. I pulled my legs under me and onto the bench and began to row.

My head felt so sensitive in so many places I didn't want to know the condition of my bruised scalp, but my hair, matted and unkempt as it was and now drying in the sun, kept the blood from flowing freely. At this point after what I'd been through, the bleeding scalp was low priority – toes were first, then fingers and knuckles, then finally scalp. It was so minor I could not care less that my scalp bled a little. My fingers, which I could see on the oars, were a mess, but at least they were attached to a live body and not something floating lifelessly in that godforsaken cave. My feet were no better, but again, I didn't care. The blue toe was twice normal size, and when I looked at it, it seemed so ridiculous I almost laughed. Ha, ha! The kids on the island will laugh when they see that giant toe. It would be hard to wait to show them. I hoped it wouldn't get smaller or heal before I'd have a chance to show them.

I pulled toward the island and realized it was just too far to get back to Uncle George's beach. Besides, I wasn't ready to talk to anyone, and his version of sanity, or lack thereof, matching my close call with insanity, was not what I needed at the moment.

It had been such a challenge to translate into his reality before, there was no chance I would accomplish it now. Out of the lee of the island the water tossed into a slight chop and the old dory bobbed like a cork. I had to be careful not to get spilled out of the boat. I wanted nothing more to do with water or swimming at that moment, thank you very much, so I rowed hard toward the beach until I caught a small wave that picked up the back of the boat and carried me to the beach.

Within reach of the warm white sand I toppled out to let it hit my face. My mouth was half in the sand, and…. who cares? I flexed my fingers and gripped the sand as if climbing a dune. I loved that beautiful, sweet, silky, pinkish-white sand that was pushing its way into my broken and bleeding skin. I wanted to eat it, it was so good. Get in every open cut there, lovely sand, and be part of me so I won't be part of all that water that almost had me. Almost. I'm never leaving you again, baby. The grit was between my teeth, and I thought I might have left something precious in that cave – my sanity – because I realized I was eating sand.

The fingers in front or face were now coated with tiny particles of sand of varying color. That did not look good. I wanted to lift my right arm, which was under me somewhere, but my body pinned it down. My left hand was directly in front of my face, and it seemed that now I'd made it to the beach I was too tired to move another inch. The warmth of the sun was motivation to crawl above the waveline on the beach, but that was crawl was a hard one.

That life-giving sun had to bring me back to my senses, so I told my left elbow to dig in so the left hand could rise, but the tiredness I felt was overwhelming. The cold and the physical exertion I'd just gotten through caused fatigue that encompassed every cell of every nerve and every fiber of every muscle. I could feel little below my hips, just a tingling on my toes, so obviously my legs were there, but it was only my face in the sand and the left hand I was trying to rise that had any real feeling. As I focused on the cuts I had a positive thought, which I savored as another small shot of reality, that this might be a good thing because if they could hurt at least I could feel them. The salt water washed over the cuts on my numb feet and that big toe that looked like a light bulb, but I could still barely feel them. Thawing out might bring new pain.

But these thoughts lasted only a second, and this encouraged me as I could tell that my comprehension of the surroundings and my condition was improving. I counted to ten, to prove to myself I could do it, and only got to six three times before finally cracking that barrier and making it to ten. With this grand accomplishment I decided to flex each finger in front of my face, twice, to prove it was possible. That worked too. I closed my eyes and rested. It was going to happen. I could see that all I had to do was to wake things up one at a time.

Next step: the wrist. I turned to dig my hand into the sand. I got the elbow down and could feel it nestle into the beach. I pressed with my shoulder and within ten minutes I had it in, and gradually I'd crept up the beach to dryer, warmer sand. I concentrated on each body part separately until, eventually, I warmed enough to get one knee at a time under me.

The sun was setting by the time I made it to my feet, but I was standing, wobbly and shaky, ready to step forward.

I started off slowly and it was dark before I made it to the shack. I paced up the narrow path to Hattie's bungalow with the last of twilight and the power for the island already shut down. Nine p.m. had struck and the kerosene lanterns were lit and the faint yellow glow from inside showed on the windows. I entered my little 8 x 6 shack in total darkness and felt for the army blanket on the cot.

My entry disturbed a few bugs which didn't bothered me at all this time, and I lay down on the softest, warmest, most comfortable bed I'd ever felt. The formerly scratchy grey blanket felt like it was spun in heaven at that moment, and I closed my eyes with a hum of contentment like the purring of a cat as I began to warm more now I had this blanket wrapped tightly around me. I let out a long sigh of relief as night fell on the island, the shack, on Hattie and her brood of bustling children, on Uncle George, and on me. I fell asleep within moments, with the final thoughts that the sun would rise again on me and this little island, which was now my little island.

`The next morning the sun did rise in all its glory over the eastern edge of the great Atlantic giving warmth and light at the birth of a new day, but I was not witness to this splendor, nor its passing beyond its zenith into the afternoon.

When I finally awoke well past mid-day, the shack was blistering hot. I looked at my fingers closely for the first time and could see fibers of the old blanket had joined the sand crusted in the scabs and were now hardened in the coagulated clots. Black dots of dried blood speckled the old grey blanket.

I was quite relieved that even though a few fingers were still bleeding slightly, it had not been sufficient to wake me. I couldn't move my legs until I'd done some stretching as well as flexing my toes, then I could begin to reach for the concrete floor with the maps of Africa and the Battle of Gettysburg, and to slowly restore some movement and get off the cot.

I stood looking at the wall, reliving parts of the day before, and horror shook my bones. Then and there I decided I was not – NOT – going to think about what I had been through. No thinking about bagpipes. No. Life was about trees and sand and earth and living and water and friends and living and growing, it was the here and now without dwelling on existential theories. I will get past the horror and focus on life.

The most immediate focus though had to be on getting these fingers and toes and matted hair cleaned up, so I stepped out of the shack, through that flimsy wooden door into bright sunshine and had to shield my eyes like Papillion stepping out of solitary confinement. I couldn't begin to imagine what I looked like, and truthfully I didn't want to project my appearance in my mind's eye for fear that floating man would be back and then I would lose my mind for sure because maybe I'd not be able to control it happening just whenever it wanted to. I also wanted to avoid having to explain or share what happened, out of embarrassment at my own part in my jangled state. I could take no pride in having found my way out – that was nothing more than a bitter consolation. As I stood in the doorway of the shack, ready to step out amongst the trees over the broken concrete doorstep onto the smooth, sandy path before me, I resolved to look ahead and not to beat myself up anymore over what I'd done. Right now I had to clean up the small wounds, plain and simple. There'd be plenty of time later for reflection and mending the bigger wounds, the mental wounds.

I made my way to the water pump and started to work. Right hand, left hand, feet and purple toe next, head and scalp, very gingerly – ouch – until they'd all been flushed with water. Bits of blanket and sand embedded in deep, red crevices were not about to be washed away without more work, but I didn't want to soak them lest they soften and open up. Well, maybe they weren't crevices, but at the moment they seemed that way. Whatever. They were cuts capable of causing considerable suffering, so best leave them alone, letting the particles of sand and blanket act as a crude dressing and base for new skin. Later, I supposed, I'd have to dig it out, and it might even hurt more at that stage, but at the moment I didn't care too much about what happened later. I worked the handle of that pump and scrubbed all over and noticed that new welts from insect bites had appeared, but these didn't bother me much, and I almost wanted to laugh at how trivial they seemed now. Like Hattie said, it was just a little cockroach, and keeping things in perspective was the lesson here.

When I was satisfied I'd done all I could to clean up, I headed off on the path to the beach to check that Uncle George's boat hadn't set itself free and to get out of sight of the islanders, not wanting to scare the children or have to explain to anyone what I'd done to get into my present state of disarray. Pity for such a mistake would be like rubbing salt in the wound, as if they'd be saying, "We weren't sure how smart you are, but thanks for confirming what we all thought: you're a fool." Like I'd need that added to my misery from having to hobble on protesting ankles trying to keep my purple light bulb and otherwise damaged toes from touching the ground. My hair was surely not stylishly done, long and matted after having gone without shampoo for six days, even if I had no mirror to confirm that. I was alive even if I looked more like old bent Aqualung than the young man who had jumped impulsively on a boat seeking adventure.

I wandered my way along the path thinking that hopefully I'd reached the figurative lowest point of the trough of a wave, the flat part, that I'd already gone up over the crest, crashed hard and had taken a long slide down with tremendously frightening speed, but now had reached a level spot and was riding along on a course of recovery. At the beach the old wooden dory remained, like a beat up Silver tied to a tree waiting for the Lone Ranger. I thought about getting it into the water, beating over the smallish but still challenging waves, and returning it to Uncle George's beach and just thinking about it was more work than I was willing to do at the moment, so I gave up on that idea.

"I'll do it later."

I said this aloud and actually surprised myself, having not spoken a word, nor heard a word spoken in many hours. How many hours?

Not having spoken in 24 hours would not be a big deal, but these past 24 hours had been a very long way from normal. My entire existence had been far from normal in an extreme way for longer than I cared to think about. Normal would assume a new face from this point on in my life it seemed. This thought surprised me, and I wondered how long the sensation of unreality would last. Would it take as long as the scabs that would eventually form and finally fall off the myriad of etchings on my fingers? Longer? Probably a lifetime longer, as if the etchings on those fingers were etchings on my soul that would be carried with me like internal tattoos as inerasable as this past 24 hours was now indelibly etched upon my soul.

At this point, I wasn't mentally prepared to reconcile all the impressions and feelings about what I'd just experienced. Remembering and reliving scared me. It made me think about someone who'd been in a train wreck and flown through the window to survive with such minor injuries that he was almost ashamed at his luck amidst the carnage of fellow passengers. I was alive and well, more or less, and I was not adding to that pile of bones I'd found in the cave. No! God, no! I'd been saved by the skull and bones of one so much less lucky than I.

I wanted to cry at that moment. No, correct that; I didn't want to cry but felt a sobbing need to cry.

My God, my good God!

I'm here like Lawrence wanted to be here. I was alive, and he'd given me salvation. He saved me. Whether that was Lawrence or someone else, that person saved me. I realized I was now grasping and understanding that I'd really made it despite what I'd been up against, and that was good. But then a huge tremor shuddered through my body, like a dog shaking water off its fur, as the fear from the day before struck me. I had to shut it down, or I'd be stuck in that fear forever. Right now; I had to shut it down right now. The fear was cold and real and so powerful that I felt almost like I was still in the cave and being out in the sun with sand under my feet was only a dream, that it was only floating me out in the sun and swimming me was still in the cave resting his neck on the forehead of a miserable skeleton fused into limestone.

Aaarrrgghhh. For the second time this short day I had to release some form of expression, and again it came out as exasperation. I dropped to my knees and clutched handfuls of sand for some form of physical stimulation to chase away the mental anguish currently running at full throttle. The question arose: did I swim out of those caves without my sanity? What the hell had I been thinking? It perturbed me deeply that my thoughts during the crisis in the cave at a life-or-death moment, were no more profound than thoughts that involved bagpipes. How could it be that such mundane and meaningless thoughts might define my life? Oooohhhhh. Could it be that my life was a total waste of time and perfectly good oxygen? Bagpipes? I was a useless and good for nothing human being. How could I not feel more than that at that so critical a moment?

I lay on the sand with my face up to the sky, and although the sand was soft and warm the back of my head was so tender I had to roll to one side. My fingers tingled as I forced new sand and grit into the wounds. It was as if I was unable to get out of my own way. My mind whirled with depressing, frightening thoughts that sickened me when I couldn't stop reliving past events that were now memories but still too fresh to be forgotten, as if something wicked could still reach up and haul me away, back into the blackness. I rolled on the sand and moaned aloud. I wondered how long would this last, how long would I have to suffer. I was out in the air but the fear was as real and palpable as if I was still trapped. I squeezed my eyes shut at the thought. Just for a minute, feelings washed over me like those I'd had in the cave when I thought that I might not get out. Again it seemed that only imaginary floating me had escaped the cave and not the real me.

"Yah. Hey! Yah."

I heard a voice from above me. I felt a sharp prod of a foot pushing at my upturned shoulder. I heard the voice and felt the shove, but it took me a long minute to understand what it was. Then the prod was repeated. It was irritating. I turned onto my back and looked up against the glare of the sun at Uncle George. At least I thought so. I was pretty sure it was him from the first, but my eyes were so blurry that I had to blink to clear them so I could confirm it.

"Yeah?" I said to him.

"Mon, what happened to you?" he asked.

I looked up at him, but had no idea what to say and wished he would go away. I couldn't even speak at all. What could I say? I was at a complete loss for words. His expression turned to one of bewilderment and he too seemed to be lost for words as he bent over to examine me. He gazed at me, but since he had nothing to say and nor did I, I just rolled away from him and nestled my face in the sand.

He must have shuffled away after that because I couldn't hear anything but the low splashing of the waves and the light breeze blowing over my ear. I had been doing so much better earlier that day. I couldn't understand what was happening to me. I was no longer trapped. I'd had a good, long sleep, and I was recovering but still ached in body and in mind. I felt immensely sore. Behind my closed eyelids, my mind replayed the yellow rings that had formed in the pitch-black to frighten me once again, so I had to open my eyes. The memory of the image of floating me, lying face up, nestled on the roundness of a smooth skull also came back to remind me of the terror I'd felt, and with it a new terror, of the thought that I would be absorbed into that reflection of myself and would be unable to return.

I was weary, so weary that despite the disturbing memories, I soon began to breathe deeply.

This helped and soon I felt my body relax. I squirmed on the sand to create a more formfitting depression and soften my resting place. The warmth of the sand seemed to envelope me, and I could feel sleep coming on as my arms and legs let go and my mind calmed. I knew I would sleep now though I experienced strange half-awake thoughts of a vaporous man floating and flying around. A skull looked at me, and its jaw filled with yellow teeth, missing here and there, moved to speak. It seemed to be trying to introduce himself or herself, "I am…. I am…." But in the complete darkness I really only imagined those yellow teeth and the voice from the skull was silent and could not tell me his name like it was confused. It seemed that the skull had no idea of its name. I supposed that without a brain inside the skull, memory would be a bit short. A brain is needed for memory I guessed.

I breathed deeply and inhaled some sand, which made me cough, which woke me fully, and I shook my head to chase away the image of a talking skull. I put my head back down and might have fallen asleep again, at least part way, and in that half-awake, half-asleep state a revelation came to me, as profound and realistic as if someone was talking in my ear. I realized that it was something I just knew, and that it was just what I'd known all along. Floating me really had not been a floating image, had not been made up partly of my sanity and partly of my life leaving me. I realized that I'd known all along how to get out of that cave, but my panic at the dark, my panic at the thought of never finding my way out, had prevented me from being able to retrace the route I'd taken getting into that final cave. That's it. When panic rules common sense fails, and it was only after I had conceded my fate that my thoughts cleared enough to remember the route into that third cave. There was no floating me, only imagined floating me. I'd needed someone to feel sorry for me at that moment and to be with at the end of my journey, but even in panic I had not been ready to die in that cave. So, it was my mind that found some device to show me the way out.

At this point, somewhere along this train of comforting thought, at my realization that even irrational thought can be life-saving in a time of distress, my overly stressed imagination grew very weary; it was as if my brain couldn't fire one more impulse or hold one more sensation or one more revelation or one more conclusion, nor even any more consciousness because it was filled to the top and ready to shut down.

I nodded off into a restive sleep, although I should more properly say that I must have nodded off because when I next looked around I was in the shadow of a tree and the air was cooler. I shook my head as I realized it was now late afternoon. I noticed a set of footprints in the sand coming toward me and going away from me and recalled that George had prodded me a few times. I searched my memory to try to decide if I had spoken to him or not and decided I hadn't. I looked to the where I'd tied the old boat to a branch of a tree, and saw that it too was gone. A fear rose within me that perhaps wave had reached the boat and rocked it until it had untied itself. I hoped not. Certainly, it was not George's only possession, he had a pair of shoes and an oil stove, as well, though that was about it, and I'd surely regret to be the cause of his losing his most valued possession.

Slowly, I gathered myself and stood. I looked at my hands, and then at my feet and looked away in an effort to un-see the mess they were in. My feet still felt numb, and I shuffled back and forth to get some circulation flowing, then turned and started to walk back to my shack. This day on the beach was over for me, and I was still not ready to talk to anyone, including Uncle George.

Back at the water pump I again worked the handle with vigor, and splashed the cool water over my head, pumping with one hand and stretching down just far enough to get my head under the gurgling stream. Hattie was in her lean-to shed preparing some food and saw me as I passed. She stopped what she was doing and stared for a while, and then without a word, piled a plate high with peas and rice and brought it to me. She didn't ask what happened, and I didn't offer anything except a heartfelt thank you as she handed me the plate. I made a little bow as I turned from her and retreated to my shack to thoroughly enjoy the peas and rice.

When darkness fell, I slept again on the narrow cot under the grey blanket.

In the morning I awoke still almost overwhelmingly groggy but no longer able to sleep. Unable to stay in the locked position allowed by the narrow cot, I swung my legs over the side and reached with my foot for the rough concrete floor. My eyes protested having to open, but the glimmer of sunshine coming under door put me in almost euphoric state. I was really happy to be up and about to face the day. The sunshine in the yard was inviting and cheerful. I stepped out into the sunshine, actually excited that my blue toe seemed to be returning to normal, but realized it was only because it looked almost normal amongst the rest of the toes.

The cuts around my fingernails and toenails were now thick with swelling and partial scabs had formed, even though they were dirty and full of sediment. But at least only a few of the cuts were still open, just a fraction of what there had been the day before. They would need attention eventually, sooner rather than later, but at least the immediacy of the need for attention had passed.

In Hattie's lean-to grocery store I could see fresh-baked bread, and took one of the still warm loaves, placing money in the box she left for payments. On a nearby shelf there were jars of preserves of some sort of fruit, so I purchased one of those too. Hattie was in the house or out somewhere on family or island business, and I was glad because I knew that sooner or later I'd have to explain where I'd been and how I'd gotten into such a state, and I just didn't feel up to it at the moment and wasn't sure I'd ever be.

I walked to the beach with the bread and preserves and ripped the loaf into pieces and poured the sweet fruit over them one after the other. Nothing had ever tasted as good as that fresh bread and thick sweet jam as I ate the entire loaf, which I soon regretted because my stomach began to ache.

With nothing else to do anyway, I lay there holding my bulging stomach until eventually it went down a bit. When I could stand up again despite the bulge, I decided it was time to go back to Uncle George's to make sure he'd gotten his boat back.

I found him on his little beach in front of his shack and approached him slowly, as he was immersed in the task of cleaning a bucket of small fish. He kept his head down, even when I was close enough that my feet had to be visible to him. He looked quite comfortable sitting in the crook of a branch on a large fallen tree, leaning over the bucket half full of fish guts cradled between his knees. Next to him a flat tray of fresh ones, sat waiting to be impaled with his very sharp, very pointy knife. Deftly he manipulated the knife into and upward, splitting open and disemboweling each little fish with one scoop of his fingers. He would not look up at me from his work.

I decided, "Yes, he's busy, that's what it is."

He was busy and had no time at the moment to greet a visitor. I sat down beside him without asking permission. How do you ask a person a question when they refuse to acknowledge you? I had something important to say, and

I'd waited a night and a day and almost another day before I tried to say it, but this man who'd set me on a course that was life-changing and almost life-ending could not respond to me.

I sat still as he went about cleaning those fish. At the moment, the lesson here was life moves, accept it and move on. I sat still and waited and waited some more, but he would not acknowledge me. I couldn't understand this at all. Here was a man who'd been so enthusiastic in the company of a stranger just two days before that it started him dancing, but now he acted as if I didn't exist.

He seemed to be in some sort of bad mood with his lack of acknowledgement. I wanted to say, "Excuse me, but I almost died in there. Do you realize that? You sent me in there, almost dared me to go in there and I almost didn't get back out."

A short distance away, once again in the tall grass just beyond the reach of the highest of the waves, was the little dinghy, the underside a rainbow of paint in the fading shades of the Caribbean. It was back here on George's beach, not where I'd left it, so he'd got it back, and I hadn't drowned. I had no idea what his problem was, and I guessed I'd never know. Maybe he didn't liked the fact I took his precious boat and hadn't returned it quickly enough, or to the right place. On the other hand, here was a man who'd seemed so starved for company that he was almost insane when a visitor showed up, and here I was willing to have another conversation in an attempt to explain what I'd just gone through, and to let him know that perhaps, just perhaps, it wasn't such a good idea to practically dare silly travelers to attempt a cave dive alone, and he, contemptuous and uncaring, wouldn't even look up. Did he know that inside one of those caves were the bones of at least one human, almost subsumed into the limestone as if it had grown there? Was I not supposed to go into the cave? I began to feel that perhaps my not returning his precious boat, leaky fossil of a boat that is was, had perturbed him somewhat and was the cause for his sullen countenance. Or perhaps when he found me the day before, sprawled on the sand, practically eating it, and I'd had nothing to say to him he took offense and this was his response.

Finally after a long sit-and-wait session, it was, "Whatever," and I gave up and walked back to my shack – Hattie's shack, I should say – my home for the past four days, and a very tumultuous four days they'd been.

As I approached, three of the island children; two with very dark, tight curls and one with tightly curled orange hair; came running to me all excited, hopping about as if they were entrants in a contest to find me, for which the prize to the first would be an unimaginable treasure. So innocent they seemed, bless their souls. They had been sent to find me by schoolmaster/grocer/caretaker and island administrator Hattie, charged with bringing me back to the house as soon as possible. They chattered and skipped excitedly around, perhaps knowing I had a penchant for disappearing to hidden places, and escorted me back to Hattie's little blue bungalow and lean-to grocery stand with its bread oven and sacks of rice and tins of corned beef with exotic labels depicting caballeros whooping as they rode on fast horses twirling bolas as they chased strays on the plains of Argentina.

When I arrived before Hattie with my bubbly and happy escort of five- and six-year-olds, she still didn't ask what'd happened, but did pause for a second to look me over. There was a long pause during which the children all stopped their jostling and teasing of each other to wonder why she'd paused, why she stood so silently, perhaps thinking that they too should be silent, lest a slap on the head was coming because her silence implied that all should be silent. She took in the state of my toes and my fingers, with a probing glance that took it all in at once, and for a second her expression implied a question. Then it was gone. Her look of understanding said that she knew the question couldn't or wouldn't be answered so the question was useless and unnecessary. Instead, to return to normalcy, to bring life back to her grocery store and relieve the children of the wonder they held at her sudden silence, she said, in a rush,

"Cap'n of de mail boat radio. He be stoppin' here today. Rudder hit a new sand bar and have big problem. He be goin' back to New Providence today, and he stop to pick you up."

What? My life was taking a serious turn, and I was now being allowed to leave? Was my lesson done? Had fate decided, now that I'd survived the caves on top of all the other unfortunate experiences I'd recently been through, that I'd been through enough, and it was time for me to go back to wherever I'd come from? I'd wanted to leave the moment I'd stepped onto the island in that storm and almost busted my toe on the roots on the path, and especially when faced with a swarm of cockroaches led by a monstrous and evil King hiding under the rack of a bed in that shack. I'd wanted to run, not walk, or swim if I could swim any distance at all, but now, strangely enough, I was hesitant to leave. It was too soon.

I was still coming to grips with my experience and hadn't had time to process exactly how I felt about everything or to decide who I wanted to talk to about what had happened. I felt I really needed to talk to someone about it. I was torn with conflicting emotions. Uncle George was no more ready to speak to me than I had been to speak to him the day before. My island adventure had turned out to be bigger and more significant than I could ever imagine, and I didn't feel ready to be done with it yet. I was beat up, torn, cut, bruised, sore, insect-bitten all over and yet was having a hard time accepting that these four emotion-packed days were coming to an end. The pages of this chapter of my life were turning, and the often difficult hours were ending, but I still felt there was something undone that shouldn't be left undone. What it was perplexed me, but as I took a moment to consider it, the moment passed, as time does, and I could only stand there without speaking.

But life and time, good or bad, torture or pleasure, suffering or complete happiness, move relentlessly forward, and so they did for me. The Lady Blanche was coming back to get me, to get me alone. Wow. All emotion drained from me as I stood silently before Hattie. I wasn't sure what to think. I asked her to repeat what she'd said since when I was dropped off on this island I was told that the mail boat was not going to come back for three more days,

"So the Lady Blanche is coming here? To get me?"

Hattie was becoming impatient,

"Yeah mon, Cappy, he come back for you. De boat hit a sand bar shifted by de storm and he go back to Nassau. Cap'py Grey feel bad, tossing you out in de storm dat night."

"When?" I asked.

"He be here in one hour, or maybe two, or more."

So, within some number of hours, one, two, or more, the Lady Blanche would be nearing the island, which meant we would be crossing open water in the dark over a choppy sea. Here we go again, I thought to myself. Hattie was looking at me, once again taking in my hands and feet, and seemed to be waiting for my explanation. I was still at a loss for anything to say. There was too much to say but maybe nothing to say and between the two I stood before her with a blank look, in fact embarrassed at what I'd done. I could take no consolation from having found my way out of that cave because it had been my own foolishness that had gotten me into that situation. In time I might be able to discuss the events of those days, but for now I just couldn't explain to Hattie. I carefully closed my hands to hide the cuts on my fingers, which she noticed but chose not to question. I felt that she accepted that I couldn't talk about how those cuts got on my fingers and didn't need to ask for details about what she'd noticed. I said to her,

"I'll get my things from the cottage and settle up my bill."

I turned away and walked down the path and into the darkness of the shack, which my reluctance to leave the island now had turned into a tropical garden cottage. It took me all of 30 seconds to grab the four or five things I had and stuff them into my red leather bag. I set it down on the scratchy grey blanket, thinking that I was taking part of it with me in the coagulated scabs on my fingers and in my lungs from having breathed in fibres trying to sleep under it, and that that was all I wanted from that coarse rag. If it would have helped me feel better to kick it into the corner, I would have, but that would have meant that I'd have to do the same with the rough striped mattress that had been inhabited by who knows what all, all of which would have been dislodged if I did kick it into the corner, so I just left it alone. An evil stare at the two would have to be enough.

I stepped out of the shack and found the island children there to escort me again, eager to have a late evening run about the sandy paths that led through the trees between the little buildings of the hamlet of Staniel. Hattie was there, still wearing an expression of curiosity. I approached, as she waited, and I paid what I owed, counting out my last dollars, obviously short of funds. I counted the last note three times, emphasizing the act of placing it down on the previous ones, adding it after counting it three times to the little pile of crumpled and water stained bills and arriving at the total of the hotel bill as if paid in full. She looked sideways at me and picked up the bills, then repeated my charade, this time counting the last note five times. Acting out that I had paid her two notes too many, she made a show of picking up the last dollar bill and holding it high before reaching down, folding it in two and stuffing it into the top of my pocket.

I was shocked at this. I actually did have money, just not there. I didn't have a lot, but I wanted her to know that I knew she could use the money, and she should accept what I wanted to give her. I took the bill from my pocket and reached out to take her hand to open it, but she wouldn't let me take her wrist to open her hand. I smiled at her, and she smiled back.

"Thank you," I said, "but you shouldn't take less."

She smiled, replying, "No problem. I ask too much for dat little shack wit all dem bugs. You pay by stings and bites, sorry for dat." With that she thrust out her hand, wanted to signify by a handshake that the account was settled. I took her hand, closing only my palm and part of a thumb over her offered hand, not able to curl my fingers lest they split open right then and there. It was an awkward handshake, and I looked up at a tree over her head for something to focus on so there would be no opportunity for the subject of wounds on my fingers and toes to be discussed. Then Hattie grinned as she reached over and handed me a brown paper bag containing something fairly heavy. I smile back, deciding that I quite liked this mother of ten, round of girth, with smooth brown skin and sparkling brown eyes under long lashes. She read the thought behind my smile and blushed, her cheeks colouring as if the sun illuminated them. In that moment we understood that we could be friends. It was one of those rare moments of silent understanding shared between two people who were still strangers.

Then the moment passed, as she turned and said to her

large group of children, "OK now, chil'un, make sure mister get to de boat at de dock. Go now. Show the young man de way." The group of mixed-age children, six or seven of them, boisterous and grinning, as cute a picture of innocent youth as there could be, gathered around us, ready to obey, but I really didn't want to move. Regardless that I'd been a reluctant visitor to this island when the mail boat left me here, at this moment I felt a similar reluctance to leave and grappled to find an excuse to stay, perhaps for another week. Perhaps my fingers and toes needed time to mend, or my scalp or the welts from the bites, or my blue toe. More likely, I just didn't want this chapter to end.

As I dithered, the children frolicked in the dappled sunlight that fell between the palm fronds and sang happily for no reason that I could discern. Apparently they felt the kind of good you feel when life is simple and you have nothing troubling you. These young versions of Uncle George – was there an Uncle George among them? Probably – had not a care in the world but the teasing handed out by bratty Willy or bully Simon who might have caught a bigger fish that day, or could swing higher from the rope hung from a branch over the lagoon to jump into deep blue water teeming with tropical fish. What had started as my island prison had become, at least in my mind, an island paradise with lessons to be learned from every experience. How could I reasonably want to leave this? Not reasonably. No, not reasonably at all. I couldn't.

The choices were to continue with my life the way I had been living it, or to try life like the one Uncle George lived. But thinking about everything that had happened and my former life and what could be my future became overwhelming and I snapped. Mimicking the children around me, I raised my arms over my head and laughed a great roar of laughter, hard then harder, again and again. The children stopped their playing, shocked and unsure for a second, then realized I was laughing, which was good. Tears might come one day, maybe soon, but only laughter was coming now, until I was almost weeping with all the emotions I felt, but the children began to laugh with me. I'd laughed hard and its infectiousness had caught the children. Six small brown island children caught my laughter as if it were a game and soon the whole area resonated with the sounds of the laughter that rang out through the branches and into the distance. It was too funny; it was beautiful and funny. I was here but soon I'd be gone, and now I'd laugh and save the crying for some later time. This was now and then would be then, and now was time for laughing.

Almost as quickly as it started, though, the laughing stopped. The prolonged heartfelt laughter had had no specific reason but served extremely well to dump a collection of strongly felt emotions. My sides ached and even the sides of my face were sore from holding such a big smile for so long. The children had been looking up at me wondering when I would stop so they could stop. Now that I could finally stop, I straightened up and used the back of my hand to wipe the tears from my face. I chuckled once more, but the laughter had finally wound down as I relaxed and my shoulders slumped like I'd just done a workout.

I said to the group of children, "OK, to de mail boat we go," and with a big smile still on my face and warm feelings in my heart I followed as they raced ahead. The smallest one wasn't even sure where we were all going, but he was racing along with his head down and at one fork ran off in the wrong direction until his big sister skidded to a stop with her bare feet on the dusty path and turned to dart after him to shepherd him back into the fold. It came to me then that this chapter of my life was closing, that my steps down this path to the dock were the first steps into the next chapter that would be new and, hopefully, challenging and exciting. These hopeful thoughts brought a spring to my step and a feeling of elation about what I had to look forward to.

Evening was coming, the sun was low and steeply angled though the shrubs and the slight haze of dust kicked up by the racing children, and everything seemed suddenly perfectly beautiful. The walk to the dock was short, and we were nearing the spot where Hattie had met me four days earlier far too quickly. My steps got shorter and shorter steps, down to inches at a time, but still the walk ended sooner than I wanted it to. In the distance I could see the Lady Blanche, chugging her way toward us, her port side reflecting brightly in the setting sun. The children ran up and down the dock, making it vibrate under their stamping feet. I wished I had something to give them as a reward for being the happiest escort I'd ever had. I'm not sure why it should be, but it seemed there was something about the novelty of walking me to the dock that made it the most fun these children could have. They were all racing around and jumping up and down and chattering to each other and shouting and giggling, and the girls screamed shrilly when the boys ran past and caught hold of braided pigtails.

I reached the end of the dock, where I sat down to wait, letting my feet hang over the edge. The children milled about me for a minute, and then one by one they darted off toward the shore end of the dock, where soon they were all gathered at the entrance to the trail that led through the trees. Then with elaborate and animated waves, each trying to outdo the one before, they bade me farewell with smiles and a series of, "Bye, bye, bye, Mister," disappeared through the gap in the trees onto the path with the high tree root made perfectly for stubbing a toe on. It was the same path that led to the little road that circled the island and passed the school and the blue church and Hattie's bungalow with the "guest cottage" resting crookedly in the front yard, past the fork that led to my beach and the fork that led to old George and his solitary existence. The road went all the way around to the landing strip and the cluster of small houses that dotted the other end of the narrow island.

I looked for a long moment at that gap in the trees and the entrance to the path, and when the sound of the rambunctious goodbye had faded completely I turned back toward the sound of the diesel engine approaching. Through the pilothouse window, I could see Captain Grey's white-haired head across the top of the wooden wheel. Did I detect a smile? No, probably not, but that didn't stop me from smiling as the boat approached. The old mail boat looked clean and neat and perfectly sound to me this time. My impressions of it before were obviously mistaken. The captain pulled alongside the dock and deftly manipulated the boat to nudge ever so gently against the wooden rail, and I stepped aboard without a line being tossed. The engines roared once more and the Lady Blanche slipped away from the dock in a second.

I went to the aft port rail and looked back toward the island. The children were gone, and the setting sun made the greens of the palms and shrubs seem greener, much greener, and all the colors seemed more vivid. The little grey dock looked ridiculously small with the backdrop of tall trees and the thin strip of white sand along the shoreline where mangrove roots were exposed in tangled knots of brown and grey. The water, churned to foam by the prop, hissed in a trail behind us, lengthening quickly. I gripped the rail with my tender and scabbed fingers and sucked in a gasp at the pain, which brought me back to reality, though it was tinged with melancholy. One particularly deep cut in the middle of the end of the index finger was causing grief and I looked at it closely, hoping the dried scab was not cracked or bleeding.

I held my hand up to the breeze to stop any bleeding,

to dry it in the wind. This gesture, my hand raised alongside my face, was my simple though unintended wave goodbye, which is how it would have appeared to anyone seeing me then. Goodbye island, children, Hattie, George, shack, cockroaches, beach. Then I thought about the cave and the other cave and the last cave and was quite sure I didn't really want to think about cave and cave and cave and skull and bones of – could it be? – perhaps, my soul mate Lawrence or some pirate, or treasure hunter. Better to say skull because I'd never really know, and please, God, let it not be Lawrence that gave me respite. But no, it's still too soon to be thinking about all that, and who knows if it would ever be possible to say a final goodbye to that episode or even recall that episode without a cold, chilling sense of horror. I was fairly certain the horror would live in me at the thought of those caves for some time to come, but at least I could try to stop thinking about it. Trying to say goodbye to those memories was simply not necessary – or, even an option – right now. Then, as the sun touched the water, I turned my back to the island and moved forward to find a place to sit and perhaps watch a game of dominoes.

Night fell quickly as the sun dipped below the horizon. Twilight lasted only as long as the flash of cobalt blue that signaled the final setting of the sun and within seconds, pinpoints of twinkling stars appeared and the rich blackness of the night sky became a sparkling dome above me and the little mail boat. Long, rolling swells each spanned a hundred meters or more on the surface of the open water, and with each swell the boat rose to starboard, crested for a second, teetered at the top, then slipped down the face of the long bank of water. At the bottom of each long swell was a flat area, and then we'd begin to climb again as the water rose toward the forward rail until my feet were mere inches from the water. Up we went and at the top of the crest I was high in the air and could see over the tops of endless wave caps, some white as they turned over, like little whips of meringue on a pie.

After an hour or so, the moon rose behind us, full and round and clear, lighting the tops of the waves and sparkling through the whitecaps, the polar opposite of the sun, similar in size and shape but ghostly white and a pleasure to observe. I chose to take it as a sign that better luck was returning. It was a treat to see the long trail of white sparkling across the water leading to me from the moon that rose like a white balloon floating in slow motion straight up away from a child's hand. It took only a dozen or so dips on my teeter-totter ship before it had risen high in the sky and appeared much smaller. It was just as bright, but growing smaller by the minute.

Chapter Nine

MYSTERY WOMAN

It was quite late when I left my place at the rail. I stepped up the narrow ladder to the upper deck and looked into the wheelhouse. Only one crewmember sat in the complete darkness at the table behind the captain, whose face was illuminated faintly by the greenish glow of a backlit compass. The crewmember looked over at me without speaking as I entered the wheelhouse and sat down next to him. He was second of the two-man crew standing watch. Watch for the captain to stay awake, watch weather changes, watch for anything. The captain stood like a cardboard cut-out he was so still and quiet at the wheel. The boat rolled from side to side, but he maintained his perfectly plumb position at the wheel, moving only his hands arms and eyes as the boat moved, but his body always staying vertical.

I opened the bag Hattie gave me and was pleasantly surprised to see two rather large, thickly filled corned beef sandwiches wrapped in wax paper. It was as if she'd watched me prepare similar sandwiches for myself, and she'd made them exactly as I'd made mine with lettuce, tomato, onion, mayonnaise, and the entire tin of corned beef in just two sandwiches. They were things of beauty, really. They were each cut in half, and without saying a word I offered half of one to the mate, and another to Captain Grey at the helm. They each looked them over suspiciously, like cats sniffing a new food before eating, as if these sandwiches were strange and foreign things, but after a minute each began to slowly munch away. We ate without speaking, the drone of the diesel engine filling the small teak wheelhouse.

After the mate finished his sandwich his look at me conveyed gratitude that I'd shared my dinner with him, and asked, "You want to sleep?"

"Sure," I replied.

He gestured with his head, "Come on." We left the wheelhouse and walked down the passage until we reached a door that he opened. He said, "You can sleep dere," as he pointed into a dark cabin. "Dere's a bunk on de wall, you share dat bunk with Lindy." He spoke softly into the cabin, "Lindy, move over."

Lindy? Share a bunk with Lindy? I stepped inside, and the mate door closed behind me. I felt my way across the room as my eyes tried to search darkness as deep as I'd experienced in the cave. My chest tightened as small but intense wave of anxiety, almost panic, washed over me. I took a deep breath and soothed it away with thoughts of the sunset and the moon and the deep greens and browns of the island as we'd departed, and assured myself that I was not floating in a cave or resting on a skull, but just in a very dark room. My seeking hands found the metal frame of a bunk bed and then the softness of a thin mattress on the upper bunk. I turned and started to lower myself onto the lower bunk.

In the dark a soft voice spoke: "Not here. There."

It was a woman's voice coming out of the total darkness, and then fingers touched my knee. I had been about to sit down on her head. She nudged me toward the other end of the bunk.

"Sorry," I whispered.

"I am Lindy," came a soft whisper. I introduced myself and decided not to reach into the darkness lest my hand touch down on the wrong place.

The bunk was narrow. I could feel her moving to make space. Island hospitality. Like the sandwiches Hattie gave me as I was leaving, as a gift without having been ask, and most importantly, something she knew I would appreciate, nourishment and comfort given freely, given because she could tell I was having a bumpy journey and was finally able to exit this part of it. I lay back and put my feet on the edge of the metal bed frame, stretching out as close to the edge as possible, most of me still hanging over the edge. I tried desperately to stay up on the metal frame, but the cot was narrow and the mattress was depressed by Lindy's weight. I couldn't stay teetering on the bedframe for long, and soon couldn't help but roll back into the softness behind me made up partly of the mattress but more so of Lindy's arms, thigh, and even her breasts. I held myself as rigidly as a statue, filled with uncertainty about the propriety of this situation. This was her bunk at the moment, though in reality the crewman's bunk. She must have felt as uncomfortable as I did with this total stranger pressing suddenly so closely.

It was hard to hold my body so tensely and tiredness started to wash over me as I was soothed by the rhythmic sounds of the water and the warmth and the rocking of the boat until I finally began to relax.

At the same time I could feel Lindy soften too. The rocking of the boat caused the two of us to bump gently against each other which, I must confess… began to feel quite nice. She was soft and warm and I was tired and now fed. I was lying on a steel bunk bed with a thin, worn-out mattress and the two of us caused the wire springs to sag considerably, but the softness of the woman behind me was making this one of the most comfortable bed I'd slept on in years.

Then, just as I was almost completely relaxed, the boat suddenly lurched up and down rather than rolling from side to side as if the Captain had turned into the waves and the bow had risen. Given my position precariously perched on the edge of the bed and being half asleep the change in motion threatened to tip me out of the bunk onto the floor, and it would have, but before I could fall, a hand gripped my shoulder and pulled me back into the deep hollow in the little mattress. I breathed a sigh of relief at being rescued.

"Thanks for that," I said through my teeth, catching my breath, suddenly very awake.

"No problem, we gotta hang on good," she whispered in my ear, raising goosebumps on my arms and neck. Her thick accent made her words only barely decipherable, but I was catching on quickly. The hissing of her whisper and the warmth of her breath stirred heavy blood within me. Her hand was on my shoulder, pulling me just a little more firmly than need be, maybe for just a second longer than it needed to be, which seemed more of a one-armed embrace.

My mind raced and the touch felt intense, almost hot and somehow – I don't know – it messed me up. She was letting me share her small bunk, which was very gracious of her, and I had to be gracious in return, and a gentleman, but, but, I was a man after all, and a woman's touch, as innocent as it might be, was still a woman's touch. I turned slightly to face up instead of out, and she worked her shoulders to the side to create a space. She'd noticed my turn and asked, "Why you on dis boat?"

I wasn't sure if her question was meant to discharge the emotion that seemed to be gathering at the moment, or if she really wanted to know, but I had to say something.

"I don't know," I said, "I got lost a bit."

Silence reigned for a moment, and I wondered whether she'd have anything more to say, or if she'd just give up and go to sleep, but she wasn't done, saying, "How you get here?"

Although sleep was a past due ticket, I had to say something, so I told her the truth, "I went to eat flamingo on Eleuthera, but couldn't find one so I got mailed to Staniel Cay."

I'd meant to say I'd caught the mail boat to Staniel, and telling her I'd gotten mailed wasn't the most brilliant answer, but I'd said it, much to my dismay. Obviously my time alone had not done my wit or mental sharpness any favors. She seemed to squirm a little, maybe trying to turn her head to look at me incredulously. Then, maybe it was my imagination but to me her next words were spoken soulfully – as inept as I might be at describing it, trust me, it was soulful – as in a soft voice, breathy and sing-song, she said,

"How much was de stamp?"

I could feel that she was chuckling as her chest, and those woman things upon, those things I was mightily trying to ignore, vibrated on my back. Then, again practically purring with her lips just inches from my ear, she said, "Dere no flamingoes on Eleuthera. Dere no flamingoes anywhere on dees islands."

Her words settled into a long pause, mainly because I was savouring the sounds of her voice, and I got lost in the savouring for a long moment. My spine tingled as goosebumps rose again. Almost totally lost in these sensations, but grasping for something to say to keep her hot whispering coming, I sputtered out the only thing I could think to say, "I know that now."

My voice sounded like I was a long way from home, almost as strange to me as she was to me, surely as strange to her as her accent was to me. This mystery woman lying beside me in the dark was foreign but the gift of her presence was very special because I'd been so much alone and my craving for something special made her that to me at the moment – everything to me at that moment. I was only answering with what my muddled brain could manage as too many thoughts were going through it at once.

This mystery woman and I moved together with the motion of the boat as it rolled like a big cradle in the long waves. There was silence between us that we let take over, broken only by the muffled growl of the engine two decks below. It was strangely comforting, as if the warmth of the air, the dark night and the rocking of the boat combined to create a soothing calmness. I was nestled into the soft, warm, curving form of the woman in the bunk with me who was pliant as only a completely relaxed person could be. That I was a total stranger, one she hadn't even seen in the light, didn't seem to matter, which contributed to the sense of ease that overcame everything else in that narrow little bunk. We were two strangers at a masquerade ball sharing something that would have been impossible had we been unmasked in the light of day. We spoke softly, as someone – or several someones – occupied the upper bunk, causing the springs of the upper bunk to sag to within a few inches of our heads. Whoever was up there was surely fast asleep as evidenced by the sound of gentle snoring, and any conversation that might take place in our bunk wasn't likely overheard.

She whispered, "You like…?"

I turned my face upward in the dark, more or less in her direction as my gesture of non-comprehension.
She could feel my confusion.

"…the islands?"

I got it. I whispered back, "Yes, beautiful."
"Me," she asked, "me, beautiful?"
Yes, perfect mistake for what I'd said, I wished I thought of it intentionally. "Yes, that is what I meant, you beautiful," I said.

"The beach?" she asked.

I replied, "Oh yes, of course. The sand is pink in some places."

"The food?" she asked.

I nodded twice before realizing it was a futile gesture since she couldn't see me in the dark, so I kept whispering, "Yes. The food is beautiful too."

Then, it might have been my imagination, or my craving for it, but I thought I felt her move, as if nestling her body closer into mine.

Her next question was as a warm caress to the back of my ear, damp as if in steam, "The women?"

The women? Her whispered question, was warm on my ear, but brought a heat in my chest. What was I supposed to think about this? The way I heard it, this was a leading question with multiple exciting implications, and I had to ask myself, was I up to this? I had only a moment to frame an appropriate response. Previously, when the opportunities presented themselves, I couldn't speak to Uncle George, nor to my newest friend Hattie. I couldn't find words for either of them. My words had been stolen by the depths of a cave system and emotions almost beyond description. Now, again, I was being required to speak. This could be my redemption, the salvation of my confidence. I had to say something smart – even just one word – as an appropriate response to this question, one that would seal the deal and lead us, perhaps, to memories of an interlude in the dark between two strangers when the moment was right for spontaneity. I needed just the right word, right now, or my lack of response would leave me, especially me, and hopefully her, too, wondering what might have been.

Her question conjured thoughts of Little Sister, so cute but afraid of me, and of sister herself who only had eyes for Buddy, and of Hattie, round and soft, with a big smile, her island existence, and her complete devotion to her swarm of happy children. It was Hattie in particular that her question made me think of. Hattie was special. I'd made a deal to rent her shack and couldn't pay her in full in the end, but she'd still sent me off with a sandwich and, more than that, she'd sent me off with understanding, with care, and with kind thoughts to take away with me. The only thing I could say about the island women, considering the experiences I'd had with the few I'd known, and particularly Hattie, in words I had to choke back as I becoming a blubbering mess with the thoughts of the past week, was a deeply heartfelt,

"Yes, especially the women, beautiful."

With that, though she was unaware of the reason for my response, I felt her squirm. She was pressed tightly into my back, and I could feel her softness as precisely as a surgeon's scalpel, that was the state I was in at this point. I rocked my shoulders, trying to determine if she was moving closer or attempting to move away in the confines of the bunk. I really wanted to touch and feel; I was intensely craving to touch and feel, to squirm around and put my arms around her and my hands all over her. This caused me to flex my hands, which made my fingertips sting sharply with pain that I tried but couldn't ignore. The ends were crusted with dried blood.

Out of embarrassment I'd not asked Hattie to dress them, and now the scabs would surely crack open if I didn't protect them. Leaving my fingers curled into my palms had served well enough, and I picked things up and moved them very carefully even when I'd held the sandwiches I'd shared earlier. But now by some strange stroke of luck, here I was, practically a handicapped man, temporarily at least, lying next to a soft, warm island girl, and my mistake of being in the cave was still haunting me, not just mentally, but physically.

There was no chance I could touch her with these scabbed fingers, especially knowing that one even slight touch would in a heartbeat lead to a million more slight touches, and many thousand more not so slight touches.

The abuse these fingers had endured scraping against the walls of the cave and the tops of the passages, gripping the sand on the beach and forcing it into the cuts, was done and over, but was not the most excruciating. That abuse hurt, and still hurt, but this topped it. A long minute had passed, and I had to move or do something or the moment would be lost.

Regardless, there was nothing I could do – nothing – and that was sad. I sighed deeply, and she was very still. The time to continue our chat that might lead to something more was passing very quickly, and she had to think that my lack of response meant I didn't want to continue. If only she knew how much I did want to continue but couldn't. Such a disappointment, certainly, it was to me. I don't know about her because only a minute later I could feel her warm even breathing on my shoulder and knew she'd fallen asleep. She was sleeping and I was frustrated, already beginning to wonder what could have been.

I consoled myself with thoughts of having been a gentleman, small consolation that it was, considering that if she wasn't really sending the signals I thought she was, and I had misread the situation, in which case any advances I might have made would have been rebuked, I would've had to sleep on the floor or even outside on the rolling deck. This way, I was at least in a soft bed and I would be thought of as a gentleman traveler and not a roving hound.

What nonsense!

Had it not been for damaged fingers I would've been all over that smooth skin like flies on rice and I knew it. Stupid consolation gentleman crap anyway.

Her breathing was long and slow and even, and the boat rocked like a giant cradle. Someone in the upper bunk shifted and the springs near my face squeaked, and I listened to the drone of the engine for a while, until I felt my eyes closing. Sleep was coming, and then I felt nothing.

Some indeterminate amount of time later, something woke me. I wasn't sure where I was except it was in some dark space. Lying wondering, half dozing, I knew I was alone, and there was something near my face. I was fully clothed, sweating, on a thin, worn out mattress. Finally, in the dim light, I could make out the upper bunk and realized I was in the cabin aboard the mail boat. All was quiet. The engines were not running. The boat was not rocking. We were tied up at the dock. We'd arrived somewhere, and for a second a cold fear raced through my body as I considered that perhaps we were back at Eleuthera.

God No!

We had to be back in New Providence. We had to.
I crawled my way out of the depths of that bunk bed and
stood up, straightening up despite the protesting of the
muscles in my back. I'd been so tired when I finally fell
asleep that I must not have moved even if I could have in
that narrow bed. I'd been so tired that I'd not woken even
when my unexpected island friend, Lindy, sleeping behind
me on the bunk, somehow extricated herself to leave.

It was a good five minutes before I could straighten up
fully. I moved to the door of and looked out. I had to
rub my eyes, but I could see that we were at the dock
under the toll bridge to Paradise Island and beyond this
long concrete dock was the road that led to the center of
the town of Nassau.

Where is she?

She had to be within the folds of that colonial town, within
the streets and narrow twisting roads. She was in a house, a
building, a car, a bus, somewhere. Where is she?

Who is she?

She was gone. Gone from my life forever. Forever.

A long sign escaped my lips as my chest and shoulders fell
in resignation.

She was gone, and I knew I would never see her face.
Impossible. How could I search faces in a crowd with only
a sweet whispering voice to go by?

But, I was back. I'd made it. But my heart longed for and

I wondered what she looked like. In my imagination she was so beautiful, so perfect, and now, so gone, so gone away.

The boat was quiet, the dock was quiet. I looked at the cabin in the light and realized it was tiny, and the bunk bed was narrow for even one person. She was no longer in that bunk and I'd not even had the chance to see her in the light or say goodbye. Too bad, but probably just as well, I suppose.

Captain Grey was gone as well, which saddened me. I would have liked to say goodbye and thank you, but I was alone. They'd let me sleep, they'd left me alone, and now it was time for me to disembark the M.V. Lady Blanche, oldest and still finest mail boat in the Bahamas.

Chapter Ten

BE...ING LAWRENCE

Mrs. P. opened the door wide for me. She caught sight of my sandaled feet first, of course, that was almost all she caught sight of anyone, and I could hear her involuntary gasp. She was looking straight at my blue toe with swollen up nail and saw the crisscrossing, scabbed-over creases on my toes that looked like they could break open at any moment. She angled back so her eyes could peer over the rims of her thick glasses and equally thick frames to look at the rest of me, and this didn't impress any more than the feet. A shudder shook her narrow frame, which at that moment seemed even smaller than I recalled. I hadn't shaved in a week, hadn't had any shampoo for my hair, and hadn't spent a second in front of any mirrored surface for that same amount of time; there was no useful purpose served by scaring myself, too, I figured.

Mrs. P was no more than four foot six, and tiny, as if receding into childhood. Her head dipped at the end of her curved back and looked as if it was covered with grey straw. I wanted to bend at the knees to get down to her level to save her from having to force her eyes up to look up at me. I shuffled on my feet to break the silence. There seemed to be something much more than simply my return to the plantation house at play here. It was very much more, as if something was changed by my return.

She didn't move, but stood very still, this small, bent lady who had to be close to a century old. All that she'd been and seen, the glory and sadness, the victories and losses, were hidden behind her eyes but at this moment I could see the losses reflected there. Unshed tears cried out to me. I felt it like my return was more than that of a boarder returning to a room after an unexplained absence. Standing there it came to me that I'd left one morning a week earlier without even telling her I was going or if or when I'd be back, and that I'd left most of my goods and my bag in Lawrence's room just like poor Lawrence would've done some fifty years before. I hadn't considered, when I'd gotten onto that rocket boat with Buddy, that it might be many days before I'd return, or that I'd left her not knowing and sitting with a loaded shot gun on her knee for those surely long nights waiting to lock the door behind me, or what feelings could have returned to her, revisiting on her the same horrible uncertainty as when another son had walked out the door to never return.

Unlike poor Lawrence, though, here I was at the door. I had returned. I may not have been her son returning, but perhaps close enough. This made me think again about the skull and bones in the cave. Had it indeed been Lawrence? Had he saved me so I could come back to relieve his poor mother and her unrequited love and heartrending loss?

Had that smooth skull on a limestone-crusted skeleton that saved my life, that skull that I'd found could keep me afloat when I was near the point of exhaustion, been there to save me so that I could save them, these two poor, desperate parents of a missing son?

Was it now up to me to explain that I had found their son, or at least his resting place, his resting place that had been my resting place?

Was I supposed to tell them that he was a true and pure man that she given birth to and raised to be a noble man and who'd saved me from a certain death in a watery grave? Had all of this happened just so I'd be able to stand before her in the doorway of this once great house, and explain to her that he'd loved her and had died with her in his thoughts and had promised with his dying breath that he would somehow get a message to her to explain and say once more that he loved her?

Was this now my responsibility?

Such were my thoughts as I stood before this little lady. I had seen in her eyes that for just a second she thought she was answering the door to her lost son. I'd seen a grainy, faded, black and white photo of Lawrence, in track and field outfit, arms draped over teammates. Yes, he'd been my age when he'd gone missing, and yes, undeniably, he and I bore some resemblance to each other, same height, same hair, same eyes, same smile.

Then a sound from deeper in the room penetrated the silence that had been heightened in intensity by the slowing of time by the thoughts unspoken between the two of us on the doorstep. It was a slight, scratching sound. Mr. P's fingers were working hard. He knew someone was there, poor Mr. P who could not speak, but who was aware of his surroundings. The slight scratching grew in level and intensity as we, Mrs. P and I, lingered in the doorway.

He had to know. He had to know who was at the door.

'Is it you, Lawrence? Is it really you?'

'Have you returned, my boy?'

'My dear Lawrence, have you returned?'

I could feel his thoughts, 'or could those just be my thoughts?' from behind Mrs. P. Then she noticed as well, and the long searching moment between us ended. Her gazed returned to me and then a shiver seemed to coarse through me as I could see her grey eyes clouding over.

I could only imagine that she hoped this would have been the last time she'd ever have to do this, to answer the door in case it was Lawrence, and then to have to once more turn and face the man in the chair with disappointing news that could only add to the sadness that seemed never ending. She looked up with a question,

"Is that you? Have you come home, son?"

I was not in control at that moment, of what I was about to say or do. I nodded slightly. "Yes."

I looked into her eyes and then saw something I'd not recognized before. The harshness she projected was an illusion. The look she greeted the world with was not her true personality, but a defense mechanism, or perhaps, her protection.

The little grey pools that were peering at me over her glasses held tears, ever so slight, but tears nonetheless. She was relieved to see me, and though not outwardly happy at my return, at least satisfied that I'd come back. I felt as if she was releasing a breath that she'd been holding, as if in anticipation of bad news as she'd opened the door. She been holding it just as little, as she was a hard and weathered soul with a tough exterior, but it had been noticeable to me in the silent moment we shared at the doorway.

She dipped her eyes back to my feet and my open-toed sandals, and seemed less bewildered or confused than Hattie had been when Hattie looked at them, saying sharply, in a rather shrill scolding tone, "What happened to your feet, young man?"

I became like I had been when Hattie asked the same question, confused as to how to answer, not having expected to have to explain to anyone their condition, not having an answer prepared, and under the influence of the strange greeting I was still trying to understand. All I could do was stand there quietly and then I put my hands out, spreading my fingers wide and putting them where she could see them too. She examined each finger on the right hand slowly before moving to the left. She said, "You been fighting with broken glass?" in a high-pitched tone more like a command than a question.

That explanation was close enough to the truth for me at the moment, so I said, "Well, sort of. It was a fight with some limestone. Rough limestone."

Her voice was raspy, as she ordered, "Get inside. Go to the kitchen," then stepped back to allow me to pass. Mothering her son had awakened in her.

I made my way past the room where Mr. P sat in his armchair, the fingers of his right hand working as usual on the stuffing, little tufts collecting between his fingers. He looked more ashen and gaunt than I remembered, and it was only five days since I'd last seen him. He stared straight ahead, seemingly not noticing me, looking slightly downward, eyes open but staring almost lifelessly. His jaw was slack and it scared me to look at him. I felt a clutching in my chest that I recognized as acute fear of getting old and being similarly incapacitated, so I moved past him with two quick steps.

"Wait for me. No use rushing," Mrs. P. said with irritation. At the kitchen she had me sit at the grand oak table as she retrieved a medical kit, and set it down on the table near to hand. She brought warm water in a basin, cotton swabs, and – God, no! – a small bottle of tincture of iodine, some tweezers and a pair of scissors.

What ensued was 45 minutes of pure agony, as she poked and prodded and dug bits of sand and sticks and wood and army blanket out of the previously scabbed over cuts. Each of them bled and she coaxed that along, wanting the fresh blood to rinse the wound. After each toe or finger was free of debris she swabbed it with iodine causing searing pain to race up my arm or leg to crash into the back of my skull then bounce back down and then repeat. It was torture, plain and simple, torture. I was being tortured as my penance for being so stupid as to go into a cave, and to pay the price for being still alive.

At some point, after I don't know how long, she granted me reprieve just long enough for the sweat to break the crest of my brows and run into my eyes. The brief respite gave me just enough time to decide to gladly accept this penance, to relish it, to say, "this ain't no big thing, I can handle this. I love the pain," and hope that turning it onto itself with a vengeance would reverse it. But then she got back to it, sadly for me and my bravado. My give-me-pain attitude dissolved in a flash and became: 'give me peace, give me peace, give me peace on earth, give me love, give me love, but, please, please, momma, make it stop'.

I was practically crying like a baby when she dug into a deep scab, and I wanted to scream in agony and go run and hide from this torturer. Had it not been for the fresh wrappings she had on my toes impairing my ability to run, I might have bolted like a rabbit, but I sat there for 36 or 48 hours or maybe even four days it seemed. In reality it was 45 minutes, but they were the longest 45 minutes of my life.

Again, I needed something to help put the pain in perspective, but I had little. The cockroaches had paled in comparison to dying in a cave and in the same way this was pale in comparison to the pain suffered by many others for many other reasons. I needed to try once more to find a way to convince my brain to reverse the discomfort and turn it onto itself. I tried to tell myself to think of it like every searing shot of the iodine she doused onto the newly exposed edges was pleasure not pain, and pleasure was good, give me more, you miserable pain of an open wound washed with iodine, give me more pain because pain was good if this was cleansing and who knows what the sand and grit and army blanket held.

It almost worked but I'd discovered I'm not enough of an adrenaline junkie to have made it a success.

She seemed to be doing all she could to be gentle, but she was not a doctor or pharmacist, she was a mother. A doctor would have prescribed codeine or morphine, a mother just prescribes, "Be a man. You don't need drugs to be a man. Take it like a man."

Oh, the lessons of life can be hard. I told myself again and again that the harder the lessons are to learn the sweeter the victory is when they are learned, and the greater the pain and effort required makes a success more glorious and that such were these lessons and so was this pain, as she dug deeper, to the point that I wanted to scream at her that she was a sadistic old lady with a curved spine and she was digging too deep for her pleasure at my pain and don't dig deeper, you crazy old lady of the plantation house. But I stopped before saying that because I knew the grit had to come out and the wounds had to be opened to get the grit and dirt out, and it was probably my own fault anyway for being so stupid as not to ask Hattie to do it which had allowed the wounds to close over and embed the sand.

She noticed me flinching. She was experienced and knew it was time, so to ease my suffering she got off her chair and shuffled to a cabinet from which she withdrew an ancient and, oh, so very beautiful bottle of rum. Island rum, perfect rum, life-saving rum that had been bottled 25 years before I was born and aged 20 years in oak before that. She brought out this gift of golden nectar of which I'd had not a sip, not even a wee dram, for at least six days, and this gift wasn't only the best rum I'd ever taste, it was given when I needed it the most. She tipped the bottle over an ancient tumbler and poured about two ounces. I watched the trickle from the bottle slow and the bottle tip back to end the stream and I whimpered like a baby.

I wouldn't cry when she was digging in the crevasses that were the cuts on my toes and fingers, but I did whimper at the sight of the golden flow from the bottle slowing after barely covering the bottom of the glass.

She noticed I was desperate and wanting more, much more as she filled the glass to the top and I had to wonder if she was thinking, "who the hell else am I saving this old rum for?" Well, that is what I thinking, at least.

I carefully picked up the crystal glass with my gauze-wrapped fingers and sipped slowly, allowing the flavor to envelope, surround, and drown each and every taste bud on my tongue. After five minutes of sipping warm, sugary, sweet, strong, burning, and finally graciously ever-so-soothing sips, I was glassy-eyed from having consumed five ounces of ancient rum, perhaps pirate rum, perhaps rumrunners-of-the-prohibition-era rum, having sipped with all the pretentiousness of an ascot-clad, rum-tasting guru with a goatee at a singles tasting party, sipping away with much narrowing of the eyes and many Mona Lisa smiles followed by prolonged aaaahhhs.

Thanks for that, rum, and thanks for the distraction from Mrs. P's work and from the memory of the small failure hours earlier not having accepted the offer from an unseen island girl in a bunk in a boat where opportunity was gifted. Of all the catching of waves, and the ups and downs, of surviving being lost in a cave now that it was survived, the missing of that opportunity on the boat was the most disappointing at the moment. When one is travelling chances like that don't come that often, and the rum poured waves of melancholy over me. I tipped my head back and smiled to myself as the warmth spread through my body. I was realizing that, after all that had occurred over the past few days, I must be coming back to my life when having missed that opportunity was forefront in my thoughts.

Good. Life will pick up again, maybe not where it left off, but certainly somewhere interesting. The mental wounds will heal as well as my physical ones.

But here, before me, working to cleanse and bandage my fingers and toes was this frail woman likely born in the past century. Through the rum-glow and the euphoric rush it brought, I looked down at her through my pain and was almost brought to tears. If she asked a question, I'd be unable to answer because my throat was choked with emotion at the thought that I'd somehow made it back to her, against incredible odds, through an experience that only I was witness to and unable to tell anyone about. The rum was fostering intense emotions in me, for having returned to her and to Lawrence's room, to be once again cared for by her as she would have cared for her poor lost son, to have her pick carefully at those scabs to remove the bits of that island recently departed. The rum gave me relief, as priceless as morphine on a battlefield. It took me from pure pain to "be a man, be accepting, this is part of the price you pay for what you have discovered," and thoughts about the weirdness that life, at even a most profound moment, can conjure thoughts during a horrifying experience that an additional horror would be the sound of bagpipes incessantly playing loudly in my room as I tried to sleep. How silly and fleeting and inconsequential life can be, which is in and of itself a lesson about life and how truly simple it can be if complications are not allowed to take over and swallow one up completely.

The rum-warmth enveloped me and burned inside, and regardless what expression I might think I should have at that second, I was incapable of preventing the corners of my mouth from lifting more and more, then breaking into a broad smile across my increasingly numb face, so I let it.

She was not my mother, and I was not her son, but, for a moment, it was what we both needed so it was what we would be. For the moment. I grinned and looked at the ceiling covered with blistered paint over who-knows-how-many other coats. The lead was so thick one could almost smell it. There had to be twenty coats of – arrrghhh, that one really hurt – paint up there, the thought of which I tried to concentrate on with great intensity to distraction from the pain still shooting up my leg from the toes Mrs. P was working on.

She was almost done, only a few more to go, and I'd made it past the worst of it. The toes of one foot were all wrapped in gauze dressings, as well as the fingers of both hands, and as much as I had refused to acknowledge these wounds, now that they were dressed I had to look at them and acknowledge that I really had done some serious damage. That didn't stop me from laughing. They were funny enough, even silly looking, even though they still sent pain up as far as my elbows and knees.

Finally the last toe was cleaned and wrapped, and Mrs. P set the tweezers and scissors back into their wooden box, but she didn't tip her head back and say, "that's it, that is the last of them." She couldn't. Her eyes lifted to mine and she seemed as relieved to be done as I was. The thought occurred to me that this sort of thing might have been a contributing factor to her curved spine. So much of her time as a mother would have been spent carefully preparing food, or bandaging wounds or managing an estate. And she wasn't a torturer after all, but she was effective and thorough. The white strips of cloth looked perfect and tight.

Perfect. I had nine little mummies and one corpulent mummy at the ends of my feet, and ten little mummies at the ends of my hands, and with rum-music in my ears and colouring my imagination, I considered drawing faces on them and giving them names, like John, Paul, George and Ringo finger, and the silly look of my enrobed appendages was, finally, a legitimate reason for the silly, circus-clown grin plastered across my half-drunk face.

I got up, teetering only slightly, then balancing unevenly on my heels to protect all that work Mrs. P had done on my toes, I wobbled my way into the front entryway toward the staircase.

As I passed it, and despite having inspected its details before, I looked into the darkened front room with fresh eyes. Mr. P still worked at the white tufts of stuffing, his fingers his heart monitor. I gazed at him, and my shoulders slumped with the pity I felt for this poor man. This sobered me, as it was heart-wrenching to look upon him one more time. It was as if this room, now that I had returned from such an arduous adventure, was well-known to me. I hobbled over to stand before Mr. P and the overstuffed chair. Then, I couldn't help myself, and reached out to touch the back of his hand to stop the scrabbling.

At my touched on his hand, it calmed, then stopped. For the first time since my arrival some week earlier, I saw something other than his hand move, as he turned his head and slack jaw slightly toward me.

"La, La, La…," was all he was able to get say.

The stroke had taken his speech but I understood what he was saying. I was slightly drunk to be sure, and possibly I was wrong, but then he said it again, "La…La…La…."

I squeezed shut my white robed fingers upon the back

of his right hand and lowered to one knee to become level with his eyes.

I looked deeply into his grey eyes within their pale folds of tired flesh without even thinking about what I was doing or what I was saying. I had never felt so much emotion as at that moment, and I knew that the cave, George, Hattie, Buddy, the Captain, had all been put in my path as a prelude to this moment. I could do nothing less than say what I had to say. I took his cold grey face in my mummified hands and angled his shaking head upward so I could see into his eyes and he into mine and I spoke the lie I knew that a week ago I couldn't have; now, at this moment, I knew what he wanted to hear, what he *needed* to hear, and then, I said it, "Yes." I looked in his eyes and smiled at him. Then, I couldn't help but take the next step, and as if it was not I actually saying it at all, another word came out, very weakly, less than a whisper, in another mans voice, "Father."

Then I dropped my hands from his face and let one hand rest on the blue and white transparent skin of his ancient hand. It's movement stopped once more, calmed into a soothing stillness, until finally I looked away from him.

I stood and faced the antique armoire, perplexed at what just came out of me. How could I play this sort of cruel joke on this poor old man? As soon as I thought it I was ashamed of myself. I was not his lost son returning to say goodbye, I was not Lawrence.

But, yet, in some obscure way perhaps I was.

Even if I wanted to, I couldn't say otherwise. I found myself in this situation somehow, and at that moment this is what I could not help but say. At that moment, even if my life depended on not saying it, I was incapable of saying anything else.

He looked back at me, this poor old man who had lost

his life without dying. The only movable part of his entire face was the expression in his eyes, and they watered, then they appeared to me to drift away into some far off place.

They were gone, as he was gone. He was immobile, and he looked straight ahead at nothing at all.

This was what I saw in that second and what I didn't want to see. I wanted to run away. I had to turn off my mind to these thoughts and step back into myself, so I turned back to the hallway and stepped forward, step, step, step, toward the staircase. But, while doing so I couldn't help but notice that Mr. P's fingers were no longer scratching at the arm of the chair. Slowly, I left the room, hobbling to the stairs, wanting to be numb to what had been too intense for too many long moments. Suddenly I craved more of the good rum, and would have done anything for the rum and the rum numbness it provided, but mother was not there with more of her elixir.

I made my way to my/Lawrence's room, and saw the old bed there like an invitation and fell forward at glacial pace, and the pillow greeted me and all my tired head and tired body and bagpipe tortured ears still faintly ringing Amazing Grace and fully dressed fingers of John Paul George and Ringo finger and toes, and I slept.

Quite soundly I slept.

Then I awoke to the call of my brother the seagull once more. But, I wasn't going to be fooled again, so I ignored him and slept some more.

Dreams filled the early dawn, or at least I hoped they were dreams. Maybe I was half-awake, and just recalling events in a strange reprise of colourful episodes that I wanted to wake from in case I was still caught in them: visions of myself floating above myself, of a seagull with pink feathers calling my name; of an old man with a crooked grin cleaning flying fish in a bucket, daring me to dive into caves that might hold hidden treasure and did hold the skeleton of a young man or an old pirate; of dancing girls and a racing boat pounding over wave tops with thunderous engines. There were feelings of sheer terror, first of speed then of a storm with a grey-haired captain at the helm of a floating relic with crewmen eating conch and fried fish and there were slaves and pirates and treasure and children and corned beef and cockroaches the size of small cars and obese muu muu-clad red-eyed demons inhaling crack like it was the finest perfume from heaven and exhaling a stream of smoke like a steam locomotive chugging though a frozen winter prairie under a beautiful clear blue sky that my father told me about, how magnificent it was when steam engines still crossed the winter prairie and puffed and thumped and billowed white steam through the frozen north....

And then I awoke from this half-dream sleep. It took three tries to heave myself out of the depths of the sagging mattress and over the edge to the floor. I had no idea how long I'd been asleep, as I'd had no idea of time for days, not since I'd first faced the customs agent, some interminable time ago, some eons before now.

Eventually I dressed and began the process of packing my bag, slowing, and finally stopping, as melancholy washed over me, making me think of a more appropriate use of the term 'tropical depression.' I was not ready to leave yet, but finally I did get my packing finished and set my red leather bag by the door, for some odd reason, unable to set it down anywhere outside the room.

I descended the stairs to find that everything in that house had changed and would be changed forever. The front door was open, and through the grand entrance beyond the broad staircase and the crumbling sidewalk and falling gate, I could see a white van with its rear doors open. Mrs. P. stood watching, for once not straining to look ahead, her head as downcast as her eyes, and it appeared to me she was once again even smaller today than she'd been the day before. The two attendants quietly closed the doors, and with a slight nod to Mrs. P ambled to their places and climbed in.

The van slowly pulled away, down West Street, toward the Colonial Hotel, to the water, to the morgue, to the doctor for his paperwork.

Mrs. P. stood silent, then her head rose slowly, as if to watch the van depart as best she could over the tops of her glasses. Time seemed to slow as quietness settled around the house, Mrs. P, the garden, the gate. Nothing moved in either direction on this now-lonely street. No birds, not my brother the seagull or the robins, spoke to me or sang or flew overhead. It was like my memory was being etched with a still-life image of this street, this town, this house, and these people. The chapter and the story were closing on this final scene.

Then these thoughts were becoming overwhelming and I had to put them away for later. Some distant time later I might possibly be able to recall them and revisit this vivid image. Later. Right now time was still moving and I was young, with lots of living to do. Most importantly I knew it, and as time still moved so must I.

I turned to the staircase to return to my room to get my bag and there before me was the now vacant red velvet armchair with its prominent void on the end of the right arm and on the floor a small pile of stuffing. My intention had been to get my bag, but something drew me in a different direction, urging me to turn and sit down on that chair for just a moment, a short moment.

But that idea passed in a moment with an inward shudder.

I strode with purpose up the broad and once-grand staircase, past polished spindles and over threadbare carpet, and into my room. I closed the door hastily behind me to shut out the thought chasing me. I stood with my back to the door, realizing, oddly enough, that more than seven days had passed, I'd be allowed to leave.

I scanned the room to make sure I hadn't left anything behind and saw the sweater hanging over the chair, the cardigan with the hard-won A sewn onto the left front side. I would need that and I was glad I didn't forget it, having passed many a cool evening in the comfort of that sweater. But as I lifted it from the chair I caught my reflection in the mirror of the dresser, the dresser with the photo of Lawrence in track uniform, his smile as mine, but mine in the mirror. The sweater was on my arm ready to pack, but I was stood still.

That was my favorite sweater —

but it wasn't mine, it wasn't mine at all. I laid it over the back of the chair carefully, knowing I was going away and my favorite sweater would not be going with me once more.

I zipped the bag shut and stood facing the door, unmoving for a long moment, until I had to ask,

"Am I Lawrence?"

ABOUT THE AUTHOR

Becoming Lawrence' is the second novel for Ronald D. Tkachuk.

Written and published under the pseudonym

T. H. Fortitude.

Using this name so the word *Fortitude* would appear on the cover and every second page.

The initials T. and H. represent 'To Have'.

Ronald D. Tkachuk was born in Edmonton, Canada in 1956. He currently lives in Vancouver.

Becoming Lawrence is based on events from October of 1983.

www.ingramcontent.com/pod-product-compliance
Lightning Source LLC
Chambersburg PA
CBHW070748280626
47162CB00018B/2776